I0609782

D M THOMSEN

HIDDEN SHORE

D M Thomsen
Publishing

Hidden Shore

D M Thomsen, publisher

Visit our website at www. Dmthomsen.homestead.com

First paperback edition: February 2009

Summary: In a small town in Northern California which sits on the coast down a lonely road, three young boys grow and discover love and relationships which take them in three different directrion. Set in the early 1960s, Hidden Shore focuses on two young lovers who make adult decisions that cause their relationship to be propelled like the tsunami that will surge down the coast of California on Good Friday 1964.

ISBN 978-0-578-01241-4
Printed in the United States of America

Hidden Shore

Hidden Shore

Hidden Shore

"And behold…the earth did quake and the rocks rent."
Book of St. Mathew

Foreword

Alaska - March 27, 1964

It was Good Friday and many of the residents of Alaska were preparing for the Easter weekend.

At 5:36 PM off the Alaskan south coast, the sea heaved and then the earth arched which sent devastation that would cause damages estimated as high as $750,000,000.00 which was more than 100 times of what it cost for the United States to purchase Alaska from Russia in 1867.

The downtown area of Anchorage, Alaska's largest city was devastated as splits in the earth separated streets from sidewalks and caused buildings to split and drop pieces onto the sidewalk below. 115 people lost their lives and 4,800 were left homeless.

The earthquake had an effect on Alaska that would last for years.

That was not all the damage that day. A tsunami or tidal wave was generated which skipped down just west of the West Coast of North America. Those communities farthest west were hit by this wave. Hidden Shore, California was destroyed.

Hidden Shore

1

Hidden **S**hore was a small coastal town in Northern California. By 1964 it had a dwindling population of only about 300 souls. By then, the once promising town had only twenty-two permanent homes, a post office, a bankrupt and closed Redwood lumber mill, a set of cabins built of Redwood, a bar called the Linger/Longer Lounge, Mike's Cafe, a service station, a used clothing store, a combination 5&dime/drug store, a grocery store, a bait and tackle shop, a Chinese Restaurant, a catalogue store, a used book store, a liquor store, and five other empty businesses; buildings that once held helpful businesses in Hidden Shore's recent past. Everyone in town knew they were going through a slow time. However, for the time being, Hidden Shore was just fine to the people who lived there .

On a gentle knoll, just east above the old mill site, still lay the remains of the population of a town whose hopes and dreams for growth faded with the passing of many years. Anyone not familiar with the history of Hidden Shore could walk around the cemetery and read the names on the tombstones of the people who lived in the town but would have no concept of the stories of these people or of their lives.

Behind a chain-link fence marked "Stevenson" stands the monument to James and Lydia Stevenson. At one time they worked 1,930 acres of land just south of Hidden Shore. James was highly respected throughout Humbolt County as a prominent and successful farmer.

Not far away is the monument to Albert Howard. Everyone knew him as "Howie." He was the cashier at the bank for most of its existence in Hidden Shore. Most folks from Hidden Shore knew of the time in 1920 when John Hangle robbed the bank and locked Howie in the vault. He almost died from lack of oxygen but was saved in time. Hangle was eventually cornered in Oakland and died in a shoot out with police. Then in 1930 the bank was robbed by "Curly" Taylor and his wife. Howie took after them in his Whippet automobile but they got away and were later captured in Arizona. After that bank robbery the town of Weston began to help with law protection. Howie lived to become President of the bank after it moved to Weston.

Then there are Karl and Emma Hostetler. He managed the Mill and worked hard to establish the bank in Hidden Shore. Karl was one of its first Presidents. Sadly, he died of pneumonia during the influenza epidemic of 1919. He was only thirty-four years old.

Also, there is a monument to Joseph and Una Anderson. They moved to Hidden Shore in 1888. That was the year the Mill opened. She remembered one night when the mill workers got in a scuffle downtown with some fishermen and proceeded to try to tear the town apart. Alta got so frightened that she hid under her bed all night until peace was restored. The Anderson's watched the town grow: in fact, Joseph built quite a few of the buildings and served as Justice of the Peace in Hidden Shore for fifty-four years. They unfortunately lost a major part of their money when the Brother

Hidden Shore

Jonathan sank in a fog off the coast of Crescent City. They both lived into their late eighties remaining in Hidden Shore until they died in 1947 and 1949.

Other people whose monuments are in the cemetery who contributed much to the town are Charles and Clara Breckinridge, Pardon Taylor, John Green and his three children (Maude, Claude and Clone), Cash and Mary Baker, Burke and Catherine Kilnter and many more. These people were bound together by one common thread: Hidden Shore. Though their markers sat on the hill, their stories were rarely recorded and all that remain are these monuments to their lives.

From the cemetery can be seen may geographical features. Just northwest is the town site of Hidden Shore. Directly west just below the cemetary but out of sight are the two beaches, South Beach to the north and North Beach to the south. To the west of the town lies the Pacific Ocean. To the northwest is Snake Butte and to the north is a flat coastal swamp and Smith's Fort: an area named for Jedediah Smith who was the first white man to reach this area of California. Not in view but just three miles east is still today the larger town of Weston. To the south are the coastal hills and grazing land for sheep which are still utilized for that today.

Hidden Shore has one permanent building, which though boarded up and crumbling, still remains today. That is the old school building. At one time there were many one-room schools scattered throughout the area but eventually these were consolidated into this large school which was called Hidden Shore School.

On June 12th 1938, two children of these early settlers Mary and Abner Williams, were married at the Baptist Church in Hidden Shore. Starting a marriage just prior to the depression meant that there were difficult times ahead of them. But the difficulty of the world meant little to them as Mary worked in the dime store and Abner worked at the saw mill.

Mary loved Hidden Shore and even when it became clear to many that hopes and dreams for growth in Hidden Shore was slowly vanishing, she pledged never to leave it. She loved many things about the town, but what she most loved was the beach just south of town. Her and Abner spent many hours on the beach. Often they would escape to North Beach which was just south of South Beach and when they were sure no one was around they would skinny dip on North Beach. Once, Mary and Abner were stranded on North Beach when they lost track of high tide. This was a particularly harrowing experience which Mary never forgot. She and Abner only escaped by climbing the cliff. They almost fell off the cliff to the rocks below. After that Mary would always caution her children to watch the tide on North Beach whenever they headed there.

Mary and Abner had 3 boys before the war broke out. The oldest was Gabriel, the second was Jeffrey and the youngest son was Stanley. With the advent of World War 2, Abner hired on at the ship yards in San Francisco and was later drafted in the Navy. He died at Midway when his ship went down with no survivors. Mary was left a single mom with 3 boys.

Mary and Abner had a son named Jeff. He was their middle son with one older named Gabriel and one younger named Stanley. Jeff Williams had two friends. One was his "bestest" friend Clint Johnson. Clint was the son of the chief of police in Weston. The other was Greg Callison who was the quieter of his friends. Greg always felt jealous of Jeff and Clint's friendship because he wanted a "bestest" friend.

2

One Sunday Morning in April 1951 Steve Taylor pulled his squad car to the intersection of Weston Drive and Hidden Shore Road. Picking up his car microphone he Keyed the button.

"Car three."

"Car three, dispatch"

"They've been at it again, the Hidden Shore sign has disappeared." Steve advised the chief who was working dispatch that morning.

"I don't think I have any more Steve, come on in and we'll make something up that will suffice until we get some more." The Chief sounded just as perturbed about the missing sign as Steve was.

Steve glanced at the half sheared signpost, "God Damn it, I'm getting sick and tired of these idiots," he muttered under his breath.

By the 1950s most residents of Hidden Shore did not want anyone to know that Hidden Shore even existed. They did not want any tourists or "Ne're do Well's" anywhere near their town and would have them stay in Weston or Eureka rather than finding their way to their little coastal community. There was one road, Hidden Shore Road, which led from Weston to the beach and Hidden Shore. John Johnson, the chief of police at Weston had sent his deputy Steve Taylor on a call. Someone had again removed the sign on the southwest corner of the town which pointed the way to Hidden Shore. It seemed like every week someone would remove it. They were "very happy living in our quiet little place without anyone interfering with us; thank you very much."

Hidden Shore was a very appropriate name for the town because it was mostly isolated and only occasionally would some people from Eureka or one of the outlying towns find their way there.

There was very little trouble in Hidden Shore. Occasionally Jack Purvis, who most referred to as the town drunk, would get in a fight with himself and Steve Taylor would be called by one of the local merchants and have to rush out and make sure Jack behaved himself. Usually, all it took was for Steve to pull up in his squad car and Jack would bid a hasty retreat home or into the woods where he often hid from everyone.

3

Boys build forts. It's a fact of life in a young boy's world.

Hidden Shore

Jeff and Clint and Greg had forts. They had two places that they usually built them. One was on the beach and that was always North Beach. As with all beaches at extremely high tides, driftwood gathered on the beaches and was pushed up against the cliffs. The boys would rearrange the driftwood either cooperating on one or building their own. Often they would consider themselves marauding pirates or soldiers of fortune that would attack the others fort. Other boys would join them and make it possible for them to have opposing armies with "Coo Kachoo" as they would attack the other. The stronger fort usually won the battle as the weaker fort was ravaged by the opposing army.

No two forts were ever alike, but there were certain things that every fort must have. There must be a rise either of sand or wood behind which the soldiers could hide and watch for marauders. There had to be a perimeter line. This would be an area determined by those in the fort as the area the enemy could not encroach If the driftwood was big enough, they could have a covered fort from which they would dig out of below the roof and thus have a lot of room to hide or meet. Sometimes they would cover the roof with seaweed and cardboard and anything else they could find that would seal the roof for them. These beach forts could remain around all summer or they could wash away at a very high tide shortly after they were built. But each winter they disappear, washed out to sea along with most of the sand to be replaced each spring with new sand and new building materials for new forts for the new summer and for the new kids.

The other place they would build forts was on the hills just south of Hidden Shore or along Dead Man Creek. On these forts they would either use existing enclosures of bush or tree or rock, but sometimes they would stack rocks and make impenetrable forts.

Once the boys built what they thought was "the best fort ever built." They designed an igloo. Based on igloo's they had seen in pictures, they chose the correct size rocks from the bed of Dead Man Creek and skillfully constructed a round room together with a doorway just like an igloo through which they would crawl and then be secure from invading "hombres." After building this, Jeff, Clint and Greg were talking about it at Jeff's house that evening and Jeff's mother overheard the conversation. Worried that the igloo might collapse and hurt the boys or trap them inside, Mary had Gab go up the next day and disassemble the igloo much to the boys' disappointment.

One Spring day, the boys were playing with air guns that Jeff and Stan had received for Christmas. These shot a burst of air which sounded like a bee bee gun shot. Jeff and Greg were fighting a war with Clint and Stan. Two older boys on vacation in Weston, came up the creek and asked to play with the boys. It was going to be the two of them against the four Hidden Shore boys. After a while the Weston boys told the Hidden Shore boys to hide in the fort and they would take the rifles and circle around and attack them when they were inside. The four boys did exactly as they were instructed and waited for the boys to attack. The four boys never saw the other two boys again, nor the rifles. The two Weston boys won the battle.

4

When Jeff and Clint were about 12 years old they decided one day to explore the old school. The school building had been sitting rusticating in a dilapidated condition. The walls were thick brick and the windows were boarded over. The grounds were unkempt and sitting before the eastern hills the temptation to explore became a near fascination for the boys. Years before they had heard that if they went near the school they would be arrested and fed bread and water for a year in jail. Gabe had perpetuated this fear by telling of the time that he and a couple of his friends had crawled through a hole in a board that let them into the basement. He told Jeff that Mike, Paul and him found an old skeleton where the science class used to be. Of course, the story grew until suddenly the skull had a bullet hole through it which indicated that the former person had been shot and his body donated to science. Then it grew to jars full of dead frogs, cats, and even a monkey head in a jar of formaldehyde. Whether any of these stories were true did not matter. What mattered was that generations of boys had taken it upon themselves to explore the inner sanctum of the old school building.

The monkey head became the main goal of the Jeff and Clint expedition. All the way over they talked about what they were going to do with the monkey head.

"We can put it under Sharon's seat at school and when she finds it that'll really scare her." said Clint.

"I think we ought to put it under Miss Zoover's chair and scare her." countered Jeff always protective of his best female friend Sharon.

"She's so weird," continued Clint. "every time Miss Zoover comes to class she stops in front of her locker in class and sniffs under each arm to see if she stinks. Why do you think she would not be embarrassed about that?"

"Remember the time that Celia put the thumb tacks on her chair and she flopped so hard on the chair and nothing happened?" Jeff remembered laughing.

"Yah, I looked at Celia and she said: 'girdle.'" said Clint. "those thumb tacks must have been flattened."

"Yah, and when she got up there was still one stuck in her butt."

The boys laughed about that one and that was when they decided that the monkey head was their goal. Somehow, Miss Zoover would be their victim.

The old Hidden Shore School building was never torn down because the county did not want to loose it if there ever came a time that they could use it for offices. Everyone felt that if Hidden Shore ever organized a police force, their offices and a jail would be housed in that building.

When the boys arrived at the building it looked very forbidding. Jeff felt a tingle up the back of his neck as he stood staring at the building with Clint.

"Where did your brother say the board was loose?" asked

Clint.

"He won't tell me because he thinks we shouldn't go in there."

"Well, let's get looking." ordered Clint.

They walked from board to board pulling on each until at the seventh board they were able to gain entry. They dropped into a dark room with pipes running across the ceiling and old desks stacked haphazardly in one half of the room. In the other half sat an old furnace which obviously used to heat the building.

They went through a door and began their search of the building. There were very few items of interest left in the building, contrary to what they had been told. The rooms smelled of creosol and mold. They were damp and it was obvious that the local rats had taken over the building. In one of the rooms the ceiling had a large hole in it and they could see that sea gulls and crows had also taken up residence in the attic. The boys began throwing anything they could find at the birds which only caused them to flap their wings uproariously and caused the boys to flee to keep from getting "dive bombed" by flying excrement.

It was obvious that others had been in before them when they found the cafeteria. There was a lot of trash and beer bottles and graffiti was all over the wall. Some of it read girls names, initials and not so cleaver expletives such as: MIKE & SHARON, FUCK SCHOOL, and KILROY WAS HERE. On one wall someone had been poetic: YAH THO I WALK THREW THE SHADOW OF THE VALLEY OF DEATH I SHALL FEAR NO EVEL FOR I WILL BE THE MEANEST SON OF A BITCH IN THE VALLEY. Jeff noticed the spelling was wrong in many cases but one thing was clear, everyone seemed to know how to spell the four letter words.

After an exhaustive search, the boys decided it was time to leave. They returned to the furnace room and Clint suggested that Jeff get into the furnace and see if there was anything in there.

"Not me." said Jeff.

"Okay, give me a hand and I'll get in." Cliff suggested.

Jeff and Clint worked on the handle and got it open and Clint stepped in. Once inside something came over Jeff and he reached over and pulled the door closed and latched it.

"Is it dark in there?" Jeff inquired kidding.

"Ass hole, open that door." Clint demanded.

Jeff quickly reached up to open it and it was stuck. He tried several times with Clint screaming at him in the back ground.

"Open this door Jeff. I'm gone kick your ass."

"I can't," Jeff informed him "it's stuck. I just need something to pry it open, let me look."

"Don't leave man, it's scary in here."

"You mean like someone might light it up." Jeff teased.

But the teasing stopped when Clint started pounding on the door and screaming every cuss word he could think of and some he invented on the spot.

"When I get out of here, I'm gonna kick your ass Jeff." Clint continued.

"I'm sorry, Clint. I'm sure if I could find some kind of wedge I could pry that open."

"Okay, but keep talking to me while you look. It's fucking scary in here." Clint pleaded.

"I'm walking over to the tables now." Jeff informed Clint. He looked around keeping Clint appraised of his progress but Jeff could not find a thing to pry the handle with."

"I don't see anything Clint. Hold on, let me think."

"I've got an idea. Push against the door with all your might and that might release some of the pressure from the handle." he instructed Cliff.

For over ten minutes they tried as Cliff pushed and Jeff pulled trying to get the door open.

"Why the hell did you close this Jeff?" Clint asked.

"I don't know, I guess I was just trying to be funny." Jeff called through the louvers.

"Big joke, what we gonna do." Clint seemed to be more calm now.

"I could run home and see if Gabe is there and he probably would come and help."

"Man, I can't stand to be left alone here."

Hidden Shore

"I don't know anything else to do."

Clint and Jeff thought again as Jeff continued to wander around the room still looking for something to pry with.

"I'm gonna have to get Gabe Clint." Jeff finally said having given up. "It's either that or look around the school more.

"If you wander around the school you might get hurt and maybe even killed. Then where would I be? They would find my body whenever they reopened the building all stinky and probably only bones." Clint sounded resigned.

"Go. But hurry. Please." He instructed.

"I'll hurry as fast as I can."

So Jeff climbed out of the board leaving his friend in the predicament he had brought on by doing something he now knew was stupid.

Clint was more than scared. He felt panic as if his hands and arms were tied together and he was buried in a casket. He squirmed and kicked and even began to cry as he felt more hopeless than any other time in his life. He felt that to die would be better than to be trapped. He remembered movies he had recently seen showing world war prisoners of war trapped in small hot huts and could only vision himself being trapped in there forever.

Fortunately, Gabe was home listening to a Four Season Album on the record player with Mike when Jeff arrived screaming about what happened. Gabe grabbed his tool kit and threw it in the trunk of his car and the three of them drove to the school. On the way, Gabe let into Jeff for even going to the school. Calling as they climbed through the boarded window, Clint felt immediate relief upon hearing their voices.

All Gabriel needed to do was to hit the handle upward with the palm of his hand and the handle broke loose and out tumbled Clint. Clint immediately started for Jeff, but Gabe and Mike held him and made Jeff apologize. Jeff did profusely and he and Clint shook and made up.

That was their adventure at the school, but it would not be the only time they would ever explore a deserted building.

5

About six months after the school incident, Clint and Jeff were hiking up Dead Man Creek and decided to make themselves familiar with the other local legendary building. The Haunted House. Supposedly, this was the house that the famous dead man lived in before he was found dead and the creek named after him.

The house really was just an abandoned ranch house but it had not been painted for years so it looked very rustic and forbidding. It was just after school and Jeff and Clint were walking home with two of the girls and decided they wanted to wander up the creek a while. The girls wanted to get home so the boys went up alone. They wandered a bit further than usual this time and found themselves standing in front of the old house.

"I don't think anyone lives there any more." said Jeff.

"I know no one does. This is where the guy who they found in the creek was killed and his ghost still haunts the house. I hear that if you are here at night you can see him through the window up there." Clint informed Jeff pointing to a window at the attic.

"Let's go in" was the agreement made by the boys. They approached the house looking in each direction to see if anyone at all was around. There were no cars, no mangy dogs running lose, it all seemed clear.

The first thing they did was to climb the stairs which lead to the front door. The house was one of those Victorian houses that dotted the area. There were no windows at the front door. To the right of the front steps was a bay window which pointed toward the ocean. Climbing up on the banister to peer in, Clint could not see anything because butcher paper had been hung over the window. They tried the door handle and it was unlocked. They entered the hallway just inside the door and to the right was what once was the living room. There was a seedy old couch, with trash and whiskey bottles scattered all over the place. They wandered in and peered into the first darkened bedroom to the right; seeing nothing, they entered.

"This would make a great clubhouse." suggested Jeff.

They walked back into the hall, down the hall and peered quickly into the other bedroom to the right. There was a bed in there which was piled with old blankets. The old kitchen area was trashed. There was a kitchen table but a lamp which hung on a cord from the ceiling toward the middle of the table had water dripping from it and the water splashed onto a puddle on the table and then ran off the table to another puddle on the kitchen linoleum floor. Obviously the roof leaked.

The boys then walked back to the living room area and sat on the old broken down sofa. "Wow, we really could fix this place up and have a fort here or a club. We could call it the Hidden Shore Boys Club." Clint decided.

It was dark in the whole house because the house sat among the cedar trees along side the creek facing the ocean. It never occurred to the boys to try any of the light switches, they assumed that there was no electricity in the house. But the boys were not really scared until suddenly from the back of the house they heard a noise.

"Who's in here? What you doing in my house?" came a voice yelling. The boys jumped to their feet and ran into Jack Purvis in the hallway.

"We didn't know anyone lived here," yelled Clint. "as the boys reversed direction and ran out of the house."

They did not recognize Jack because they were so afraid to take time to look at the person so they just ran.

"Did you see that? Clint said as they ran.

"What?

"He had a woman's head in his hand."

"No way."

"I saw it, he was holding it by her hair and he had an ax in his other hand."

"Oh my God." Jeff exclaimed running even faster.

The boys ran and ran and did not stop until they arrived at home.

"You know, if we say anything he might come and get us."

"Are you sure it was a head."

"Sure looked like one."

"And did you see the body on the bed."

"No way"

So the boys made a pact not to say anything at all. The secret did not stay completely between them because a new story of a mass killer of women was perpetuated among the local boys and added to the legend.

The truth of the matter was that Jack Purvis, the local town drunk, often escaped to Dead Man Creek to get away from his mother whom he lived with. Mostly the two would get along fine, but when one or the other had too much to drink they would often get into shouting matches and Jack would escape to his secluded home which he never owned but tried to keep to himself. The "head" that Clint thought he saw was simply a chicken' body dangling from his fist that Jack had just beheaded for his dinner because he had no intentions of returning home that night and had appropriated one from a neighboring ranch.

The house became the Haunted House up Dead Man Creek where the spirits of murdered women wandered in perpetuity looking for their severed heads. Notorious for it's stories Dead Man Creek remained safe as long as "you stay away from the house."

Even the story of Dead Man Creek is much simpler than one might expect. The original rancher who's land the creek ran through and who built the famous haunted house was named Joseph Denholm. Pronounced Den-hum or Den-hum Creek, the name over the years had been bastardized to reflect the name Dean Man.

6

The boys played together and had lots of adventures, just a great time as long as there were no girls around. Sometime in 1957, the boys got together for the first meeting of the Girl Haters Club.

The first motion of business was that no girls could ever belong to the Girl Haters Club. The second rule voted and approved was that any boy seen walking with a girl had to hold his face in a bucket of water for one minute. Second offense and he was banished from the club. A total of at least a dozen rules were agreed and passed on Tuesday. By Friday every member had either broken a rule or forgot what they were. The club quickly ceased to exist.

By 1959, they all had girl friends but none of them would admit it until Jeff decided to stand alone the day Ann kissed him after he first spun a bottle that landed on her. From that day on they considered themselves boy friend and girl friend.

Ann was a special little girl. Her parents were friends of Jeff's and they brought her to play at the house whenever they visited. The day of the first kiss was no different than any other day except for the kiss. The kiss sealed their relationship and Ann was now Jeff's girl friend.

Whenever the kids got together, Ann was who Jeff now wanted to play with. They never kissed again. They only needed to kiss the one time but Ann told Jeff that she loved him and that he would always be her boy friend.

In 1960, Ann's parents moved to Denver Colorado. Ann wrote two letters and in one of them she sent him her picture. The second letter told him her parents had split apart and her Mother moved her to Colorado Springs. Jeff forgot to write to her and the love affair faded into a memory. Jeff always wondered how Ann did in Colorado but he lost track of her.

7

One day early in 1960, Jeff was in the garage and just nosing around. There was this shelf that had a large array of items on it such as paint cans, oil, rags, car parts, etc. all neatly arranged but not in any particular order. The garage had a pitched roof with no attic space just an open roof with no ceiling. At the top of the shelf was a board that angled away from the front of the shelf to the ceiling of the pitched roof. Jeff also noticed that at one end it was open but he could not see what was in this spot. He found a ladder and climbed to the opening finding an old cardboard box inside that he assumed had been left by a former owner of the house, so he reached in and pulled the box out. Inside he found many magazines like he had never seen before. He pulled the box down and took it to his bedroom. No one was home, so no one saw him carry it to his bedroom. Inside were may Nudist Colony magazines, National Geographic and Playboy Magazines. He began to look at all the pictures and read the stories and educated himself on the female anatomy. The one thing that frustrated him was that he thought someone had taken a pen and colored a vee between all of the ladies' legs. He could not understand why it was so dark there and that their penis did not hang out. The men had hair and a penis, but for some reason this black vee was drawn on all the women.

Jeff invited Greg over to see his find and the boys spent hours looking at the pictures. Jeff asked Greg why someone had marked all the ladies' penises up like that and Greg laughed and told him that women did not have a penis and that they grew hair between their legs.

"Why do people take these pictures?" Jeff asked.

"They take them so men can jerk-off on the pictures."

"Jerk-off? What's that?" asked Jeff.

"Masturbate. They take their hand and rub it up and down on their penis until they cum."

"Cum?"

"Shoot off! You know!" Greg told him frustratingly.

"No, I don't know." said Jeff.

"My God Jeff, you just turned fourteen and you don't know about masturbating?"

"I don't get it!"

"Jeff, men and women kiss and then men stick their wiener in a woman."

"What are you talking about."

"Well I can't show you because these pictures don't show

what women have. They don't have a dick. Here, let me show you." He took one of the nudist pictures and explained. "A man has a dick. A woman has a pussy. You can't see that here but right here is where it opens up at." he pointed to the bottom of the vee on one woman. "The man's dick is a pole, like this one." he pointed between the legs of a man. "You know, you have one. Well, a girl has a hole that the man sticks it into. I mean a lady not a girl. Girls don't do that until their older. This is how they make babies."

"I'm really confused." Jeff admitted.

"Look, see this man? Just like you he has a wiener or dick, whatever you want to call it. The man kisses the woman who has a hole between her legs. The man's dick becomes hard and he sticks it in her hole. He pushes it in and out until he shoots sperm into her. This mixes with her egg which is in her hole and that makes a baby.

"Okay, but what's that got to do with basturbate?' asked Jeff.

"Masturbate, Jeff, masturbate. When a man sees a picture he feels the same as he does when he sees a real lady. So he plays with his thing until he shoots his stuff all over his bed or whatever. Haven't you ever gotten hard? Greg asked.

"Yah, some times in the morning it's hard and I get embarrassed that Mom or someone might see it. When I started at Weston, I worried about it happening getting dressed for gym. I asked Gabe about it and he made fun of me and told all his friends that I was worried about getting a renob, that's what he calls it. So that's all they do to get pregnant? How come none of these guys aren't hard?

"Renob, that's backwards for boner. That's what people call your dick when it's hard. I guess they get used to seeing naked woman when they are around them a lot so they don't get hard. You've had wet dreams haven't you?"

"Wet dreams? How do you know about all this stuff? I had one and Gabe laughed again and told me I'd learn later what it was. I didn't even touch myself. Was that, what did you call it?

"Sperm! Reggie at school found this book and it told all about it. And I've seen my sisters. They were getting ready once and I went into their room and Debby had no clothes on so I saw her and compared it to the book. I seen them some other time too. You don't have any sisters so you don't see anything. Haven't you ever seen your mother?

"Once," admitted Jeff, "she was getting dressed and she had her leg crossed while cutting her toe nails in her bathrobe But all I could see was black down there.

"Sometime, you need to try it. Take one of these pictures and play with yourself. If you get hard, beat yourself off. It feels good when you shoot. You get all tingly all over and you can try to hit something like a garbage can with your stuff."

"Show me!" Jeff asked.

"Well, that would be queer, but I guess it wouldn't hurt just don't try to touch me and don't tell anyone."

With that Greg sat down on the bed pushed his pants to his ankles and pulled his penis from his fruit of the looms and began playing with it shaking it every way as he looked at a picture from the magazine. Finally, he became erect but try as he would nothing would happen.

"You're just watching and it makes me nervous. Do it yourself!" Greg ordered.

Jeff reciprocated and grabbing a magazine of his own and finding a picture of a woman standing next to a sign which said "Caution nude folk near" his penis became hard also. Finally, with a gasp, Greg grabbed Jeff's garbage pail and ejaculated into it. Jeff watched him shutter and said: "That went a long ways like peeing." Greg told him to try.

Jeff pumped and pumped and pumped but nothing would happen. Finally, the feeling went away and his penis softened.

"It wouldn't work for me the first few times either. Keep these pictures and keep trying." Greg counseled Jeff.

So for the next few nights Jeff tried and it never worked. He was afraid something was wrong with him. He finally forgot to try any more.

One day the box of pictures disappeared. No one said anything to him but he saw the empty box in the garage by the garbage can. He eventually realized that the box must have been his step father Bill's and instead of embarrassing Jeff, Bill simply searched for it, found it, and either disposed of the magazines or found another hiding place for them.

8

One day Jeff was able to really put his newfound hobby to a test. Jeff and Clint and Greg and Jason were hiking in the hills west of Dean Man Creek when Clint brought out of his pocket a small box.

"See what I got?' he said showing the box to Jeff and the others.

It was a box of playing cards and instead of the regular Queen, King picture or numbers on the faces, there were pictures of naked women on them.

"I found these in a box of stuff my brother left when he went in the Navy." Clint went on.

Each boy grabbed a dozen of each and looked admiringly at the pictures.

"I like this one."

"Look at the tits on this one."

"Man, you can see the bush on this one."

Each of the boys had an opinion of them.

"This ones ugly." or "This one looks like my sister."

They each found their favorite. Jeff's was the nine of spades which showed a dark haired girl with medium sized breasts dangling a gold chain between her out-stretched arms which had a cluster of chains connected that dangled down over into her lap hiding her personal treasure.

Clint liked the ten of spades with a girl with long black hair but small pointed breasts and black boots that extended over her knees. "You can see her pussy under her butt there." Clint pointed.

"No you can't." argued Jason. "And look at those tiny tities."

"Anything over a mouthful's a waste." shot back Clint.

Hidden Shore

"I like the ace of clubs. Look at those knockers," Jason showed him "and all that blonde, I like blondes looks like Barbie."

Greg liked the brown haired joker with the elephant doll in her lap whose trunk was obviously a phallic symbol.

"Let's play strip poker." Clint and Jason suggested.

"Play what? asked Greg and Jeff but they went along.

They played until each was naked then Clint went running off gamboling through the trees. The other boys followed; all were buck naked. This was a lot of fun for the boys. Clint finally reached the highway standing there looking both ways. The other boys hid in the forest and laughed that he would get caught that way. Finally a car came around a corner and Clint ran back up to the trees, his penis flailing every where."

"That was close." the boys said when he returned.

"Damn! Look at that."

Right after Clint dove into the forest, another car came from the other direction; it was a police car.

"That might be your dad Clint." Jeff said as all the boys rolled in laughter.

"So what if it were." Clint shot back shaking his fist at the passing car.

The boys began walking back with the cards still clutched in each of their fists. One at a time the boys began looking at the pictures of the ladies in their hands and began playing with their penis'.

They reached the spot where their clothes were and each sat down still pulling on their members. They commented on the women in the pictures, and on the girls at school.

"You know Dorothy in our Math class? I'm pretending I'M with her." said Jason as he leaned back and closed his eyes.

"Yah, that's about all you'll ever be able to do is pretend with her." Greg teased him.

"Last person to cum is a queer." yelled Clint as he pumped away. This got the rest of them pumping harder.

Finally, with a "God damn" Clint ejaculated.

"I knew it," Clint said jumping up, "I'm gonna keep track."

he said watching his wristwatch.

"One minute, two minutes." Clint called the time. "Come on you faggots, can't you cum?"

The other three boys kept looking at the pictures. Jeff was afraid of being called a "queer" if he didn't ejaculate but he never had. His right hand tired, and then he tried doing it with his left hand but that hand didn't work for him.

"Need some help?" Clint yelled.

Greg came.

"Two more now." Clint called. "Let me help Jeff."

Clint kneeled down in front of Jeff between his legs. "Here." he said as he placed his hand over Jeff's hand and helped him push up and down. Jeff was in shock as eventually Clint pushed his hand aside and began jerking Jeff with his own hand. Jason was still trying and so Greg did the same for Jason who leaned back and closed his eyes.

"I'm cumming!!" yelled Jason as he ejaculated all over Greg's hands.

"Yuck!" Greg yelled with a sneer as he wiped his hand in the under brush.

Jeff began to soften as Clint continued to try. Clint became a bit kinder as he told Jeff: "come on guy, come on you can do it.

"I've never done it before." said Jeff. "Just forget it."

Jeff pushed Clint aside and grabbing his shorts and pants he started putting them back on. He was crying when Clint walked up to him and put his arm around him.

"That's okay buddy, you're not queer, you just haven't gotten the things working yet." he said comforting Jeff.

"Maybe I won't ever be able to." Jeff said.

"I don't know, I never had that problem but maybe some day. Do you ever do it at home?" Clint asked.

"I tried it a couple of times." Jeff lied. "It ain't that big a thing. Forget it."

Okay, we'll forget it." Clint said as he and the others all dressed and went back to exploring.

The boys hiked around for quite a while then they all pulled their penis' out again and walked and jerked and walked and jerked and jerked keeping their eyes on the cards.

As a "consolation prize." Clint told Jeff to keep the cards for luck. He thought Jeff needed them better than his brother ever would.

9

One episode in Jeff's life bothered him more than any other after it happened. Jeff always tried to be sensitive to other people's differences; but sometimes even he, when spurred on by other boys, could be just as cruel as them.

There was a girl in the 5th and 6th grade named Martha who had polio and wore leg braces. The boys would call her the "koody girl" and scream when she approached and ran away. When picking players for dodge ball, the boys would cruelly say: "Don't pick her, she's the koody girl." Jeff knew this hurt her but he did little to help the situation. Instead of defending her, because he feared the boys would say she was his girlfriend, he went along laughing at the cruel "joke." She finally moved away so the boys did not have her to pick on any more.

There was also the "retarded" girl that lived next to one of Jeff's friends in Weston who the boys would get to lift her dress and pull down her panties. The boys would never touch her, but it was always a fun, though cruel, game to see how much of her body they could get her to expose.

One day her father, who was slightly handicapped also, caught them in their cruel activity and would not let her play with the boys again.

By Junior High in Weston, the boys found another "koody girl." This one was a boy. His name was Howard and, whether or not he was no one knew, he appeared to be "queer." The "queer" boy was a boy with effeminate mannerisms who spoke with raised voice and protruding tongue.

Hidden Shore

At school the boy was teased, but he had a friend named George who was a large brute of a boy with a low IQ who took to Howard because of his willingness to be a friend. George stood up for Howard whenever anyone would pick on Howard, but George would not fight; he was afraid to hurt anyone.

George helped keep the boys off of Howard, but if Howard was found by himself, they would tease him, call him queer, take his belongings, and chase him away.

At school Howard was relatively safe, but there were times that he was found away from school and this produced a smoldering firecracker.

One Saturday, Jeff, Greg, Stan, Clint and two other boys were exploring and skinny dipping up Dead Man Creek when to each of their surprise, down the trail by the creek came marching George and Howard.

The call went out: "Faggot" as one of the boys spotted the two innocent hikers. The boys who were in the water naked covered up their "private parts" in fear of exciting a "faggot." They jumped into their clothes and chased the two boys; catching them near a large spruce tree.

"What are we going to do to these faggots." yelled Clint.

"Let's string them up." yelled one of the other boys in true cowboy fashion.

To hang outlaws, the boys would need a rope. Fortunately, for them, they usually carried a rope to swing into the creek while skinny dipping. The rope was procured and the boys flung it over a branch and after tying a knot in the end and making a hangman's noose, the boys placed it over Howard's head and around his neck while they held George telling him that he'll be next.

Coming to their senses, the boys pulled down the rope and tied Howard and George to the old Spruce tree.

"I'll bet he doesn't even have a dick." yelled one of the boys.

"Let's see." said another. "You got a dick faggot?"

At this both Jeff and Greg stopped the others while Stan stood by. They had reached their limit and demanded the other boys stop.

Not to be stopped, the boys pushed them aside and proceeded to yank Howard's corduroy pants down to his knees. Saying "gross," Clint pulled Howard's under shorts down also.

"look at that." he yelled.

To all the boy's amazement, Howard was uncircumcised and his penis appeared to them to "hang to his knees."

"My God, you're a freak" Clint and the other boys yelled.

"A mutation."

"You belong in a circus, queerboy." they all went off.

The other boys kicked the two helpless boys in the stomachs, and untying the rope, the boys ran away leaving the other two boys in pain rolling on the ground.

When they arrived home, Jeff, Stan and Greg all talked about what they had done and felt sorry about it. They let Clint know that they were not happy about what had happened. He just called them wimps. They vowed never again to let themselves do such a thing to other unfortunate people. Jeff and Greg both apologized together to Howard and George who told them that their apology was not accepted and that some day God would punish them for what they did.

10

Children play many games. The boys were no different. Since receiving the game SHOOTS AND LADDERS and CANDYLAND at Christmas at the age of five, Jeff enjoyed all kinds of games. He graduated to new games as the years went by such as MOUSETRAP to LIFE and then to MONOPOLY. Sometimes boys created games: Cops and Robbers, Cowboys and Indians, Doctor and Patient. Sometimes they got so bored in the summer they even played School. Girls played house and dolls and eventually were asked to join the boys in Doctor and Patient. Innocent fun, but sometimes required the exposure of body parts such as the chest to hear heart beats. Usually Doctor and Patient is simply innocent.

One game that has been played for generations by boys and girls is Spin-the-Bottle. This game usually starts on the playground or at someone's home when the children are thrown together to play while their parents are busy. The first time Jeff and Stan played spin the bottle was when Yvette and Natalie's parents came to play poker with Mary and Bill. They sometimes played with the children underfoot, but usually they would lock the doors to the playroom and tell the children they needed to stay in the bedroom and play without disturbing them.

Gabe knew Spin-the-Bottle and so he instructed the two boys and the two girls that all they did was sit around in a circle and each person got a turn spinning a bottle in the center of the circle. Whoever the bottle pointed to when it stopped spinning had to do whatever challenge the spinner instructed or they lost.

The game began with Gabe. Since he knew the game he could spin first. They sat in a circle. Gabe to Jeff to Stan to Yvette to Natalie.

Gabe spun the bottle. It landed on Yvette.

"Yvette, you must jump up and down ten times on your left foot."

This accomplished, Yvette was able to spin. It landed on Gabe.

"Gabe, you must balance this bottle upside sown in the palm of your hand for one minute."

Timed and accomplished.

It went like this until Natalie got silly one time and told Stan to spank Yvette ten times. Not bad but contact was made.

Eventually, every once in a while a kiss was ordered. But that is as far as it went.

Yvette and Natalie's parents, Mr. & Mrs. Garcia, often came to the house or the boys would go to the girl's house with Mary and Bill. They never knew exactly why their parents locked the door but Gabe thought they made a lot of noise for just playing poker.

Sometimes Celia's parents, the Valdez's would play also or

Hidden Shore

Mr. and Mrs. Richardson would bring their kids, Monica, Jason and Adam. Sometimes the Babin's brought their daughter Ann. Sometimes the Chavez's neighbor's son Greg would come to play with his best friend Jeff. Other kids would sometimes wander in and play just because that is where everyone was. Sharon and Alicia Biddle were there with the kids often. The kids would play MONOPOLY, or the game of LIFE or Spin-the-Bottle.

As the children became older they began to pair off as boyfriend and girlfriend.

This is how Jeff acquired his first girlfriend Ann Babins. They paired at about the age of ten. Greg liked Yvette but Yvette liked Adam. So Greg settled for Celia. Jason paired up with Monica. Natalie never had much of anyone to pair with. Clint had no special girlfriend. Sharon and Alicia played with the kids often, but their parents never played poker with the other parents as well as Greg's parents.

The group played all the different games. The boys began to protect their individual girlfriends. If Spin-the-Bottle turned to kisses rules limiting physical contact were adopted.

Since Clint had no one special, he liked to act as a substitute boyfriend for Natalie, Sharon and Alicia.

One warm summer day the twelve were hiking up Dead Man Creek together to the boys favorite swimming hole. They sang and waded until they reached the spot with the rope to swing into the water. The boys had worn their swimming trunks, as they always did when they went up the creek. The girls had not. Usually, the trunks came off if it were just the boys, but this time the boys dived in leaving the girls on the bank visiting. Natalie wanted to swim with the boys so she borrowed one of the boy's shirts, hid behind a bush, and took her pants off and put on the shirt. The age of the kids at this point were 10 to 14 and so the girls were not all developed yet enough for it to make any difference if they had tops or not. As the other girls saw how much fun everyone was having, swinging on the rope into the water and swimming, they slowly one at time began to remove their pants and jumped into the water to swim in their panties, those that had them continued to wear their bras. The only ones left on the bank were Sharon and her sister Alicia. Sharon was the eldest and was embarrassed about her development. Alicia started to undress and Sharon stopped her. Finally deciding it was all right Sharon allowed Alicia to do it but Sharon simply tied her skirt up around her waist and waded into the water.

After a while, the kids were sitting around on the bank drying and slowly putting their clothes back on, when Clint suggested playing Spin-the-Bottle. Everyone except Sharon agreed. Sharon had never played Spin-the-Bottle at the house and had refused other attempts to play it. When the others agreed, she said "Then I'm already out, we're going Alicia."

"I want to play." Alicia pleaded.

"No. Now let's go." Sharon demanded and the two of them left the others wishing them well and returned home to Hidden Shore.

Since they did not have a bottle with them, Jeff and Clint devised a pointer made from a stick with a balance arm secured by a shoe string. The arm was centered and the stick would spin with a designated head to determine the point.

There were now ten of them; an equal number of boys and girls.

They spun the bottle a few times and the loser had to kiss the winner but after a very short time they all decided to play a new game suggested by Clint which they called Strip-the-Bottle. The rule was that at the first spin that a person received, the spinee had to kiss the spinner or the spinner could sock the spinee.

The second time the spinee had the pointer land on him or her then that person would have to remove an article of clothes. No one could swim until the last article of clothing was gone. When everyone was in the water, except one, then the rest could throw that one in the water with whatever he or she had on and get it wet.

Jeff was chosen as the first spinner, he spun to Clint. Clint said "I'm not kissing you, go ahead and hit me." as he offered his shoulder.

Clint spun Ann. Ann kissed Clint.

Ann spun Celia. Celia kissed Ann.

Hidden Shore

Celia spun Jeff. Jeff kissed Celia.

Jeff spun Natalie. Natalie kissed Jeff.

Natalie spun Adam. Adam kissed Natalie.

Adam spun Monica. Monica kissed Adam.

Monica spun Natalie. Little Natalie was first to remove her blouse. She wore no bra so she only had two items left.

Natalie spun Yvette. Yvette playfully kissed Natalie.

Yvette spun Ann. Ann removed her blouse. She also did not have a bra on.

Ann spun Jeff. Jeff removed his shirt.

Jeff spun Clint. Clint would not kiss Jeff and Jeff would not let him so Jeff was able to punch Clint.

Clint spun Monica. Monica removed her blouse. Though she was already developed enough to, she wore no bra.

Monica spun Celia. Celia removed her blouse. She did wear a brassier so she still had three items left.

Celia spun Yvette. Yvette removed her blouse. As with Monica she was already developed enough but she did not have a bra on so she was left with two items.

Yvette spun Adam. Adam removed his shirt.

Jason and Greg felt left out. No one had yet spun either of them.

Adam spun Ann. Ann removed her pants and stood in her under panties.

Ann spun Greg finally. Greg finally got to kiss Jeff's girlfriend Ann.

Greg spun Jason. Jason refused to kiss Greg so Greg punched him.

Jason spun Greg. Greg removed his shirt.

Greg spun Clint. Clint removed his shirt.

Clint spun Monica. Monica removed her pants

Monica spun Natalie. Natalie removed her pants.

Natalie spun Jason. Jason removed his Shirt.

Jason Spun Monica. This meant Monica would be the first one completely naked. She timidly removed her panties and walked as timidly into the water. Jeff had never seen a girl naked before.

All the boys watched Monica which made her nervous.

Since Jason had spun Monica and forced her to the water, they decided that he could spin again. Jason spun Greg. Greg removed his T-shirt.

The kids became very bored with the game by this point and they decided to forget the game and they all stripped naked and jumped into the pool and played and swam for hours. The egg had been broken.

None of these kids made physical contact as they played. It was just an innocent day of swimming with their best friends. After that they often got together and skinny dipped. On later dates, Alicia joined them and got to skinny dip too. Eventually, skinny dipping just became the way to swim among the kids. They never told their parents because they were sure their parents would not ever do anything like that.

As years passed, the girls one at a time stopped going. Eventually, it just became the boys again. Natalie, however, would go any time she could. She was the one for the boys.

11

Greg had always really been Jeff's best friend. Though Jeff spent more time with Clint, Greg was the friend he could turn to and talk about anything. He could talk about girls to Greg without fearing that Greg might say something crass or indecent. Since Jeff had no sisters, he knew very little about what it was like having someone of the opposite sex that was near his age around the house. Consequently, Jeff tended to place girls on a higher plain than his other friends did. Greg had two older sisters, much older, and he looked at girls as more of a problem, more of a bother.

Greg was an unwanted child, his parents were in their late 30's when they found out they were expecting an addition. His sisters were already teenagers when he was born and his parents were looking forward to a time without children. Greg was placed under the care of these sisters who, on the most part resented the responsibility which interfered with their dating and high school activities. When the girls graduated from high school and went away to college, old habits of leaving Greg under the care of others persisted and when he became old enough to care for himself, Greg was left home alone a considerable amount of the time. Jeff was between two brothers, so to escape them he spent much time at Greg's home which gave them plenty of time to talk about everything.

Greg learned earlier from his sisters about the birds and the bees. Jeff knew very little and Greg was an encyclopedia of sexual information. Greg did not mind spending time sharing his wealth of knowledge with Jeff. Though his information was packed with some misinformation, Greg was able to give Jeff a pretty thorough knowledge of how the female body was constructed and how it worked. For this Jeff was eternally grateful.

Greg had a little secret that he did not share with Jeff though. It was his fascination for women's clothing. It began when he was only about twelve years old. His sisters had packed much of their belongings into two cedar chests and stored them in what was once their bedroom but were now a guest room. It began simply by his happening upon them one afternoon when he was home alone. He found their underwear. The panties had an aroma that could not compare with his Fruit of the Looms. He would hold the panties up to his nose and breath in the scent. It was exquisite. Immediately he would have an erection. The next step was to hold them against his erection and rub them up and down along it's length. The first time he did it, he rubbed it too long and ejaculated into them. The thrill was devastating. Afraid that someone would find out he quickly brought himself under control and took the soiled panties next door and deposited them in Mr. Chaves' garbage can. Fortunately, his sisters never gave any indication that they were missing a pair of their panties but he vowed that would not happen again.

Just in case, the next time he ventured into the bedroom, he took a paper towel with him and kept it handy. This time he became a little bolder. He took off his pants and under shorts and while he was still limp, he rubbed another pair of panties all over his penis until it got hard. He laid back on the bed and felt it's softness meld among the softness of his penis which soon grew. He stopped. Waited for the feeling to go away. He wanted to do something else this time. He rolled back his knees, stuck his feet into the leg holes on the panties and slowly, not wanting to stretch or leave marks on them, pulled them up around his crotch and tucked his again soft penis within them. He reach back and pulled his penis up and into his anal cleavage so as to not see the penis. He then found a garter belt and wrapped it around his waist fastening it. He found a pair of nylons neatly rolled together and slowly pulled the stocking up over his left leg and then his right one. Clipping the garter clips to the top of the hose, he securely fastened them and ran his hands up and down his leg reveling in the feel of nylon against his own legs.

He then took off his shirt and T-shirt. He found one of his sister's brassieres and placed his nose within one of the cups of the brassier. The same feeling occurred as did when he breathed the exhilarating aroma of the panties. He hurriedly placed his arms through the straps of the bra and pulling it back, reached around and hooked the bra into place. He located a tissue box and wadding up tissue stuffed the brassier cups with the tissue giving him the full look.

He paraded around like this in front of the mirror for a few minutes and then stripped out of the garments and neatly placed them back where he had found them.

The closets of the spare room were filled with summer clothing that his sisters left behind. For his next adventure he decided to try on a blue pleated skirt with a pink silk blouse. He loved the look and was exhilarated by the way he felt in the outfit.

The next few times he tried different outfits and combinations. His favorite was finding his oldest sister's strapless bra and prom dress.

One day he determined that he wanted to try on a girdle. His sisters had no girdles. If they ever wore one, there were none in the chests.

This meant a more daring adventure: He had to raid his mother's underwear drawer. Her dresser held whole new and varied assortments such as underwire bras, a white and pink and a blue teddy, a white camisole, even a pair or white French boxer briefs. Her shoes even fit him, so he was able to try on a different pair of pumps every time he ventured among her drawer. For a religious lady, she had some very sexy outfits.

The girdle was invigorating. The feel of the pressure against his penis and legs made him quickly struggle with pulling the girdle down enough to lower his mother's panties and pull his penis from its restriction. He proceeded to pull on it until relief came in spurts all over the firmly held towel which he held tightly around the head of his penis so as not to get any of his seaman on any of his mother's beautiful underwear.

One day; in a corner just under her pink and blueberry nightgown Greg made a discovery that shook him and made him gorge in disbelief. In a box about the size of a cigar box, he found a white plastic gadget that was phallic shaped with a switch that made it hum when he flipped it. He knew what it was. He had only seen one in pictures in magazines which showed a woman holding one up to her cheek and advertised them as stress relievers. Okay, Greg knew different, but what was one of these things doing in his mother's underwear drawer and did his father know it was there?

This was more than Greg's young mind could fathom. He quickly stripped out of the unmanly clothes and returned them to their proper places.

The next day he heard his mother complain to his father that there were a couple of runs in her stockings that she knew were not there when she put them away.

"That's strange." his father said.

12

Clint and Jeff were inseparable most of the time. Greg was

a good friend but Jeff had always considered Clint his best friend. That was why when Jeff had the problem climaxing during that day in the hills, instead of making fun of Jeff, Clint valued his friendship enough to be sympathetic. That was why they remained friends, they knew each other's limits. Sometimes; however, even the closest friendships are strained.

Clint spent the night at Jeff's house often and Jeff would also spend the night at Clint's house. Clint had a playroom in his back yard which he would go to whenever he wanted to get away. When Jeff spent the night at Clint's, they always slept in the playroom.

One night in 1960, Jeff and Clint were "camping out" in Clint's playroom. They wrestled and played Monopoly until late at night. Clint brought out a new magazine that he had found at the dump while scrounging there a while ago.

"This is a queer magazine." Clint informed Jeff.

The magazine had pictures of men without clothes and in various poses. They proudly displayed their manhood for the camera. Some were flaccid, but most were erect.

"Look at the size of some of these," Clint pointed out for Jeff, "let's see if you figure this guy is about six feet tall, then he must be eight and a half or nine inches long. How long are you Jeff?"

"I don't know, I never measured myself." Jeff responded.

"I have, I'm seven inches long and I'm only fifteen, imagine by the time I'm eighteen I'll probably be ten inches long."

Jeff began to wonder.

"Take off your pants Jeff, lets measure."

"You too Clint."

Clint pulled out a yard stick and measured Jeff flaccid.

"Three and a half inches." Clint teased.

"You mean hard don't you?" asked Jeff.

"Well, make it hard then."

Clint reached over and began to pull on Jeff's flaccid penis.

"Come on, do me; that's not fair." Clint begged Jeff.

Jeff reached over and both boys began to massage each other. They leaned against the wall and relaxed as they both became erect.

Clint pulled his yard stick out again and measured Jeff as six inches.

"No, it begins here." Jeff indicated where he thought his penis began from the underside.

"Well, that makes me seven and a half if your six and a half." Clint argued.

The controversy erupted as to the true starting point for measurement.

Clint suddenly stuck his finger in and toward the back slightly tickling Jeff's anus. Jeff jumped and told him that it tickled. Clint continued to slowly run his finger from down the area between the bottom of Jeff and his back side. Jeff became very erect.

"Clint, that's not good to do." Jeff said as he breathed with difficulty.

"It feels good though don't it?" Clint asked. "Why don't you do it to me."

Jeff timidly reach and ran his finger just as Clint was doing. Clint while still fingering Jeff reached with his other hand and pumped up and down on Jeff's penis and Jeff reciprocated.

"Have you ever shot yet Jeff?" Clint asked.

"Yes, once." Jeff answered with difficulty. The boys kept the play up until Jeff finally ejaculated all over Clint's hand.

"Oh man." Jeff proclaimed.

Clint told him to lay on his stomach. "I haven't shot yet." Clint protested.

When Jeff laid on his stomach, Clint began running his finger along and up to Jeff's anus. "I've already done it." Jeff protested.

"Wait," Clint cautioned.

Clint then took a jar of Vaseline from a drawer he had and brought some out and rubbed it into the palm of his hand.

"What are you doing Clint." asked Jeff.

"This will help me." Clint responded.

Clint covered his penis with the Vaseline and fingered some on Jeff's behind.

"No, Clint. What are you doing." Jeff loudly protested.

Clint jumped on Jeff's back holding him down and slowly tried to insert himself into Jeff. Jeff continued to protest. Clint pumped up and down into Jeff.

"Stop!!" Jeff protested.

"Just for a minute Jeff."

"You jerk, what are you?" Jeff accused Clint of being gay.

Clint then took himself in his hand and began pumping away while Jeff sat incredulous about what had just happened. Clint finally ejaculated and laid back exhausted.

"What the fuck is wrong with you?" Jeff yelled.

Clint began to cry. Jeff was left speechless. Clint cried and gagged as his crying was so fitful. "I'm sorry Jeff, you just don't understand."

"I know that was a queer thing to do. I thought you always hated queers."

"Jeff please, I have to explain. Your my best friend aren't you?"

"Well, yes but you just kind of raped me."

"I'm sorry Jeff, I'm sometimes out of control. Jeff my father has been doing that to me for years when I'm in trouble. I've never told anyone. I used to think that every father did that to his kids when he took them out to punish them. I can't help it. I started thinking it was good, because instead of getting a beating he made me feel good and then he made me swear I would not tell anyone."

Clint broke out in fitful tears and Jeff put his arm around Clint and held him.

"Clint I don't know what to say, that is not how parents do things. You shouldn't let him do it again."

"I don't know how to stop him."

"Come and talk to me when it gets bad. Thank you for telling me, but if you ever try to do that again to me, I'll kill you." Clint and Jeff began to laugh knowing that Jeff was only kidding but Clint was genuinely afraid that if Jeff got mad he could hurt him.

They never discussed the situation again. Jeff never told anyone else what Clint had done except some day he would later confess to a girlfriend about it. Afterwards Clint and he were no longer close friends, but since Clint's father was the Police Chief in Weston and a respected man in the community Jeff could not see telling anyone about what Clint's father was doing to Clint.

13

January 13th 1962 was one of those beautiful mid-winter summer-like days when the sun actually gave off enough heat to make sitting in it pleasant. These kind of days often happen on the north coast of California.

Greg showed up early at Jeff's house and told him to call Clint to go to the beach.

"I've go a date today." boasted Clint

"Who with?" asked Jeff.

"None of your fucking business Jeff."

"Damned secretive, huh?" Jeff responded, "Must be ugly."

"Get off it. Gotta Go." said Clint as he hung up.

"That's weird! Almost like he's seeing someone else's girl or something." worried Jeff.

"Maybe it's a married woman." Greg joked

"I don't know, he's weird anyway." remarked Jeff, "Forget him, let's go."

It really never takes boys long to get over disappointment when it stood in the way of accomplishing a goal. Today's goal was to hit the beach while it was warm and pretend that it was summer and "have a blast."

So the boys took off and again walked the whole distance to the beach: Up the levee, down Railroad Road, to the bridge, across the bridge, past The Mill to South Beach.

The beach was totally empty of people even though it was a nice day. It always seemed that most people stayed away from the beaches in the winter, even when the weather was summer-like; so a beautiful day gave the boys lots of freedom to do as they wished on the beach.

They headed for the tide pools and spent an hour, or so, teasing the muscles and other crustaceans, as well as poking at the urchins like they had for years.

After a while, they headed to North Beach as soon as the tide was low enough to gain access. Their fort from the previous summer had obviously disappeared during one of the early Fall storms, as well as most of the sand. The rocks on the beach gave them new areas to poke and prod. Stripping naked, they waded and body surfed, and swam for almost two hours.

"The water seems a lot colder this winter," said Greg as they laid next to each other in the sun after their swim.

"It always seems colder when you ... wait! Did you hear that," Jeff exclaimed.

"What? All I hear is the surf!" Greg listened.

"No. Listen!"

"FAGGOTS."

"He's such a jerk, Jeff."

"I hear a girl laughing too."

"Shit." Greg exclaimed as he ran for his pants.

"See them?"

"No."

"It's Clint. I know it is." Jeff determined.

So the days swim ended as the boys never heard another word and again walked up the beach, past the tide pools, up South Beach, past The Mill, and across the bridge carrying their shirts and shoes and socks the whole way.

The next day was a repeat of the previous day. Greg showed up that Sunday morning, but this time told Jeff his mother could take them across the bridge in her Buick since she was heading to Weston for church.

"But we gotta hurry or Mom will leave." said Greg.

"The ride meant they would have an extra hour or so to explore their over explored beach.

"Hear from Clint last night?" Greg asked.

"No, I'm still a little pissed off at him for yesterday. You know, if he was going to the beach with this girl they could have joined us. Well, forget it."

This time there were two family groups on South Beach. If there were ever anyone on South Beach, the boys would not skinny dip on North Beach even though very few people hiked the distance to it.

This time the sea in its ever churning, dumping motion, retreating and depositing, had deposited what appeared to be a seal body on the beach.

"Watch out, there's a seal down there." warned Greg.

"Gross. But no flies yet. Must be a new kill. Probably a shark."

"Wait!! That's not a seal! That's person!!"

A sudden and uncontrolled spasm shot up both boys backs as they twitched and danced around on the sand shaking their arms about.

"Damn!! It is!!" yelled Jeff. "Let's get someone."

So the boys ran faster than they ever had, past the tide pools and when they arrived at South Beach they approached Mr. Chamberlain, the Fairbury High Librarian, who was sitting on a lounge chair reading a murder mystery.

"There's a body on North Beach." the boys yelled as they continued to twist, crossing their legs hoping to squeeze the shock out of them as they shook their arms in disbelief of what they had found. It was only then that they realized the putrid smell that had come from the body was human rather than the smell of rotting seal flesh which they had become accustomed to over many years.

Mr. Chamberlain ran with the boys after sending his wife and kids to town to call the police.

"Shall we get an ambulance?" she asked.

"It was dead. Right?" he asked the boys.

"I don't think anything that smelled like that could stand up and walk," Greg said sarcastically."

So they returned to North Beach with Mr. Chamberlain in tow and returned to the body.

As the boys held their noses, Mr. Chamberlain softly inserted his foot under the body and gave a heavy lift to turn the body over. It was a girl, nearly naked and bloated. It was probably the worst thing the boys had ever or would ever see.

After about thirty minutes, Clint's dad, the Weston Police Chief, arrived with a deputy. He questioned the boys and told them he would contact them if he needed them.

For the next week it was all they could talk about.

Jeff celebrated his 16th birthday that Tuesday, and when the boys saw Clint at school, they asked him if that was him at the beach. He denied it. Later, they asked him what happened on his date and he said: "The bitch stood me up."

The body turned out to be a Eureka girl. Nobody in Hidden Shore, Weston, or Fairbury knew her.

14

James Madison Abraham Lincoln Munro lived about a mile south of Dead Man Creek. He never was welcome to the social functions of Hidden Shore. His father had owned many acres of land and had kept sheep successfully on the land. His father's father had been freed by the daughter of his owner and had migrated to California spiriting away the teenage daughter of one of the other slaves.

Abe (which everyone called him) Munro was born prior to and had been raised during the depression. He inherited his father's land during World War 2 and slowly began to sell portions of the land to live off the sales until he finally had only an acre and a quarter left on which two houses sat.

Abe was a large built, small framed black man. He wore a beard because his kinky hair would curl when short and irritate his skin. If he shaved the course beard hairs would create puss pockets and in-grown hairs would irritate his face unbearably. Abe was barrel chested and thin waisted with a large rear end. His skin color was black; very black. He stood only 5'9" but weighed 225 pounds.

Hidden Shore

He was a hard worker on the land but most of his attempts to make money off of it failed. He simply had no mind for ranching.

His father died in a farm accident when a farm tractor fell on his head crushing him. This left Abe alone with his mother who died two years later leaving Abe alone. He buried both of his parents at the Hidden Shore Cemetery on the north east corner which was the only place that the cemetery operators would allow "people of their sort" to be buried; right near the pauper graves.

Abe had a younger brother named Jacob who joined the navy in World War 2. He did well for himself and never bothered Abe. Jacob had a son and a daughter who seldom saw their Uncle Jim. They lived in Oakland.

Abe perpetually suffered from the itch and pain from his hair. He found that Vaseline softened the hairs and this attempt to soothe the itch caused Abe to keep a complete covering of Vaseline all over his whole body. When anyone would condescend to shake his hand, it would be accompanied with the "slimy" feeling of Vaseline.

Abe walked to town twice a week; he always made four stops. First to the bank to withdraw the money he needed until his next trip; Second to the grocery store for food and chew; Third to the pharmacy for aspirin and Vaseline and finally to the liquor store for his Thunderbird wine. He drank only Thunderbird wine.

In March 1961, Abe ran out of the money from his land sales. All he had remaining was his acre and a quarter. He applied for an equity loan and to his chagrin the bank only would loan him $12,000.

Angrily, he withdrew all twelve thousand dollars refusing to deposit any money in his account. The bank closed his account without regret.

Abe always wore a pair of blue mechanics coveralls, a filthy red jacket and a navy blue stocking cap over his well Vaselined head. He stuffed the $12,000 in the inside pocket of his coveralls and whenever he made future purchases he pulled his fat fold of twenty dollar bills out and everyone in town now talked about all the money he had with him.

Abe had two houses, a barn, a chicken coop and two pheasant coops on his property. One of the houses was a small one and the other was the old family house but after his mother died, Abe moved out of it and just used it for storage.

Abe was always fearful of cougars coming on his property and killing his pheasants or chickens. He set up a trap in which he extended a cord across between the two houses at night which if a cougar would hit the cord, a shotgun would fire and he hoped would kill it. Twice he managed to kill a doe so he had venison for dinner for the rest of the week and jerky for the next month.

One night he heard something out on his property. He disconnected the cord from his shotgun and ran out to confront the intruder with a second shotgun. A shotgun blast was heard by one of his near neighbors but the next day it was discovered that Abe had tripped over the cord and accidentally shot himself.

This was the version determined by the police. However, no second shotgun was found and his cash had disappeared.

No one knew that one of the local boys had witnessed Abe making a purchase at the drug store and followed him to his property, hid in the woods until just after nightfall and then shot Abe near his trip cord and set it up to look like the accident that the police had bought into.

The bank laid claim to the property. What was left of the twelve thousand dollars was never discovered.

15

On December, 27th 1962, a bus pulled into the depot in Eureka and a 14-year-old girl stepped from the bus to be met by her Uncle Jim and Aunt Peggy. Her name was Melody Pruite. She had just arrived from San Francisco leaving her Mother, Grandmother, and Brother there to live because of an incident that had occurred the year before that had so upset the family that a need to separate precipitated her moving to Weston for a time. She was shuffled to her Uncles home in Weston for what her mother called "your own good."

Nervous about the change of residence she wanted to be home. She knew her Uncle who had visited his sister a couple of times in San Francisco. Though her Mother and her Uncle were not close, her Mother felt it was better to have Melody there. He was a good man and she liked her Aunt also, but they were not her Mother.

Her Aunt registered her into Weston Junior High and she began attending classes after the start of the semester. This was difficult for her. She had trouble finding good friends and stayed mostly to herself. Eventually, she did find a boyfriend for about a week named Leonard, but she did not like a lot of things about him. She told him she did not want him any more so the relationship ended. She had left a boyfriend in San Francisco but she never heard from him after she moved.

She did begin to feel more comfortable after she began to go somewhere with her Aunt and Uncle on a regular basis; however, she still wanted to return to San Francisco and be with her Mother again.

16

One day in January, when she was having breakfast with her Aunt Peggy, her Aunt approached her about something while sitting in the kitchen talking.

"Melody, your Uncle and I have been wanting to talk to you about something for a long time, but we have had trouble figuring out how to approach you about it."

"You can talk to me about anything, but why the mystery?" she asked.

Her Aunt reached across the table and placed her hand on Melody's.

"Do you know what a naturist is Melody?"

"No, I don't." was her reply.

"A naturist is a person who believes that the natural way that

Hidden Shore

God created people and all other things is the most beautiful. People ruin God's gifts by disguising them and that is what a naturist believes ruins people. They dress in clothes which disguises their natural beauty. Naturists believe that the nude body is a beautiful thing and just as with the beauty of nature, people should share their beauty by living without clothing."

"Don't they call them nudists?" asked Melody.

"Some people do. We do sometimes but we prefer to call our selves naturists rather than nudists."

"So you and Uncle Jim are naturists." she shot back.

"Does that bother you?"

"Well,...no, but I couldn't..."

"Are you sure?" Aunt Peg pressed.

"I'd be too embarrassed."

"It's really not embarrassing when there are others who are the same Mel. Can I show you?"

"What do you mean."

Peg began to undo the buttons of her house dress and asked Melody "Can I take my clothes off and show you how I prefer to live?"

Melody sat in shock averting her eyes not quite sure of what to say. Recognizing how uncomfortable Melody was about her undressing in front of her, Aunt Peg stopped and asked her: 'Would you rather I not do this?"

"Well, this is kind of embarrassing Aunt Peggy, it seems kind of strange. I'm not used to this kind of thing."

"Let me go into the bedroom and I'll return after I'm ready."

She left Melody alone and after a couple of minutes returned fully undressed. "Does this bother you."

"A little, but that's okay." Melody laughed embarrassed.

"Your Uncle and I have always lived nude in the house, but we started dressing for you. Now we would like to do it again but we want you to be comfortable.

"You mean Uncle Jim will be like that also?"

"We'd like you to feel comfortable about doing it also." she shockingly told Melody. "What do you think."

Hidden Shore

"This is really strange, Aunt Peggy."

"Melody, when I was a little girl my folks moved to a farm in a mid-western state. There were no neighbors near. The closest was better than a mile away. The back half of the farm was in timber. No ax had ever come near the woods as there was plenty of fire wood closer to the house. Through the middle of the woods ran a stream of sparkling water. As a very little girl I loved to go back to this stream and wade. Then one day my sister and I were wading and we decided to try a part of the stream where we had never been. We found that it was too deep for us to wade with our clothes on. So I said 'Ruby, let's take everything off and wade.' Without a moment's hesitation we climbed out on the bank and removed the last stitch of clothing. We were used to being nude together in our bedroom so thought nothing of seeing each other's bodies. We sure did enjoy that experience with the sun shining on us through the trees, the warm water playing over our bodies."

"We had such pleasure that afternoon that we decided to come back the next day and spend the whole day, if we could coax mother into giving us a lunch of some kind. Sure enough, mother gave us the lunch. No sooner had we gotten to the stream than we took off our clothes and proceeded to get in the water. After a while we came out of the water and, having climbed up on the bank, we ran through the trees in the sheer joy of childhood. Neither of us gave a thought to the fact that we were naked. We were enjoying life to the fullest. All that summer we spent as much time as we could in our retreat. Several summers passed with us going as often as we could to our pool to swim and play with the warm breezes gently caressing our bodies."

"Then came the spring when I was twelve and Ruby was thirteen. My aunt in the city wrote and asked that Ruby come in and spend the summer with her. My aunt had no children. She wanted Ruby to stay on with her that fall and go to high school. As there was no high school closer to us than the County seat my folks let her stay on. From then on Ruby never came home except for short stays of a few days. So I went to the woods alone. But I still got a thrill out of it. Though I was getting larger all the time, the joy of being naked was still with me. Whenever duties in the home did not require me I was out there with myself and the glorious summer air."

"The summer I was thirteen a family moved to the farm joining ours on the north. They had one child - a boy of just my age. I shall never forget the first time I saw him. I had gone back to the swimming hole one afternoon. I had removed my dress, which was the only article of clothing I had on, as soon as I came to the woods. When I came to the pool I dropped my dress on the bank as I had done so many times before and went headfirst into the pool. How long I was in the water I do not know. I recall that when I raised up to shake the water out of my eyes I became conscious of the presence of someone else at the other end of the pool. There was the neighbor boy. He was standing in the water as though he were undecided whether to run or what. The water was above his middle so I could not tell for sure whether he had on trunks or not. But I rather thought not from the way his body looked through the crystal clear water. There we stood and looked at each other. At the time it seemed like hours, but in reality it was only a few seconds. Where I was, the water was up to my navel. At first I wondered if he had been there and seen me as I came down the path with my dress over my arm. Then on second thought I said, 'Well.'"

"That single word seemed to break the spell. All of a sudden I came to realize that I did not care how much of me he had seen. There was nothing about my body of which I needed to be ashamed. People told me that I was the best formed girl of my age in the community and I recalled that I had never been sick a day in my life, except when I had the 'three-day measles.' I attributed my good health to my nudity in the summer time."

"But there we stood in the water. A naked boy and a naked girl: each of us keenly alive. I could see from his well tanned body that this was not the first time he had been nude. So I said to him, 'Ever been nude before?'"

"He looked at me and replied, 'Lots of times; and I like it. That is the only way to swim and it's lots more fun to play out doors while nude than with a lot of clothes on.'"

"'Yes,' I agreed. 'Why shouldn't we swim together and play together this way?'"

"'This is the way the Lord made us and He must be wise.'"

"With those words he came a little closer to me and said, 'There has always been a great question in my mind and you can give me the answer right now if you are willing. May be you have the same question.'"

"'What's that?' I said."

"'Why my people make such a hushed up and secret matter out of the body. I have asked my parents lots of times as to what the difference is between girls and boys. Of course being on a farm, I know in a general way from seeing the stock. But, as you can imagine, my parents have always given me some evasive answer. I have been too timid to talk to any one else about it. But what's wrong in that?'"

"'Well, I don't know where any wrong could come from a question like that.' I replied. 'I have always wondered about those lines, too. Maybe this would be a good time to answer our questions for ourselves.'"

"His eyes met mine in a clear, understanding way and they plainly said, 'Do you dare?'"

"'Yes I dare,' I said, as I began to climb out of the water. 'Let's get up here on the bank where we can see better.' And there we were - boy and girl thirteen years of age, the age of natural inquisitiveness. We stood apart for a while looking at each other. There was not an inch of my body that his eyes did not cover and I missed none of his. Then I asked him to turn around. This he did. I saw his well tanned shoulders and back. He was well formed for a boy. Then I turned that he might see my back. In a few minutes our curiosity was satisfied. We each knew what the other's body was like. We asked various questions of each about the sexual parts. Then he said, 'Let's swim,' and like a flash he dived into the water. I followed."

"We swam, dived, and chased each other in and out of the water until the sun was well down. Then we realized that we must be going home. We had learned more about sex in that afternoon together than in all of our years before. Yet neither of us had the least thought of anything impure. We were interested in God's creations. We agreed to meet there again the following Saturday at one o'clock."

"At one on Saturday afternoon we were there. I reached the place a little ahead of him and had already put my dress on the grass. He had undressed as he came through the woods, for there he came naked and unashamed. He had left his clothes just inside the woods gate. His folks and mine had gone to the County seat and would not return until late; so we knew that we were all alone for the rest of the day. We ran, climbed trees, swam, laid in the sun, and in general enjoyed ourselves. There was not one word of sex that day. Our minds were satisfied the day before. We were just young animals enjoying ourselves just as we were intended to be - nude. The rest of the summer we met at the pool at least two afternoons a week. As I look back on it now, I believe that those were the beginning of the happiest days of my life."

"The next spring, as soon as the sun began to warm things up a bit, I went back to the pool. As soon as I was well in the woods I came out of my coveralls which I had been wearing about the stable. I was going along enjoying the gentle breeze on my bare body when I heard Jim whistle. I thought that it would be fun to hide behind a tree and jump at him as he came by. When he came alongside, naked as he was born, I jumped and said, 'Boo.' He started to run for the pool saying, 'You can't catch me.' I did not catch him but I did hit the water about the same time that he did. The water was so cool that we soon came out. We ran about on the green grass for a while. Then we sat down on a log together and began to talk."

"There we sat, a boy and a girl fourteen years old. There we were talking about life and the joy of life. It was our first trip to the pool that year. We had seen little of each other during the winter. He had to tell me about his colt and I took great delight telling him about my chickens and ducks. Every day that we could not get together that summer was a day lost. So we passed the months and another year went by. Then came the spring when we were fifteen. We met just inside the woods that day. There we undressed

Hidden Shore

together. During the winter it seemed that I had developed into womanhood. To me it seemed that my whole body had undergone some kind of change. I knew that I was different from what I was the last time we had been nude together. I wondered if he would notice the difference in me. But in a moment I saw that he had changed also. During the winter months he had taken on the build of a man. I noticed with pride how his shoulders had broadened out and how his arms and legs were filling out from what they had been. For a moment we stood and looked over each other in utter frankness. There was nothing of which to be ashamed. We were together nude once more and that made us happy. We joined hands and ran for the pool."

"Summers came and went. Your Uncle Jim went away to college and I went to a school in the city. We knew that we were in love with each other. We were counting the years, the months, the weeks, and then the days until we should be out of school and back on the farms. Our folks were aware of our plans to marry and they had told us that when we were ready to go to housekeeping they would move to the city and let us have either of the houses we wanted to live in. We decided on a new house to be built in the woods where we had enjoyed ourselves so much. I shall never forget the day after the folks had all left. We had been in our new home about ten days. Jim's folks and mine had become a little too old and wanted to get away from the farm. We stood by the gate of the north farm and watched the two couples drive away together. As they turned the bend in the lane, Jim turned to me and said, 'Let's spend a while in the pool.' Right there we removed our clothing and raced for the stream. We spent that summer almost in a dream. I wore nothing about the house and Jim went the same way on the farm except that when he went over toward the lane he carried his overalls with him."

"Five years later we lost the farm and moved here to Weston. We have never been dressed at home ever since. Whenever we are indoors we are naked. We think that we are healthier because of it."

Peggy began to do her normal routine of cooking dinner. And invited Melody to help. Melody helped feeling some at ease from the pressure of the moment as they began to talk and prepare dinner as they always had.

When Jim arrived from work he walked in and placed his lunch box on the kitchen table and looking delightfully at his wife, he kissed her and asked: "So you talked to her?"

"Yes Jim, she's nervous right now. Do you mind if he does the same Melody? asked her Aunt.

"Have you ever seen a man without clothing before." her Uncle asked.

"Just once." she shyly responded.

"Well? Do you mind Mel?" he asked.

"Ah, No. Do I have to?" she countered.

"No, absolutely not. Only if you wish. We want you to just be comfortable as we would like to be. If you ever want to walk around undressed feel free, but if you feel more comfortable with clothes, then you wear them. We sometimes do but sometimes we don't. We do whatever we wish." Peg explained.

"And I'd like to get ready for dinner." Uncle Jim announced and went into their bedroom."

Dinner that evening was very difficult for Melody. She did not say much but her Uncle and Aunt did not pry either. Uncle Jim had returned with no clothes on and she felt it was not as bad after all. She just did not know what to say.

A coincidence was that the first man she had ever seen naked was her Uncle about five years before. When she was younger he and Aunt Peg had visited her Mother in San Francisco and she and a friend of hers had peeked at him when he was in the bathroom taking a shower. The friend wanted Melody to see what a man looked like and so they had sneaked a peek one morning when her Uncle was there alone and she was playing with her friend. So unknown to her Uncle Jim, when he walked out into the kitchen nude that evening, Melody already knew what to expect.

This is how it went for about the next month. Sometimes her Aunt and Uncle were dressed around the house, sometimes not. If there was any possibility that someone might come over they were always dressed. Things began to change for her. When she got up in the mornings she began not to wear a robe. Then she would begin to walk to the bathroom in her underwear and finally she even began to feel comfortable enough to undress and then walk directly to the bathroom for a bath without any clothes. She even tried sleeping nude but she missed the warmth of her bedclothes and quickly reversed that; always dressing for bed.

One day she was preparing for a bath in her room and she headed to the bathroom undressed. Peg and Jim walked out of their room equally undressed and they met in the hallway. This was the first time they were all nude standing together. She stopped, looked at them, smiled, and Uncle Jim motioned her to go in to the bathroom. As they walked by she called to them:

"Uncle Jim? Aunt Peggy?" The two stopped and faced her. "Thank you for making me feel so comfortable. Next time that you go to your camp, can I go with you?"

"You betcha" they said in unison.

17

The first trip to a nudist (or naturist) camp was difficult for Melody. They arrived pulling a trailer into a parking area where there were many other trailers. The camp had everything: stores, picnic areas, food stands, swimming pools, tennis courts, archery range, and many other things. What stood out for her were the different people of all ages from babies to obvious Great Grandparents. None seemed to care whether they were fat or skinny or bald or hairy. No one was ugly because they were comfortable with their nudity. They had beauty contests and played games such as Twister and three legged races and all other kinds of fun things to do.

There were several girls and boys her own age whom she was introduced to and who took her under their wings and made her feel comfortable. Soon she played and swam and had more fun than she had ever had in her life. One girl in particular, named Linda, became her best friend. She found friendships with boys and girls unlike any she had ever developed in school. May of the love games played between teenagers were forgotten as each one enjoyed just being together. These kids bonded as they shared their common interest: Naturism.

Melody went to the camp several times with her Aunt and Uncle on the weekends. That March, she met another person, somewhere else, that would make her life outside of the camps just as wonderful.

18

Jeffrey Williams was usually a fine student. He was not an A student but he occasionally brought A's home. He never got into trouble. Therefore it was out of character that on Monday March 26th 1962, Jeff was late for school. He took the bus as usual in the morning but when he arrived, he went across the street from the school and bought a donut and milk in the Beanery.

He did this quite frequently. It never created any problems but this time he became so involved in the book he was reading, On The Beach by Neville Shute, that he failed to hear the bell ring for the start of Home Room.

When he finally looked at his watch and realized he was late, he ran as briskly as he could to class. The teacher asked him why he was late to which he replied:

"I got off the bus and was walking by the Beanery when I suddenly noticed that my shoe was untied. I didn't want to trip and fall so seeing a delivery truck parked in front of the Beanery, I set my books on his rear bumper and proceeded to tie my shoe. Well, gosh I didn't know that the driver had finished his delivery and was about to take off. So, that's just what he did because suddenly the truck took off forcing me to slip onto the pavement. I stood helplessly watching my books as they went down the street hanging precariously on the truck's back bumper. I jumped as quickly as I could to my feet and proceeded to run toward the truck as fast as my feet could carry me. About two blocks down the street I saw him stop at Ruth's grocery so I laid on with the pumping of my feet knowing that my time was limited and I had to be to school shortly. Just as I began to reach the rear of the truck, it took off again. I chased it for a another couple of blocks before it stopped again, but unfortunately I again was not able to reach my destination before the truck took off again. Finally after it's third stop I was able to hail the driver as he began to gain entry into the truck and the gentleman was kind enough to wait until I caught up to him and retrieved my evasive books. Mr. Skowran: by then I was over five blocks from school and pretty darned tuckered. I'm here now, though."

Mr. Skowran, of course, would not buy the tall tale. Jeff was sent to detention which meant he had to report to the Dean of Boys: Mr. Harding.

"I see you were late, Mr. Williams?" the dean asked.

"Yah, I'm not sure what happens now?"

"We'll let's see." Mr. Harding pondered, "I haven't ever seen you in here before. Is that right?"

"Yes, sir."

"I'm supposed to call your parents but I need some help tomorrow during the second half of school for an orientation meeting for next semester's incoming freshmen. If you'll "volunteer" to help, I'll give you a pass back to class and this won't even show up on your records."

Jeff pondered the choice for a moment and then agreed. He would have really rather had the dean call his folks, but he had no idea what would happen if he did not reach them, and he was sure they were not home.

So on March 27th, right after lunch, Jeff, who was a sophomore at the time, helped Mr. Harding orient some "Junior High School brats."

It turned out that this chore was not such a burden after all. The kids were pretty nervous about actually being on the grounds of the school.

His job was to help with any students that seemed to be

confused about anything and answer any questions they might have concerning location of cafeteria, rest rooms, assembly hall, gymnasium and anything else. He liked the job actually. He felt older some how, and he noticed that some of the girls seemed to take special interest in him, so he tried to be as helpful as he could.

One girl in particular made quite an impression on him. She was obviously very shy but also very intelligent. Since he had no girlfriends at the time he began to follow just close enough to hear her conversations, hoping to harvest away enough information that would be helpful just in case she was free. Jeff thought she was about the nicest looking girl he had ever seen. She was short, had just longer than shoulder length hair. She wore a pleated skirt and blue blouse with knee socks and tennis shoes.

Suddenly he heard someone call her Mel. "Mel, what a funny name," he thought.

What next? Jeff was not really experienced at "the move" that seemed to come natural to other boys. He stealthily meandered amongst the kids, waiting for the chance, like the fox to his prey, to pounce on this innocent creature that had so effectively began to monopolize his attention.

Finally his opportunity occurred. Mr. Harding guided the young students into the assembly hall and there was to be a coordination speech from the principal Mr. Chelsea.

As everyone took their seats in the hall, Jeff made his move. He asked the girl standing next to her if she had any questions and she answered in the negative. He then, for good measure asked a boy the same question, but seeing that this all important girl named Mel was about to enter a row of seats, he cut, turned abruptly from the boy and asked her: "Do you have any questions." His voice did not crack, but deep within his gut he felt a shudder and was perspiring and shaking and was sure everyone could see it.

She paused for a second, started to speak, and then looked up at him. When she made eye contact, he was bit. He was sure that this was how love at first sight felt.

Without hesitating, he followed her into the row of seats and sat pretending that Mr. Chelsea's speech was just as informative to him as it was to the new students.

The speech and the rest of the doings in the auditorium lasted about 20 minutes. The next part of the tour brought them to the study hall. Jeff stayed as close as he could to his new found friend. In the study hall sat Sharon. Seeing Jeff, Sharon asked him why he was with all the "kids."

"I'm helping Mr. Harding for orientation." Jeff answered, trying not to let this Mel out of his sight.

"See that girl over there?" he whispered, trusting Sharon not to do anything to embarrass him, "Her name is Mel, do you know her."

"Nope," was all she replied.

From study hall they finished in the cafeteria. Jeff actually did well there.

"So, gonna be here next year I assume?"

"Yah," she said, "What grade are you in?"

"My God," he thought, "a question."

"I'm a sophomore now but by the time you get here I'll be a junior of course." Jeff replied to her question.

"How do you like it here in high school?"

"Much better than I did in junior high. Everyone's so much more mature here." he said worrying immediately whether she would be offended by his calling junior highers immature."

"I can't wait, I haven't liked Weston since I first got there in January. I was new and when we start here, we will all be new, then I might be more comfortable."

"Yah, and you'll have a head start, you'll have me as a friend already." damn, he thought as he said it, that was good.

"Yah, I'm Melody, but everyone calls me Mel."

"Hi! I'm Jeff, everybody calls me ... Jeff."

They laughed.

Sitting down, they began to talk. Found out they both liked history, but Melody liked Science which was Jeff's worst subject. Melody hated PE but loved to run.

That twenty minutes before the teachers began to gather everyone together went faster than any twenty minutes Jeff had ever lived.

Quickly he shot: "Got a boyfriend."

"Nah, I had one but, well you know!" she said with a grimace.

"Bye, see you in September!"

"Nice meeting you, Jeff." she said as she walked away.

All Jeff could think of on the way home on the bus was that the last word she said to him was his name. It will forever be etched on his brain. "Jeff. Jeff. Jee...ef. Nice meeting you Jeff. I don't have a boyfriend, Jeff. I love you, Jeff." It all kept going around and around in his mind. "Nice meeting you Jeff."

"Oh my God!!!!! I won't see her again for... SIX MONTHS !!!" he suddenly realized. "She'll get a boyfriend. She'll forget me. Oh my God, what do I do now."

19

Jeffrey **E**dward **W**illiams was now in a terrible quandary. He had to devise a plan to see MELODY again. "I really have to see... my lovely Melody. I really have to see... my lovely Melody." He kept singing over and over again as he walked marching to the cadence.

It only took two more days for an answer to come to him. Thanks to his best friend Sharon. On the bus on the way to school that Thursday Sharon said: " How you doing Casanova?"

"Casanova?" Jeff laughed.

"Yah, Alicia said that Yvette was talking to her and she knows this girl in her school that was asking if anyone knew anything about a guy named Jeff from high school and Yvette said she knew you." Sharon filled him in. "Seems she's pretty interested in who you are and Vette told her you lived in Hidden Shore. Seems she wants you to ask her out or something. Know what her name

Hidden Shore

is?"

"Melody?" said Jeff.

"Yah, that's the girl you pointed out to me the other day, Right?"

"Yah."

"Well, what you gonna do now?" Sharon asked.

" I don't know." Jeff answered confused. "Whadda you think?"

"I guess I'm gonna have to fix you guys up somehow since I'll bet you don't have the guts to just go knock on her door and ask her out yourself."

"Ah, wow; could you?" he pleaded.

"Nah, I don't have any time to fool with chasing little girls down for you." she teased.

"Well I guess I'll have to do something." Jeff retorted.

"Get out of here, I've already made some plans, I'll drive over to your house tonight and we'll talk about them."

The plan was made; It was a simple one. Sharon discovered that Melody went to the public library in Weston and read and did homework every Monday, Wednesday and Friday. So Jeff was to get off the bus in Weston and go to the library. It worked well. The first time Jeff walked in on the next Monday and saw Melody reading by herself. He nervously approached her.

"Hi, how are you?"

"Hi Jeff!" she lit up having seen him.

There it was again. All Jeff could think of was how much he loved the way she said Jeff; more like Geee-ef.

"What are you doing here?" she continued with a smile broad enough to assure Jeff that she wasn't disappointed.

"I come here all the time." Jeff lied, "Maybe we didn't notice each other because we hadn't met yet."

Melody doubted the facts but did not care because she was so happy to see him.

"I'm studying your favorite subject." she teased showing him her science book. "Want to sit and study with me?"

"Sure."

Hidden Shore

And that is how it all started. Jeff would ride the bus only to Weston and walk home about an hour after. He would always get home late telling his Mother that he was at the library doing his homework to Mary's obvious pleasure.

The first Monday they studied. Wednesday they studied. Friday after "studying" they went behind the library where there was a playground and they swung on the swings together.

The second week went about the same: Monday "study," swing. Wednesday "study" swing. The second Friday; however, after the "study" session, the two walked to Randy's Soda Shop and to Melody's surprise, and Jeff's pretended surprise, Sharon was there and they sat with her.

Sharon had contributed to this "romantic escapade" so she felt she needed to meet and , hopefully, pass approval on Jeff's new-found love.

"Guess you know I'm Jeff's girlfriend." Sharon said with a stare of disbelief from Jeff.

"April fool." she said. "I know, it's Friday the thirteenth but still seemed appropriate."

So Jeff sat and nervously listened as Sharon and Melody talked as old friends. It was amazing how easy it was for them to open up. He was a little jealous because Melody and himself had not got along as well yet.

"Well, I gotta go" Sharon finally said. "I think I approve."

"Now come on you guys." Sharon continued as she reached over and grabbed Jeff's right hand and Melody's left and placed them among each other. "This is the last help your gonna get from me."

Sharon walked away. Jeff held tightly to the hand that meant more to him than anything in the world at that moment. He did not let go when they got up. He did not let go when he paid for their sodas. He did not let go as he walked her home for the first time.

When they arrived at her house, Melody said: "I think I'll need this back now." she pulled her hand from his gentle grip.

Jeff said goodbye and slowly walked away as she watched from her porch. When he got to the sidewalk she assured him: "You

Hidden Shore

can have it back next time Jeff." and went into her house.

Jeff. She said Jeff again. The last word she said to him was Jeff again. The three mile walk was definitely a pleasure to Jeff as he walked vowing not to wash his hand when he got home. He placed his right hand to his nose and noticed he could smell her perfume all the way home.

So now their relationship progressed to Library and walks home. Holding hands, the locals in Weston began to get used to seeing those two "love birds" walking down the street.

Eventually, Melody invited Jeff in to meet her Aunt and then her Uncle. This was done on Monday April 30th. On Friday it was arranged for Melody to go to Jeff's house to meet his mother and brothers. To do this, Jeff asked Gabe's girlfriend Stephanie, who lived next door and went by the name of Stevie, to meet Melody's Aunt and Uncle so that Melody could stay at her house that weekend. Gabe drove Stevie to Melody's house and Stevie made such a good impression that the arrangement was approved.

From then on, besides the Monday, Wednesday and Friday meets at the library, most weekends Melody stayed at Stevie's to visit with Jeff in Hidden Shore.

The weekends became very special for Jeff and Mel. Walks mostly. Holding hands. They walked on the beach most of the time with April turning to May and then to June 1962.

On Saturday June 2nd, Jeff finally found the courage to progress in their relationship. Melody liked the tide pool area of the beach and she and Jeff spent many hours there; sometimes with Greg or Stan or Stevie and Gabe. But on this Saturday they were alone sitting on a small precipice over the pools when Jeff told Melody that he loved her.

"I really enjoy it here Mel." he said.

He had his arm over her shoulder and she was leaning back on it. Suddenly, without hesitation, he leaned over to kiss her and she turned her head away. A sound had distracted her at this very inappropriate moment.

She looked back and Jeff said: "I hope you don't mind... I love you, Mel."

Melody looked into his eyes and tears began to form in both of their eyes. Melody began to breath harder as she realized Jeff had just said the words she had wanted to hear for a long time. She very appropriately said: "I love you too, Jeff."

Her first I love you ended with Jeff. Jeff leaned over and this time planted a kiss squarely on her much desired lips. The feeling permeated his soul. His hand wandered to her back and he rubbed it up and down as she encircled her arms around him.

They backed off, looked again into each others eyes and again fell into a kiss that only true lovers would ever understand. This was one of those kisses that poets write about. Both Melody and Jeff were truly in love. This was not simply infatuation.

That was how it happened. It ended after the brief kiss then the passionate kiss. They walked home together arms behind backs, with their feet never touching sand on "wings of love."

That night Melody had to be home so they walked all the way to Weston and one more kiss was exchanged on Melody's porch before they parted.

Jeff walked, or precisely flew, to Sharon's home. He could not go home yet. Sharon was just sitting and watching Casablanca on television. Jeff proceeded to kiss and tell but it was all just out of joy; not brag.

During the airport scene on Casablanca, Sharon, who was sitting right next to Jeff on a sofa, remarked " I can't imagine you kissing anyone."

With that and Jeff's new found confidence, he leaned over and kissed Sharon for the first time squarely on the lips.

"Well, I'll never say that again." Sharon laughed as she wiped her lips with her wrist.

20

June 9th, 1962 - Jeff had been working on something a long time. Neither he nor Melody had ever been on a real date before.

Hidden Shore

Everyone suggested that they double for their first date, but Jeff would have none of that. He asked Melody out and asked her Aunt and Uncle for their permission. It was given.

He decided: dinner and a movie. He had saved all his money from chores he did for people and swung a loan from his Mother for the rest. He did not want to take her to the Loeb in Weston because he knew that people they both knew would be there. Days of Wine and Roses was playing at the Eureka Theater in Eureka. His mother called and made reservations at the Eureka Inn for dinner. This was going to be special. His mother also agreed to chauffeur them around since she had a good friend she could visit while they were busy and it was only a couple of blocks from the Eureka Inn to the theater, so after dinner they could walk to the theater.

Mary drove Jeff to Melody's home and waited in the car while Jeff went to the front porch to get his date. Melody's Uncle answered the door and said she would be right down but to have a seat while Melody continued getting ready.

They talked, with Jeff nervously fumbling with the box containing the corsage that his mother had insisted he purchase, when suddenly Melody walked into the room. Jeff had seen Melody in a skirt, but this was the first time he saw her in a dress. She wore a baby blue dress with a slightly low neckline. She wore make up and her hair was ratted in back which made her look much older; not just the girl he had fallen in love with. She wore slightly high heels which brought her closer to his height but since she was so short it did not make her too tall. His breathing became labored as he stood and handed her the flower.

She handed it back telling him: "It's your job to pin this on for me.' Jeff nervously took it from it's box and tucking his finger just slightly inside the bodice of her dress, he pinned the flower in place.

Melody's Aunt insisted that they allow her to take pictures of the "lovely couple." She then handed Jeff Melody's jacket which for the first time he chivalrously aided Melody by helping her on with her coat. After hugs from Aunt and Uncle, Jeff walked Melody to the car, opened the back door for her to enter and sit down, and closed the door running to the other side to sit right next to her. Mary was already making a fuss about how beautiful Melody looked.

"Don't you think so." Mary asked her son.

"Of course I do Mom, she's the most beautiful girl I have ever seen in my life." Jeff answered with a wink to Melody.

The date went wonderful. The Eureka Inn had a fancier restaurant than Jeff had ever eaten at before. They each had a Shirley Temple to drink. Melody ordered ravioli fearing the mess trying to eat spaghetti. Jeff ordered the frog legs; something new for him. Melody ate slowly countering Jeff's hurried consumption of the legs. He was not sure whether he could eat them with his fingers or not. The waiter told him: "Fingers are appropriate."

The movie was enjoyable; though the subject matter was romantic, it was one best understood by an older crowd. But the movie was superfluous. Although Jeff watched, he would not take his arm from around Melody throughout, and could not take his eyes off of this beautiful person that he felt he was the luckiest person in the world to have as a girlfriend.

At the end of the movie, Jeff and Melody walked holding hands, back to the Eureka Inn. There was a feeling in the air which permeated to each of their collective souls. It must have been the romance of the evening. The air seemed a little fresher. The chill of the evening gave Jeff the opportunity to hold Melody close to him as they walk to help to warm her. With her nestled in his arms, he felt her soul meld within his. These two individuals were hopelessly in love.

Jeff and Melody finished with an ice cream sundae at the Inn. Mary arrived before they had finished their sundaes. Jeff was happy for the delay because he could tell his mother had a drink or two at her friends and the drive back would take about a half hour.

On the way home, Melody and Jeff rode with the shine from the street lights passing periodically as Jeff could see Melody's illuminated face which would then fade to dark only to illuminate again with the next passing light... fade... illuminate. He held her hands firmly and about half way home leaned over and told her that he felt that she was the "most beautiful girl in the whole world." She kissed him, placing her hand at the nape of his neck.

Mary dropped them off at Melody's house. Jeff wanted to walk home. They kissed on the porch just before her Uncle turned on the light.

"Have fun?" her Uncle asked after opening the door.

"Yes." they both replied with a collective sigh.

Jeff walked home after Melody went inside. About half way home Gabe was driving to find him and picked him up.

"I thought you might like to talk." said Gabe

"Thank you." Jeff replied.

So Jeff and Gabe bonded like all brothers should at such an important time. They talked about love, they talked about girls, they talked about school; they talked about everything that meant anything to either one of them.

Gabe told him about Stephanie. He told him how much he loved her and how much he loved making love to her.

"But don't rush it squirt," he advised, "love too quickly developed can burn out just as quickly. I worry about you kid. If you love a woman too much you can't keep the fire always burning. Those that burn too brightly, like a lantern's wick, quickly consume themselves."

Jeff was not sure he understood completely what Gabe meant, he only knew he wanted to spend the rest of his life with Melody.

21

Melody and Jeff carried on a letter writing routine. Whenever they had time at school they would write to each other and when they met at the library they would exchange notes. These notes were written during class and in them they expressed their feelings about each other. Phrases such as: "All I could do today was think about you." and "Do you miss me as much as I miss you?" permeated the letters. But every once in a while a letter contained important information such as the one Jeff wrote to Melody on Monday, June 18, 1962:

Dear darling Mel,   June 18, 1962

I can't wait to get out of school to talk to you about what my Mom told   me last night. We're going to San Francisco on vacation for two weeks this   summer. We'll be leaving on July 2nd and will be at my Uncle Bob and Aunt   Irene's for two whole weeks. You said you were going there sometime this summer and I thought it would be great if we could be there at the same time.   My cousin Mike knows a lot of great places there to go and I don't think I would enjoy it as much without you. Find some reason to convince your Mom that July is the time for you to come if you can and want to. I'm so excited. It would be so   much fun. I would not enjoy myself if you weren't there with me. All I think about is you. I miss you. Lets talk about this tonight.

I miss you

Jeff XOXOXOX

22

Thus began the process toward going to San Francisco. When they met in the library that afternoon they discussed all the details.

Wednesday was Melody's 15th birthday, and Jeff wanted to get her something special. He found just what he wanted at Mitchell's store in Weston: A necklace with a heart shaped pendent which was split in half. The necklace came with two chains. One person wore the one chain with the left side of the heart on it and the other person wore the other chain with the right side of the heart on it.

Jeff handed Melody the gift in a little box and when she opened it Melody was so thrilled.

"This means as long as we're together and wear our hearts, the heart is full." Jeff told her.

" I could not have wished for a better gift from you Jeff," Melody told him, "I guess this means we're going steady, Hugh?"

"I kind of figured we already were." he answered.

Jeff opened the clasp on Melody's half of the necklace and holding the half-heart he pulled softly on the neck of her blouse and dropped the heart between her breasts.

"This will keep my heart at your heart." Jeff told her.

He handed the other necklace to her and she placed it around his neck and following suit dropped his half to his breast.

"Happy Birthday Mel, I really love you." Jeff said in commitment.

"I love you too Jeffrey." she replied.

And they kissed.

"Well? Any thoughts about Frisco?" Jeff asked her.

"Not yet much, Mom wants me to come but if I do it would also be for two weeks and it looks like the second week of your trip." Melody responded, " You know, July 9th or so? Then we would be apart for two weeks anyway. First the week you get there, then the week together there, then the last week I would be there without you. I don't know if I could stand that much time away from you. ....Jeff? How did I live for over fourteen years without you?"

"I certainly don't know Mel, I lived over sixteen years without you." Jeff said as he cuddled close to her. "I don't think I could handle that much time away from you very well either, but that week in Frisco would be great. I could meet your Mom and Brother."

"I don't know if you'd like that." Melody cut him off.

"Why did you ever leave there anyway? Why don't you live at home with them? Not that I would rather it any different."

"Someday maybe we can talk and I'll explain it to you," Melody replied, "for now let's talk about better things."

"Well, I think I would like to meet your Mom. You know my Mom, I'd like to know yours, you know my brothers, I'd like to know Carlos."

"I doubt it."

On that Friday, Melody had exciting news:

Dear Jeffrey,

It's all arranged. Just as I said Wednesday. I'll talk to you later.

Gotta Go,

Love ya,

Mel XOXOx

On this letter Melody planted a kiss with lipstick.

So it was arranged. That Friday was the last day of school for the summer and San Francisco was next.

The week between school and Jeff's inevitable departure for San Francisco was unendurable. Both were excited to go; however, but, both dreaded the imminence of their separation. It would be the first separation since they found each other.

23

Hidden Shore

July 2nd 1962 arrived; a clear sun drenched morning. Jeff had said his good-byes to Melody. The family: Mary, Bill, Gabe, Jeff and Stan with Stevie in tow, climbed into the station wagon. Gabe had signed up into the Army and was to report to Boot Camp soon after the trip. Stephanie and Gabe were inseparable at this point.

They all drove to Highway 101 and then south until they crossed the Golden Gate Bridge entering San Francisco. The majesty of this structure confounded Jeff's imagination. He had never seen anything of this proportion in his life. The sweep of the cables, the dignity of the towers, the clamor of the automobiles and trucks on the road bed with vehicles heading north or south to destinations into or away from the city which was San Francisco, not Frisco as he was informed the first time he said the word Frisco to his cousin Mike, thrilled him to his very soul.

Jeff's Uncle Bob and Aunt Irene lived in the Excelsior district on the south side of San Francisco, just about five miles from where Melody had grown up. Though away from the center of town, Jeff and his family quickly learned the bus connections to take or city streets to drive to get to anywhere they wished.

Cousin Mike was a perfect host. Jeff and he were only days different in age. Mike was an organizer. The first thing, Mike set to do was to schedule an itinerary for Jeff and the rest. Then he decided Jeff needed to be "cool." Looking at Jeff's Levis, he told him that they had to go. So the boys headed to a shop on Mission Street to find the right kind of pants for San Francisco. A perfect pair of slacks were chosen, but this was not enough, they needed to be "pegged." Pegged pants were all the rave for high school kids in 1962, according to Mike. To peg the pants the legs were stitched at the leg openings, just wide enough to slip on. They were stitched all the way to the crotch as tight as the legs could handle. Then there was the hair. Jeff was taught to grease his hair with hair cream and then using the middle three fingers, pull the center of his hair by hooking those fingers among the hair and grease, pulling forward to make the hair over the forehead form a puff with a curl hanging over the forehead. On Mike it worked great, but on Jeff it looked stringy and fell in his eyes, but Mike assured him that his hair would "train" and then the hair would look fine.

Jeff was now "IN." It was time for them to venture out into the great municipality of San-Fran-Sisco.

On Tuesday July 3rd, Jeff, Mike, Gabe and Stevie all jumped on a 14 Mission bus and transferred to a 10 Monterey bus to ride to Golden Gate Park. With them came a friend of Mike's who was to him as Sharon was to Jeff. Her name was Sophia who lived down the street from Mike. On the trip over Mike pointed out a house that the Monterey bus went past and informed them gleefully "That's Willie Mays' house, we need to go to a Giants ball game before you guys leave."

He also explained to the others about "beatniks." "The Park is full of them, especially in the panhandle." he informed them. The panhandle was an area on the east side of the Park that extended about ten blocks and was a city block wide. To the area around the panhandle were drawn a bohemian class of young rebellious adults of who the characterization was to dress in casual clothing with goatees and sit around playing bongo drums. Their interest was jazz or folk music. They preferred to work as little as possible and to simply enjoy themselves rather than stress over life. Their characterization was personified in a television show that Jeff and the others at Hidden Shore watched called <u>Dobie Gillis</u> in which Maynard G. Krebbs was a beatnik. Those in Hidden Shore found him funny but more of a ner-do-well. This same area and these same people were the seeds of another major bohemian movement that would come five years later and were to be given the name "Hippies" by a San Francisco columnist named Herb Caen to reflect their "hip" personae.

The visit to Golden Gate Park began at the Museum and Aquarium where the Monterey bus dropped them off. There were two things in this area that Jeff and the others were fascinated by at the Aquarium. One was a full skeleton of a humpback whale assembled and on display. Jeff had seen a humpback whale spewing it's plume of water from it's spout from Hidden Shore. But he never had seen anything like this except for some pieces of bone on the beach over the years. Once he had found a femur of a humpback and had it hanging on his wall in his bedroom at home. A vertebrae on the skeleton looked identical to the one on his shelf and he was excited to see the completed set. The other thing that excited him was a cross cut circle from a giant redwood tree. On this cross-cut was a listing of years and historical data of when certain events occurred during the life of a Redwood. Though he had seen many Redwood trees near his home he had never seen one which gave him such an understanding of the age of these trees. This gave him a new perspective and respect for these gigantic behemoths of the forest. Jeff determined that this was one place he would have to come with Melody when she arrived.

The group spent the whole day walking through the Japanese Tea Garden, playing at the Polo Grounds, taking off their shoes and dipping their feet at Stowe Lake, staring at the tame Buffalo's, and inspecting the wind mills at the west end of the Park. They then proceeded to Playland which was a permanent fair set up across from the beach. There was a roller coaster, a tunnel of love, and other rides. There was also a fun house which to enter they had to go through a maze of mirrors. Inside there was an indoor slide which each of them had to climb to the top of, carrying a gunny sack to slide down on because the slide was made of hardwood. There were also other things to climb and rolling barrels to run through. At the end of one there was an air gun set up and when girls ran by an operator in a booth would shoot a shot of air and the girl's skirt would fly up to their screams. When Stevie went by she was confident because she was wearing peddle pushers but she forgot that the air could blow a blouse up too. Stan and Jeff stood near watching girls go by, but obviously when boys did that the operator would not shoot the air out of respect for the girls.

Jeff's favorite device was a full sized dummy of a fat lady clown who laughed in
a glass cage outside the fun house. She laughed and laughed and laughed and her laughter was contagious. She would be the most memorable thing at playland for him.

The group returned home that evening and Jeff determined

that he was going to return the next week with Melody to Golden Gate Park and Playland.

24

Wednesday July 4th.

So far so good. Jeff had survived two days without Melody and now he had only five more days before he would see her again.

The big excursion of the day was to the Zoo. They were all going to take swimming gear because right next to the zoo was the beach and there was also a large swimming pool right between the zoo and the beach.

This time they rode on a Streetcar which took them downtown from where they took another one to the Zoo. The Streetcars were very exciting. They ran smoothly on a track and in both directions, downtown and to the zoo, they rode through a tunnel and the cars whizzed along at a rapid speed, click click, click click, was the sound they made as they raced through the tunnels which had a rather putrid smell to them. The smell was kind of a combination of wet earth, creosol and urine. Not very pleasant.

At the zoo there were many animals of various types and shapes as at other zoos. They paraded around and gained a lot of information about the animals because Mike had a plastic key shaped like an elephant with it's trunk sticking out that when you inserted the key into a box that was placed in front of each cage it would tell everyone facts about the animal they were viewing. They then went to the pool.

Fleishackers Pool was an Olympic size pool of salt water. The pool was huge and since it was a holiday it was full of kids and adults. Everyone enjoyed their time but soon had to head home because they had to join their parents.

The whole group, kids and adults, were going to go to Chinatown for dinner and then to the Marina Greens to watch a fireworks display. They all rode downtown in three cars and parked so they could ride one of San Francisco's famous Cable Cars to Chinatown. Jeff really enjoyed hanging out on the step of the car and feeling the air pass over his body. The air was chilled by a early evening fog. They rode to Chinatown and had dinner. During dinner they all decided to forgo the fireworks show because of the fog. They knew they would not be able to see the show with the fog. They decided to go for a drive around San Francisco but Sophia wanted to show Jeff the city. Jeff asked permission and received it.

Parting the rest, Sophia and Jeff walked the length of Chinatown down Columbus Street to the Fisherman's Wharf. They talked about everything. Sophia had a boyfriend in the Air Force and she planned to marry him when she graduated from High School the following June.

Jeff told her all about him and Melody. They found out that they had a lot in common.

With the developments of the last couple of months with Melody and now the trip to San Francisco, Jeff was maturing rapidly. Still just sixteen years old, it was obvious that he was no longer the scrawny kid that skinny dipped with his friends at Dead Man Creek. He had gone beyond the companionship of boys to relationships with girls. He did not want to be with any other girl than Melody, but at this time there was something special about being out on the big town with Sophia.

Sophia knew a special place that she wanted to show Jeff. The two of them walked along the waterfront and at the foot of a hill she said, "Feel adventurous? Think you can climb those with me?" She pointed to a set of steps that climbed a hill. "I want you to see what's at the top."

So they climbed, and climbed, reached a driveway at a house, reconnected to some other stairs and climbed and climbed, finally reaching the foot of a concrete obelisk "This is Coit Tower Jeff." Sophia informed him.

"This tower was built to commemorate the firefighters that died fighting the fires after the San Francisco earthquake in 1906."

"Lets climb the stairs to the top." Sophia suggested.

"More stairs Huh?"

"Not too many more, it's spectacular up there."

By this time the light of day was beginning to fade and the lights of the harbor were coming on to the north and the lights of the city were shinning to the south and east. Jeff stopped as he approached the top of the tower and exhaled in disbelief of the beauty of the city lights.

"I have never seen anything like this in my life." Jeff ejaculated.

The chill made him shiver and Sophia wrapped her arms around Jeff from behind and held him close. He could feet the press of her breasts against his back. Instead of pushing himself away he leaned slightly back to accept her warmth. To his surprise he felt a tinge of love for this older girl. How could that be he asked himself. He loved Melody. This began to scare him and he finally pulled away from Sophia's embrace.

"I'm sorry if that bothered you," she said "it just seemed you were cold."

"I was, thank you." he responded.

Whether they wanted to admit it or not there was something special beginning to occur between these two.

They walked down from the tower and back to Chinatown.

"You've got to see the Fairmont, Jeff." she told him.

"Okay, let's go"

From Chinatown they climbed the two blocks to the top of Nob Hill and entered the Fairmont Hotel, the queen of hotels in San Francisco. They walked through the front door like they owned the place. The elegance was above and beyond anything as had so much of Jeff's San Francisco trip been so far. She took him to a garden area from which again they could see the city below and Coit Tower in the distance.

Again Jeff was mesmerized by the lights and said "I have never seen anything so beautiful in my life." They then walked out of the hotel and spent the next couple of hours walking and talking in the cool fog shrouded night air. The chill seemed to surround them as they walked passed the Crocker Mansion, passed churches,

Hidden Shore

houses, bars, stores with a myriad blend of types of peoples. They walked to Union Square and back to Market Street, but somewhere in the middle of it all Jeff and Sophia joined hands and walked hand in hand for the rest of the evening.

From Market they walked to Mission Street and caught the 14 Mission home. As they walked the final few blocks Sophia decided it was time to say something to Jeff that was real important.

"You know Jeff, we have had a very special evening. I think I have found a soul mate in you, but I love Ken and you love Melody. We're not going to mess anything up. We're going to continue to be friends and always remember the special night we have had."

They stopped and faced each other at Sophia's front door. "I love you as a best friend Jeff, now you may kiss me if you wish, but I would really rather just have a hug."

Jeff reached out and hugged Sophia closely. Sophia lowered her hand to Jeff's buttock and ran it over his left cheek then slapped it.

"Shame on you Jeff." she said, and went into her house.

Jeff was ashamed. Obviously she had felt that he had developed a erection. This really bothered him because he had never yet had an erection from Melody. Yes, he and Melody had kissed and held each other, but it never was as passionate as it felt with Sophia. Could he feel the same way about her? When Melody arrived, would he be able to take her to the places Sophia had and feel the same stirring in his body? Would he feel as ashamed with Melody as he did at that moment? Had he been unfaithful to Melody that evening? Jeff was ashamed and confused. He really felt lost now.

25

Melody sat in front of her mirror at her night stand and stared at her reflection. It was early Thursday morning and she could not sleep. A soft light filtered through the blinds of her room casting a mixture of shadows and light that softened her reflection.

This was the morning that Jeff had arranged to call and she was nervous about hearing from him. She was sure that he was as miserable as she was. She missed him so much. Her hand gently slid into her night gown and she fingered her heart pendent contemplating her loneliness. She opened her gown top and dangled her charm to stimulate her aereola. Her nipples became firm and she stared in glazed concentration on them. She remembered when her breasts were no more than soft little buds mostly nipple and when she first started to go to the camp she had developed breasts that she felt confident about, but now they had grown just enough to look pleasing to her. She concentrated on their size and structure; turning from side to side observing their reflection in the diffused light. She wondered if Jeff would like these or preferred bigger breasts. She worried that maybe they would grow too large; she hoped not. Slowly she drew her index finger to her left breast and began to tweak it ever so gently. The sensation felt nice, they itched sometimes and rubbing her breast seemed to ease the itch. She wondered if this was why girls allowed boys to rub their breasts because the sensation felt so good. She began to rub a little harder and then she felt another sensation between her legs. With her right hand on her breast, she slowly lowered her left hand between her thighs and softy began to rub her fingers between the curls of her soft down hair slowly fingering the lips of her soft flower pedal lips. Her breathing became labored as she stared at her reflection and rubbed both of her hands. Suddenly she stopped. She was embarrassed at herself; a little ashamed. She shook abruptly and awakened herself from her altruistic contemplation.

"That's nasty, I can't do that." she thought.

Her thoughts returned to the impending call from Jeff. There were things she needed to tell him and she knew she should do it soon. She needed to explain about her mother and brother and about why she had come to Weston. She needed to tell him about where she had gone with her Aunt and Uncle on weekends. Even more imminent was that she needed to tell him that she and her mother had discussed returning permanently to San Francisco.

26

Jeff awoke early, much like Melody. His mind still spun from what had happened the night before. He was not in love with Sophia but he had felt love for her. He wondered if people could love more than one person at a time. He thought they fell in love and that was the only person that mattered and that they could not love another person the same way, at the same time. In addition, he awoke with an erection. He lowered his right hand to it and began to stroke it gently, then feverishly until he spewed all over his bed sheets.

"Damn, what a mess. I'll have to clean this up myself." he said stripping the bedding.

Now he was even more upset. His mind had pictured Sophia , not Melody during his self absorption. He had never even done that while thinking of Melody before.

"I love Melody, how can I do that." he thought.

Suddenly he remembered he was to call Melody. He dressed, gathered up his bedding and carried them to his Aunt Irene's laundry room. He ran into Gabe on the way.

"Wet dream little brother?"

"Get out of here." Jeff snapped embarrassed that his brother would say that loud enough for others to hear.

At 10 o'clock, the appointed time, Jeff telephoned Melody.

"I miss you so much, Jeff." Melody told him.

"I love you, Melody." Jeff said and suddenly he began to cry. He felt ashamed that his mind had wondered at all from Melody.

"I can't wait to get there Jeff, I talked to my Mom and she looks forward to meeting you. But my Mom's really strict so we can't give her any indication that we are steady or kiss or anything.

"Okay, I know."

"No you don't." Melody said harshly, "You have no idea. Just watch it or that could be the end of it. She won't let us go out at night so don't think you can ever ask her permission, she'll stop us immediately, but she'll let us do things in the day so go ahead and make plans."

"I have a lot of things I want to do." Jeff went on. "We've gone to a lot of places. I want to go with you to most of them. We're going to a baseball game today, Giants and Phillies, I wish you could go with us."

"I do too." Melody responded, "I miss you so much."

The rest of the conversation was filled with the "I miss yous" and "I can't think of anything but yous."

As soon as he hung up, Mike walked in with Sophia.

"I hear you two had a good time last night." Mike said.

"Yah." was all Jeff responded hoping that Sophia had said nothing about what had happened the night before.

"We'll have to do it again before you leave, kid." Sophia cut in winking at Jeff.

"Such a tease." Jeff thought.

27

The baseball game began at noon so the boys had to leave soon after that. Jeff, Mike and Stan were the only ones going. Stephanie wanted to go to a friends house with Gabe; a girl who once lived in Fairbury and had attended school with the two of them. So Gabe drove the boys in the station wagon to the game, but they were on their own afterwards.

The boys arrived on time for the game and entering the stadium, they took their seats after purchasing their tickets, buying the required catalogue on the teams and score sheets. Mike filled them in on the fine art of baseball attendance. He held his glove in his lap "to catch foul balls." he told them.

He helped them learn to flag down a "hawker" for hot dogs

and sodas. This was easy because they were everywhere yelling "hot dogs!!", "get you ice cream!!", "hot peanuts!!", "cold beer, ice cold beer."

Mike was very disappointed that Willie Mays only played a couple of innings. But Orlando Cepeda hit a home run and Felipe Alou made an amazing catch in left field. Tom Haller got beamed by the pitcher Robin Roberts who then got beamed by Jack Sanford which precipitated a bench clearing. Sanford was ejected from the game and Billy O'Dell pitched from then on with help for one inning from Gaylord Perry.

"That's the rookie," Mike informed them, "They say he pitches a spitter" which necessitated an explanation from Mike.

The Giants lost this game 5 to 3 but they would go on to the World Series that year losing to the Yankees four games to three which Jeff, Stan, Greg, and Clint would watch at home together in Hidden Shore.

Candlestick Park was located on a land fill in San Francisco Bay. Between the Park and home laid a notorious area of town called Hunter's Point which was a Naval Base bordered by the Negro ghetto. White boys did not wander into that area often unless they did it at their own risk, but Mike had walked home from games before. He advised them not to look around but to just walk "as if you have some place to go" and to just walk straight and not stop because lingering made them easy targets for "toughs."

It did happen. As the boys were walking along Palou Street heading home they were approached by about three black kids (boys) who gathered around Mike, probably because he was the biggest one, and they had an exchange of words. The boys then gathered around Jeff and asked him: "Do you got any money?"

"Not for you." he stupidly responded.

Suddenly all five boys were on top of Jeff, pounding and kicking at him. Jeff thought his number had come up as more boys came from all over. Suddenly, like the parting of the Red Sea in the movie Ten Commandments the boys seemed to fly off of Jeff. Mike had jumped into the pile feet first knocking the boys off of Jeff. The crowd scattered and they remained standing back as Mike, Stan, and

Jeff began to regroup. One of the boys was more bold and began to threaten Mike and the three of them were sure this was it as the boys regained their confidence and began to close in on the three. A siren suddenly sounded and the crowd dispersed momentarily. As the three looked up there was a Police car sitting and the officer had flung his rear door opened. What luck. The boys ran for the cop car and jumped in.

"What the hell were you guys doing walking alone through there?" I don't even come through this part of town unless I have to."

The boys were grateful to the officer. He took then to a bus stop outside the dangerous area from where they rode home. Jeff would never forget how helpless they had felt, he imagined how scary it must have been for Howard that day at the Creek when they had been even worse to him. "Maybe this was the punishment Howard meant when he had refused to accept their apology."

28

Friday, July 6th and Greg had nothing to do. With Clint being his obnoxious self he did not want to do anything with him. With Jeff and his brothers in San Francisco, Greg really was alone. He went to the place that always gave him solace when he was depressed, that was North Beach. The tide was down so he crossed the tide pools and went on the beach. He took a book with him and sat to read.

Not long after he saw the faint figure of a girl cross from the tide pools. He knew who she was, it was Mary Woo one of his classmates and daughter of the couple who owned and ran the Chinese restaurant in town. He waved at her and she approached him. He had always liked Mary. She was the smartest girl in class. Always a straight "A" student. Played violin in the orchestra at school and belonged to the chess club. "Brainy" he always thought. Somehow she was very attractive. Thin and short and today she wore a pee coat just like the ones that him and Clint and Jeff wore on cold days.

"Miss school?" she asked outrageously.

"No, You?"

"Not really." she laughed. "Where's your buddies? I sometimes think you're all joined at the hips I never see you guys away from each other."

"Clint's home, Jeff's in Frisco, they both have girl friends now so I don't see as much of them."

"Yah, me too."

"You don't have a boyfriend?" Greg asked.

"Nah, my parents wouldn't have it. If I did he would have to be Chinese."

"Oh, I see."

They sat, just idly kicking the sand with their feet and stirring it with a piece of driftwood; just anything to disguise the fact that they had run out of things to say.

"Just out for a walk?" Greg finally broke the silence.

"Yah, I come here a lot."

"You do? I've never seen you."

"That's because if I get to the tidepools and you guys are on the beach you're usually buck naked."

"You see us?'

"Of course I do, everyone in town does. Boys have done it for ions. You guys are just the rulers of this beach now. Someday you guys will leave and other boys, very much like yourselves but younger, will claim the beach and swim naked just like you. And there will be girls just like me who will always refuse to enter your sanctity."

Greg was really embarrassed; but he got over it and after a time he walked back to town with Mary and when they got a couple of blocks from her parent's restaurant, they lived next door, she suggested they part so her parents would not think they were together. Greg cooperated saying: "see you in school." Mary said: "That's still a couple of months off away, maybe I'll see you on the beach again. Unless your naked of course."

29

In San Francisco, Jeff, Stan, Mike, Sophia, Gabe, and Stevie, had big plans for the day. One of Mike's favorite things to do was to take the bus to the Marina Greens, where they were supposed to go to see the fireworks show two days before, hike through the Presidio, hike across the Golden Gate Bridge, and then hike down to the Bay coastal town of Sausalito, have lunch and then hike all the way back.

The first part of the hike was nice for each of them. They talked about movies they had enjoyed, books they had read and other things such as school and how much they were enjoying their trip so far.

Gabe was fascinated with the Presidio. Since he would be entering the Army shortly after the trip he wanted to explore the whole open base. The Presidio had a section with barracks, offices, theater, Officers and Enlisted men's Messes. He hoped he would be stationed there some day, but he knew he could be sent just about anywhere. "Maybe even over seas," he said to Stevie's chagrin.

After the Presidio, they walked down to the foot of the Golden Gate Bridge. Fort Point was located there. This was an old brick Civil War fort that was closed and boarded up looking as forbidding as the old school house at home but on a much larger scale.

Mike told them of about how many people jumped from the bridge to commit suicide but that just recently, a man had jumped short of the water. Water does not break on impact as quickly as solid ground. It's a fact that a Physics teacher could probably explain to them. Mike certainly could not. But Mike told them that this man had survived the jump, only one of the few who had, by falling through the roof of the old fort.

The majesty of the bridge, standing below it like that, again peeked Jeff's imagination with things like "gateway to heaven." He noticed that the cables that suspended the bridge went into a concrete warehouse looking structure and Mike explained that from the main cable there were smaller cables that went into a turning device that tuned each cable individually like a guitar string.

"I hear that if you fired a gun, just a handgun at these cables where the tuning devices are, you can snap them. So they're guarded closely." Mike informed them.

They then climbed the hill and entered the pedestrian sidewalk that ran along the roadbed. Stevie was scared to approach the edge looking down at the water and Jeff had to admit to himself that he was timid at the altitude. That was to the right. To the left was the road bed at such a close proximity that when a vehicle, especially a truck went by, the sidewalk shook. This forced Stevie to walk in the center of the side walk holding tightly to Gabe's arm.

Jeff threw a quarter over the side and watched it fall. All the way as it fell he screamed: "Ah, Ah, Ah,..." as if he was a leaper trying to imagine the time that free fall off the bridge would take.

"I would probably be dead by a heart attack out of fear before I hit the water" he said to Mike and Sophia."

The hike was tiring but enjoyable the rest of the way to Sausalito. On the water front at Sausalito, Jeff finally saw and heard what Mike had told him about in Golden Gate Park. A group of beatniks, two guys and a girl, were doing just what Mike had said: Playing bongos and strumming a guitar. Jeff liked their casual appearance, they seemed to enjoy themselves as they gamboled to their music.

Lunch in Sausalito was nice. The whole group sat and talked for about two hours. Jeff had never done this before. In the past whenever he ate, of course, he ate and then just took off somewhere. Here, Jeff learned the concept of eating slowly and enjoying his meal and the following conversation in a composed, reserved fashion. He had seen "grown ups" do that many times, in fact that seemed to be all his Mother, Bill, Uncle Bob and Aunt Irene did; somehow he better appreciated the quality of "slowing down" and enjoying good food and good company for the first time. He remembered his dinner with Melody and the rapidly nervous way he had eaten the frog legs. He vowed to do better next time he ate with Melody.

Another thing that became obvious as he sat across the table from Sophia was that there would never again be the same sexually charged play that occurred on Wednesday night; much to his relief. She seemed to tease as sexually with Mike and Gabe as she had with him. Jeff realized now that that was just how Sophia was.

Though mesmerized by the presence of Sophia, Jeff suddenly realized the presence of a woman at the table behind and just to the left of her. The woman was sitting facing Jeff with a gentleman in front of her and another couple beside them. The woman was about twenty five years old and had ordered a marguerita with her lunch. Jeff noticed that every time she raised the glass to have a sip she hesitated and slowly holding the glass just in front of her mouth her tiny tongue slid from between her lips and touched the very tip of the glass rim accepting a small bit of salt and then retreated into her mouth and then she sipped from the glass. She performed this act nearly a dozen times each time in what seemed to Jeff like slow motion. Raise the glass, tongue comes softly into view, tongue retreats ever so slowly, sip of the marguerita. Over and over again ever so slowly. This was one of the sexiest acts that Jeff had ever seen. He was not sure if she was at all aware of his watching her performance but she did it with such deliberateness that he felt she must have and he watched so intently, how could she not have noticed even though he tried to remain unobserved.

The hike back to the Marina was pleasant but more rapidly executed than the hike over had been. Thoughts of Melody began to cloud his mind as he realized that soon she would be joining him.

30

Saturday and Sunday became "the beach days." Uncle Bob did not work those days so everybody had time to spend the day

Hidden Shore

together.

Mike, Sophia, Gabe, Stevie, Stan and Jeff wanted to go to the beach. It was very warm that weekend and they had not been on the beach since they had arrived in San Francisco. The adults told them that they just wanted to drive down the coast so they would take the kids to the beach and pick them up when they got back. Two picnic baskets were packed and they all piled into the station wagon and went to the beach near the zoo. They did all the beach things. Mike told Jeff that his parents really had a special beach that they liked to go to and that was why they had gone south alone.

"I've been there two times, but your parents wanted to see it without us." he explained.

"What's so special about it?" asked Jeff.

"Well, I'll tell you later, but I'm not sure I should tell you now."

This seemed so mysterious to Jeff; "What was it? A nudist beach or something?" he thought.

The next day Mike confirmed his suspicions. Mike told Jeff, Gabe and Stevie that he needed to talk to them and sat them down with Sophia to propose what they might do that day.

"I've kind of been elected by Mom and Dad and your folks to tell you where they went yesterday." Mike explained. "There is a beach at the Devil's Slide area, south of town, which is a nudist beach. My folks have been going there for years and I never knew it, then when I turned sixteen this year, they told me I was old enough to go with them. Anyone can go, but they have this sixteen year old rule of their own. Well, they took Aunt Mary and Uncle Bill there yesterday and they liked it. I guess your Mom has been nudist before but not for a long time. Last time I went Sophia came with us so she's been there too. They want all of us to go today, but Aunt Mary thought it would be hard to approach you guys.

"Okay with me," said Gabe. "Jeff you and I have often gone nude on the beach at home on North Beach."

"You have?" said Stevie.

"I used to," said Gabe, "when I was younger. Before we started going out,"

Hidden Shore

"I just think it's funny that you do it on North Beach. No wonder nobody goes there."

"Why not?" said Jeff nervously trying not to look at Sophia. This would mean she would be there.

"I don't know....I've never done it before," Stevie said hesitantly.

"We also have to decided what to do about Stan," Mike interjected, "My folks have that sixteen year old rule."

"We can just spend the day here with him and go somewhere." said Stevie.

"Ah come on, It'll be fun." Gabe retorted.

"You know, it's not as bad as you think once you get down there. I was real nervous but I wanted to try it real bad so I went and as soon as I got down there I felt fine." Sophia assured Stevie.

Stephanie took Gabe aside.

"Gabriel, come on yourself, I can't do that."

"You sunbathe topless all the time in your back yard."

"That's different, only you have seen me do that."

"Hey Mike," Gabe called out, "do you have to go nude?"

"Nah, it's clothing optional. There's some that don't. Sometimes guys'll go down with pants on just to stare at the ladies."

"How about if you wear your suit and just see how you feel."

With a little more prodding, Stevie was convinced it would be all right but she was nervous all the way down there. So was Jeff, though he had skinny dipped on the beach and at Dead Man Creek, this was different. Though he had even skinny dipped with the girls when he was little, this was different. Here he would see his brother's girlfriend. Here he would see Sophia, and adults, and his Aunt and Uncle, and Bill and his MOTHER. This was going to be different. "Oh my gosh," he worried, "WHAT IF I HAVE A BONER?"

The beach at Devil's slide had a parking lot across from Highway One. The family parked among other cars parked in neat rows as if they were all going to a church social. Being Sunday, Jeff wondered if some of these cars had come from church directly to the beach on such a lovely July day. They entered a gate where Mike informed them that the owners of the parking charged for parking and to cross their property. Uncle Bob explained that for years the owners had chased nude swimmers off their property and finally gave in and decided to make it a money making opportunity. They built a stairway to provide safe access to the beach so they would not have to fear law suits for injuries.

Climbing down the stairs with ice chests full of soda's and sandwiches was tricky. As they ascended a beach full of nude people began to come into view. At the foot of the steps, against the cliffs sat a woman with her husband and a daughter approximately ten years old playing in the sand. It immediately became comfortable to Jeff because there were people in all shapes and sizes in exactly the same condition: nude.

After choosing an appropriate location to sit and setting the ice chests, the group all laid out their towels. Everyone in the group, as were other people just arriving, began to peel off their clothes. Jeff nervously unbuttoned his shirt, pulled off his T-shirt, kicked off his socks and pulled his pants down quickly. He then pulled at his swimming trunks, lowering them to the ground as he felt the familiar feeling of air among his manhood. He averted his eyes from most of the group as they did the same...NO BONER. No more nervousness. He watched clandestinely as Sophia, wearing a maroon blouse with an extremely low neckline that circled the edge of her bra began to join the rest. She wore a necklace which sat well defined about one third of the way down her exposed neck area. She had on dark blue Levis. When she pulled her blouse off she crossed her arms to the bottom of each opposite sides of her blouse and raised the blouse over her head exposing her flowery decorated white bra against her tanned skin. Through the bra there was just a hint of the dark nipples visible through the pattern. The brassier hooked at the back. To remove it she hooked her thumbs on both straps and pulled her bra almost seductively down exposing the nipples and then turned the bra at her belly to unhook the back.

Her panties were white; Pure white with no design. She removed them by hooking her thumbs again on both hips within the strap of her panties and pulled them down bending at the hips. With her perfect posterior pointed at Jeff she turned slightly, lowered herself to her towel and pulled her panties from her feet.

All this Jeff just happened to notice.

They all were now set comfortably on their towels; some sitting and some lying. They began to talk as if it was no different than any other beach. Stevie even felt immediately comfortable as she said to Gabe: "What the heck." and removed her bathing suit top.

After about 20 minutes of conversation and sun bathing, Mary said: "Lets all go for a walk."

The whole group arose and began to walk together as casual as if they were dressed. Mary came up and put her arm around Jeff and asked how he felt about all this. He replied: "S'okay." He observed that there was an equalizing effect at nude beach. People arrived dressed in different quality of clothing which identified their place in society were suddenly indistinguishable after shedding their clothes. The only thing that set them apart were hair styles and, of course, their natural differences. These differences were proof that all men were not created equal. There were long ones, short ones, skinny ones and fat ones. Circumcised and uncircumcised. Jeff was quite surprised how many uncircumcised men there were considering the shock the first time he saw one.

Women were just as variable. Some had big ones; some were small. Some with huge aureoles some with none. Some with breasts that were firm some that hung.

But no one seemed ashamed. One woman was walking alone just at the tides edge and she was pregnant. To Jeff this was an amazingly beautiful thing to see.

Jeff wondered if Melody would someday come to a beach like this with him. He tried to separate what he was doing from thoughts of her. She was so innocent and he could not imagine her even considering this. He hoped their relationship would progress but he feared Melody was above this kind of thing. She did kiss him and he knew there was passion in her, but they had not progressed enough for him to truly know her.

As they walked Jeff was cognizant of the four women that

were with him.

Sophie was not one of the most beautiful girls to Jeff but she had one of the most perfectly proportioned bodies of all the women on the beach. With her Mexican tanned skin she looked to be a natural for nude frolic. Her hair was longer than shoulder length, her eyebrows were narrow. She had a fairly large nose that flayed at the nostrils and very full red lips. Her eyes were brown; dark orbs deep set into their sockets with high cheek bones.

Her hair cascaded down past her shoulders framing a neck which was decorated by a diamond entrusted gold necklace which Jeff figured was a gift from her boyfriend Ken. Her breasts were taught as was all her skin. Her skin seemed to fit her body to a perfection with no loose spots, no perceivable imperfections. The areolas were brown on the outside changing to a stark pink at her tiny nipples. Her breast stood out without any droop. She had a birth mark that ran from just below her belly button and extended until it disappeared among the dark curls of her short pubic hair.

When they returned to their spot on the beach, two things had changed while they were gone. Three young women had arrived together and placed themselves squarely in front of Jeff. One a blonde, one a brunette, one a red head. They were now lying on their stomachs with their feet pointed directly toward Jeff's towel. When her sat down, he could see directly up the channels of their slightly spread legs.

The other thing was that some of the other bathers had set up a volleyball net and were trying to get players. All the kids jumped at the chance. Before joining the game, Stevie looked around and feeling much more comfortable with the nudity around her; actually feeling uncomfortable with her suit bottoms on because she was the only one wearing anything and feeling freakish because of it, she pulled her suit down and felt the sudden rush of air on her special spot. She was amazed at the euphoria it generated in her and she was ready to play volleyball.

The games were fun and very aggressive. The players dived and served without concern for their flailing body parts. Jeff thought it felt pretty good as he ran and jumped just as he did on the beach at home. What was really difficult to get used to was when he would bump into one of the other players, whether male or female, and have his penis slap against another persons body. Over a period of time, new teams were assembled and new games played, each time with different combinations of players.

Jeff took a break and sat out one game. He sat a little further away against the cliffs with his behind and testicles firmly planted in the sand. He studied his mother for a moment. No Freudian mother/love thing here just interested to see that though not taut, her stomach was well shaped with stretch marks evident from three pregnancies and two miscarriages. Her breasts drooped a little and her aureoles collapsed a bit around her nipples.

A thought occurred to him as he stared unashamedly longer than he knew he felt really comfortable about; he realized that from amongst that tuft of hair between her thighs, his life had begun. He seemed somehow at peace with this thought and comforted in knowing that even his parents had obviously had the same desires as he now had for Melody. He focused on the soft folds of her lips that shone bright crimson among the black heavily forested place. He suddenly felt a stronger love for her now that he could almost share in her conception of him. He never knew his father so he could, or would not try picturing his father with his mother. His attention quickly focused on Bill sitting next to his mother and he suddenly shook his head and his thought out of it.

Stevie was on of those kind of women who seemed to have a perpetual smile.

Stevie had arrived wearing a white sleeveless blouse that buttoned down the front. As always she wore pedal pushers. Her hair was brown and about the same length as Sophia's though Stevie was much taller, just about the same height as him. Without much of a perceptive part, her hair hung full and wavy. Her eyebrows rose from the center out and as he looked at her now, he noticed her breasts seemed spread outward also more than Sophia's; they were flat in the middle, more full on the outside. Where Sophia's blouse could not have been lower without exposing breast, Stevie could have worn a blouse cut to the navel without exposing any indication of breast down the middle. Her nipples were larger and longer on the sides almost like they had been gently bitten to flatten them. They were bright red as were the cheeks of her face. She had very little aureola which splayed out from the nipples in an imperfect arc. Her teeth were bright white and her lips were red but thin with little pucker below the nose. Her nose was also thin and came to a downward pointing slope but was petite. Her eyes were blue. She had thick pubic hair with curls that frizzled up Jeff thought to tickle her abdomen. The tan lines indicated that she only wore a swimming suit bottom when she sun bathed. After being in the sun so much today, her posterior was now becoming bright scarlet. She had another tuft of hair at her rear. He noticed when she bent over with her legs tightly locked and her behind pointed at him that her womanly place protruded in a sort of sphere with a cleft down the middle. He knew his brother had enjoyed the pleasures of this intriguing woman before him.

This was more than he felt he should be thinking. He wondered if noticing these attributes turned what was supposed to be innocent frolic into something soiled. He thought or at least hoped not. The people on the beach had to be there because they loved the human body and if admiring it was not allowed or seen as sordid, then how could someone say they love it?

Mike, Sophia and Jeff took another walk. They walked to the extreme north side of the beach. Suddenly, the crowd turned more male. Mike informed him that this was the men's side of the beach where men preferred to be with men.

"Oh." Jeff responded noticing that most of them were circumcised also. This changed a horribly implanted falsehood for him.

Just before the air began to cool and the group lugged their gear back up the stairway, Jeff and Mike wearing only their T-shirts and Sophia wearing Mikes shirt with the tails hanging down and slightly opened at the front, took a last walk and after passing a group of women Mike pointed with his thumb as nonchalantly as he could.

"Did you see that?"

"Yah, I'll bet she doesn't have to ever shave her legs either." Jeff mistakenly concluded.

"No Dummy. That's the point: she does shave it."

"Never, I would never shave that." Sophia exclaimed.

"You shave your legs, don't you? Not much different." Mike returned without waiting for an answer.

"How would they do that? You'd have to be a contortionist to do that. No, someone else would have to do that for me and I ain't never lettin' anyone near me there with a razor." Sophia responded.

"I think it's kind of clean. I wouldn't do it either. I'd be afraid it would slip and cut me off." he said reaching for his penetrater but thinking different suddenly saying. "OOPS!"

"Guys do it sometimes." said Mr. Pubic Hair Expert Mike.

The day was done. The sun was setting. The family headed home in the beautiful mid-July twilight. Jeff felt a little lonely on the ride home. He wished he could have had Melody with him but knew he couldn't even tell her about what they did that day.

They arrived home and were not there long when the phone rang.

"It's for your Jeff"

Jeff came to the phone.

"Hello?"

"Jeff, where have you been?" It was Melody.

"To the beach." Jeff answered not being too specific.

"This is the third time I've been out. My Mom says "Boys call girls, girls wait for calls." She said sarcastically imitating her mother's voice. "She won't let me call because she thinks its improper."

"What are you talking about?" Jeff asked.

"I'm here, silly. I left a day earlier. Yesterday I went with my Aunt and Uncle to this place we go to a lot which is on the way here and they brought me here today." Melody had gone to the camp again with her guardians.

"I really wanted to see you, I could have gone to the beach with you guys if I had gotten here soon enough."

"Well, that would have changed things." Jeff thought.

"I gotta get back now, I'm at a pay phone." Melody went on. "I just wanted to at least hear your voice and say I love you, Jeff."

"Oh God, You have no idea how much it means to hear that. I miss you so much Melody. I love you." Jeff responded.

"Call me tomorrow, we can talk longer but I won't be able to tell you I love you with my Mom there. Better make it after 4 o'clock because other wise she'll know I called and said I was here. I'll visit with her tomorrow. Then we can do something Tuesday. I can't wait to see you Jeff. Bye"

They hung up. He knew then that tomorrow would be the worst.

31

Monday July ninth arrived. Jeff spent the day at St. Mary's Park playing baseball with Mike and Stan and some of Mike's friends. They were a little late getting back and Jeff did not call until around 4:45.

"Hello?" came Melody's voice from the other side.

"Hi, Melody. Sorry I'm late."

"Yah, Mom says that that's men for you." she said but it was obvious that she was not the one upset.

"Mom's invited you to lunch tomorrow. Can you come?"

"Of course." he said laughing amused by the absurdity of the question.

"11:30 Okay?" Melody said still serious.

"Fine."

"See you then."

"Wow," Jeff thought, "What a difference. She almost sounded cold. I hope there's nothing wrong between us."

32

Monday dragged to Tuesday. Jeff had the address near the corner of 16th and Valencia. Valencia was one street over from Mission, so Mike told him to simply catch the 14 Mission again but ride to 16th and walk to her house.

Jeff dressed up as nice as he could and caught the bus. The 14 Mission was not a typical bus as most think of them, it was an electric trolley car. Trolley cars were just like buses. They looked similar and both ran on tires but the Trolley had two poles which extended about ten feet from the top of the Trolley to two wires, one positive and one negative that were strung overhead and made contact with the two poles. He was amazed when he reached his stop that he had gone within a block of her house on the 4th of July. He walked slowly to Melody's house. He had left at 10:30 so as to not be late again, but now he was early so he watched his time and walked around a little in San Francisco's Spanish American area.

At precisely 11:30 he walked up three steps to the front door or the duplex, her door was on the left. He rang the bell and heard Melody's voice on a microphone ask "Is that you Jeff?"

"Uh, Yes?"

The door miraculously opened itself and Melody called to him from a walkway at the top of the steps just inside the front door.

"Come on up Jeff" she called.

After climbing two steps he swung around when her heard the door automatically close.

"It works from a lever up here Jeff. Come on up."

The stairway was dark and had a thin carpet tacked up the mid-length of it. On both sides of the carpeting was hardwood. At the top there was a larger step, then two more steps to the right and he was at the top with Melody.

Behind her stood a portly but friendly looking lady, much different than he had pictured her.

"Jeff, this is my Mom." she said introducing them, "Mom this is my friend Jeff."

Mrs., Sanchez stuck out her hand and accepted his

handshake.

"Hi Jeff," she said pleasantly, "nice to meet you."

Jeff suddenly felt much more comfortable now that he saw that she was a very nice lady. He wondered why Melody had painted such a bleak picture of her for him."

"Like taco's Jeff?" asked Mrs. Sanchez.

"Sure do." he answered.

"Come on in, I've made some up."

So Jeff followed the two ladies into the kitchen and sat at the table, and with his best manners, ate lunch with his sweetheart and her mother. With her mother looking in the other direction, Melody reached out and squeezed his knee letting him know she was proud of him.

About halfway through lunch an older lady walked into the kitchen and over to the refrigerator, got milk out of it, crossed to the sink, pulled out a glass, filled it and walked back to the refrigerator.

Mrs. Sanchez yelled loudly. "Mama, this is Jeff."

The lady seemed to ignore her and returned out of the room.

"She's deaf." Melody explained. "That's my Grandma."

Near the end of lunch the front door could be heard being opened by key and someone walked up the stairs.

"Que Pasa, Mama." he said kissing Mrs. Sanchez's cheek.

He then went to the refrigerator and just like Melody's grandmother retrieved the milk and an apple and reached for a couple of tacos. He appeared not to even notice Jeff.

"Carlos, this is Jeff," Melody said.

"Hey man." he responded and left the room.

"That's my brother, or half brother I mean."

"Yah, Melody's my only gringa, that's why she's a Pruite. Only descent one I had; God rest his soul." Mrs. Sanchez explained. No more husbands though. Mr. Sanchez was number three, Mr. Pruite number two, and Carlos' padre Mr. Martinez was number one. That's enough for one life."

When lunch was concluded Mrs. Sanchez laid down some rules.

"Melody tells me you two are good friends. I don't mind that but she knows I have rules. Since your only going to be here this week, I'll let her go with you but you must have her back for dinner at 5 o'clock. Of course I know my brother makes you follow these same rules at home. Now, late once and no more. Don't you dare touch my daughter, she's too young for boyfriends. Be a gentleman to her, mistreat her and you'll have me to account to. And lastly, I don't ever want to see her cry because of something you have done to her. Follow these rules and we'll get along fine, defy them and you'll find I am someone to reckon with.

Melody sat through the instructions almost as if she had been through this before. She stayed calm and smiled but Jeff knew there was an intensity within her that was about to explode.

"Mama, can I walk Jeff to his bus stop?"

"Well, I guess so. Girls shouldn't be walking boys, boys should be walking girls."

The second they were on the side walk, Melody let out a huff of air and screamed shaking her body, flapping the pleated skirt she was wearing.

"Some times she just drives me craaazy." Melody exploded.

"She seems all right, just a little strict."

'That's not the word."

Melody changed the subject. "lets walk over to the park. I always go there to get away."

They walked over to Mission Dolores Park which was near the old Junipero Serra Mission Dolores. Once Jeff tried to put his arm around Melody and she pulled away. Looking at him paranoid like she said: "Too close to home, someone might see us."

How different Melody appeared to Jeff. She was in her own environment but seemed so much less comfortable, almost a different person. They walked for about ten minutes until Melody said she had to get back. "You can walk to the bus stop alone, can't you? I better get home." She lit up: "Where we goin' tomorrow?...No! Surprise me. What time?"

Jeff asked her: "How about ten ... or nine?"

"Nine o'clock will be fine." she said.

Suddenly she stopped. There was a young man walking

toward them.

"Oh God." she said. Obviously trying to avoid him.

"Melody?" he asked as he approached. "What are you doing here."

"Just visiting." she said "Bob, this is Jeff."

"Hi, nice to meet you Bob. Did you go to school together?"

"Oh, Yah" he said ignoring Jeff and turning to Melody. "I'm stuck in summer school this year, that's were I'm coming from." He then walked away.

Melody abruptly acted like none of this mattered. She leaned over and whispered. "I love you Jeff, I wish I could kiss you. Take me somewhere that I can tomorrow." She then ran away leaving Jeff standing there. He could see the back of her skirt bounce up and down hitting the top of her knee socks as she left.

33

Jeff was up plenty early on that Wednesday, July 11th. Mike was up with him and shaving and they were talking and listening to: KYA Radio twelve-sixty, DA, DA, DA, San Fran Cisco went the jingle, when a song softly came on the radio. Jeff sat and listened to the words as best he could and then his head began to spin. It was as if his body was separated from his mind as he stood above and watched the room spin. The song touched him to the very center of his soul. He began to cry.

"What's with ... oh boy, you got it bad." Mike said to him.

"Do you know the words to that song?" Jeff snapped, "I need to write it down."

"I think I do, or at least I'll try."

For the next few minutes Mike struggled with his memory and understanding of what the song said and Jeff wrote the words. When they finished, he gently folded the sheet of paper and tucked it into his shirt pocket.

To get to Melody's house, of course, Mike had to ride the

bus; however, he had not taken into account that this would be during "rush hour." The first couple of buses passed him by; filled to capacity. Finally, when one stopped he pressed himself in and squeezed among a sardine-can like packed vehicle. He held tightly to the overhead bar that extended along the walkway falling slightly this way and then that as the bus jerked forward and then stopped, forward and then stopped. At one point he was thrown violently into a girl about his own age and he apologized telling her he was not used to this sort of thing.

"Well just hold on; if I think your gonna fall, I'll grab you." Jeff thanked her feeling helpless.

His timing was fine; in fact perfect. When he arrived, Carlos, her brother was sitting on the front stoop with the door opened smoking a <u>Camel</u>.

"Hi!" Jeff said.

"Hey! Jeff right?" Carlos asked. "Hey hermana, its your boyfriend." he yelled up the stairs.

"I'll be right down," Melody yelled.

Without looking away from the stairway, Jeff stood nervously not knowing what to say to Carlos as he shifted his feet back and forth. Suddenly, Melody bolted down the stairs. She was wearing pants this time which he had never seen her in. She had a jacket slung over her shoulder.

"No coat, Jeff?" she asked.

"No? It's warm." he replied.

"You don't know San Francisco, do you? You have to dress just like you do at home because it's not the same everywhere and it can cool off fast." Jeff had not even thought of that.

"Let's go." she blurted.

Today Jeff was going to take Melody to Golden Gate Park and Playland. As they walked to the bus stop he glanced over at her and thought of how young she seemed; like she was a little girl here. At home she had seemed more mature but this may have been because she was in her childhood environment and back with her mother.

Jeff knew which bus to take. The 14 and then transfer to the

10.   This time they caught the 14 going outbound (away from downtown) so they were able to get a seat and sit next to each other. Melody quickly grabbed his hand and then leaned over and kissed him on the cheek.   "What a difference from the way she was yesterday." he thought.

"So what is this knew look?" she asked, "I'll bet you didn't think I noticed yesterday. I'm not sure I like it."

"Mike said I had to be cool if I was going to be here."

"Yah, but I like my country boy better. You look like all the boys around here now." Melody scolded, "but I'll take you any way I can get you." She said as she wrapped her arm under his nestling his upper arm against her breast. This was the first time he actually felt her breast pressed against him and even though it was subtle, it felt nice.

"You seemed awfully nervous yesterday." Jeff broached the subject he had worried about the last night.

"Jeff, we have something to talk about, but we have lots of time, lets have fun and forget my mother for now."

"She seems nice." Jeff interjected.

"I love my mother. Don't take me wrong."   Melody confessed.

They dropped the subject and just enjoyed being together for the rest of the trip to the Park.

When they arrived, Melody told him she had been there a couple of times on school field trips.

"A couple of times. If I lived here, I'd be here at least once a week."

"Oh Jeff, your so innocent some times." Melody told him.

Jeff showed her the whale, the tree cut; they walked among the taxidermied animals on display; they went through the museum, and each place Melody graciously made Jeff feel like it was the first time she had ever been to any of them, because, to her, this was the first time with Jeff, so it was the best time.

Melody and Jeff both loved the Japanese Tea Garden. The high little Japanese ornamental bridge over the pool with the goldfish was special to them.

Hidden Shore

"They say if you throw a penny in the pool and make a wish, your wish will come true if your heart is pure." Melody told Jeff. "Got a penny?"

If he had not had one he would have ran anywhere to get change so Melody would have her penny; he had one. Melody held the penny in her hand, closed her eyes and wordlessly mouthed her wish. Kissing the penny, she tossed it effortlessly into the pool.

"What did you wish for?" Jeff asked.

"Oh, you know!; if you tell, it doesn't come true." she replied.

What Melody did not tell him was that though simple, her wish was the most important thing to her at this time. She simply wished to return to Weston which meant Hidden Shore and Jeff.

There is a spot in the Japanese Tea Garden that is a porch which overlooks the gardens and had a large Buddha statue. Jeff had his camera with him and he had to have a picture of Melody in front of the Buddha. There were also some benches and Jeff and Melody sat at one holding hands and taking pictures.

Jeff suddenly decided this would be an appropriate time to pull out the words of the song which were still tucked securely in his pocket.

"Melody, I heard a song on the radio this morning. I think it should be our song."

Jeff tentatively handed her the paper after unfolding it for her. She cautiously read the words he had written. They were the words to the song "I Love How You Love Me" by the Babys. He sat cautiously waiting for her reaction.

"I hope I got it close to right." Jeff told her as she suddenly erupted into fitful sobs.

Through the sobs, Melody struggled to say: "Jeff, those are the most beautiful words I have ever heard. That is exactly how I feel about you." She wrapped, or precisely engulfed him in her arms, still sobbing. "I love you Jeff, I love you with all my heart."

She composed herself and then said: "Jeff, I will die rather than let anything come between us." Again she melted into his arms as they stood and walked from the garden holding on to each other as if nothing would ever be able to pry them apart.

"Jeff, there is a place here in the park our science class came to once and I want to show it to you. It's right next to the Aquarium. It's really pretty but this is the wrong time of year. It's called Rhododendron Dell."

"Sure, let's go."

They walked to the orchestra pit and to the back of it and there was a trail that went under the road and emerged at the entrance to Rhododendron Dell. The trail took them through a large collection of bushes that Mel explained were all different colors of rhododendrons. After what had happened in the Garden this was a calming excursion for them. There was a wooden bench in the middle of the Dell upon which the two lovers sat. Jeff looked over toward Melody and surprised that it was the first time that day kissed her on the lips. She responded to the kiss that she had asked him the day before to make possible for them. She initiated the tongues. To Jeff's surprise he felt the gentle initial probing of her soft and thin tongue as she first slowly ran it over the his top lip and then around to his lower one. Responding, he casually allowed just a bit of opening which made it possible for Mel to stealthily maneuvered her innocent arrow into the damp confines of his oral channel. His teeth parted and for the first time in his life, a woman had invaded him in this much desired way. Melody proved quite capable at what is commonly called a French kiss. The adulteration of excretion between them was pleasant rather than revolting. Most people find it repugnant to drink from a glass after someone else has, let alone to play joyfully in each others slime. The kiss was sensual and loving at the same time. This was a very adult step for the young lovers. Jeff softly placed his hand on the side of Melody's lap and began to rub her leg on her pants as they kissed. Melody made no effort to stop him. She knew where she would call him off. She had already found it necessary to say "down boy" to others before. This was not her first French kiss, but it was only the second.

Jeff felt the tongue go into his mouth and he proceeded to follow suit and eventually the kiss was terminated by both at the same time as they pulled away and looking into each other's eyes, breathing heavily, Jeff kissed her again softly this time, just a sealing peck.

"We need to mark this. Damn, I don't have my knife." complained Jeff

"Why asked Melody. What do you want to do make us blood brothers or something?"

"No, I want to carve our names in this bench."

"Oh!...I have a nail file."

'That'll work." So Jeff carved their initials which were not too fancy. Looked like this:

Jw + MP
7-11-1962

The bench is still there.

As Jeff and Mel walked from the dell to begin the long walk to Playland, Melody felt those wonderful sensations that had begun to creep into her whenever the two began to kiss. Jeff had only played at petting in the Dell, but she wondered where her cut off point really was. She knew she should not let it go much further than it already had, but she also knew she loved Jeff and wanted to show him how much. Letting him do as he wished would not be showing love, but she wanted to do more. She had to set her perimeters. She knew that the girl needed to set the limits.

The walk through the park was not bad since they had walked from Hidden Shore to Weston so many times and the park was about the same distance long. At Playland they rode the tunnel of love, ate a local favorite that was invented there at Playland called an Its It, which was two cookies with ice cream in the middle. Melody laughed with Jeff at the Clown. She had never been to Playland before and could not believe that she had been so deprived.

When they entered the fun house, Jeff explained to her about the air gun. "How did you know to wear pants? I probably would have seen your underwear!" he teased as they entered. He was right,

Hidden Shore

her tightly tucked blouse and pants were not challenged by the air monster.

After the fun house they bought a ticket and rode on the roller coaster, and then bought another and rode again, and then bought another and rode again. This was the funniest thing they had ever done together. Melody would scream and grab for Jeff and he would hold her so chivalrously. They kissed on the free fall and they kissed on the climbs, and they kissed at the tops. During the sharp turns it was hard to stay connected. Jeff reached over once and accidentally brushed her breast but it really was an accident. Jeff got very cold without having a jacket so Melody cuddled up to him to keep him warm.

The ride home was difficult, arrival meant parting again. When they arrived at Melody's house she informed him that he could not just drop her off but had to come up and say hello. This was another of Mama's rules. Jeff did that, Mrs. Sanchez thanked him for taking such good care of her daughter and he left.

Melody went into her bedroom and sat at the edge of her bed and thought hard of the events of the day. All she could think of was: "I love how you love me."

Melody wandered into her mother's room the next morning looking for something to tie her hair. She felt like pigtails today so she wanted two bands that matched. Mrs. Sanchez had left for work at six A.M. as she had every Tuesday to Saturday for the last fifteen years. She felt cheered sitting on the edge of her mother's bed taking in the warm feelings that to her the room had always provided. When she was unhappy her mother would hold her on this very bed. When she was small and frightened, her mother would let her crawl in bed beside her and sing to her or talk the fear out of her. She loved being her Mama's little girl. She missed having her mother do all the special things she did. But she had grown older now. She was no longer her Mama's little girl.

Mrs. Sanchez built a shell around herself and her children that no one else was allowed any more to penetrate. Mr. Martinez, who was Carlos' father had beaten her incessantly. The marriage was short and divorce was quick; Carlos was his son but he left him with Mrs. Sanchez. Then she met and married Mr. Pruite, Melody's father. He was so wonderful to her. He treated her like a queen. There never was a harsh word between them. Their marriage was also short. Her world caved in around her when she received the Western Union telegram from the government that he had been killed in Korea. She found the job as a housekeeper at the Sir Francis Drake Hotel downtown, moved her mother in, and went no where except to work, to church on Sundays and then to Mr. Pruite's grave taking Melody with her after church on Sundays. She would dress Melody in her Sunday dress with a little white hat. After 8 years, Mrs. Sanchez met and married Mr. Sanchez. He was the janitor at the church. He treated her well. Then he disappeared; it seems he returned to his wife in Mexico.

Melody knew it had been tough for her Mama and when the incident with her brother happened, it had destroyed the stability that was her mother's little world.

In the top bureau drawer she found her mother's clips right where they had been for as long as she knew. She chose two small green bands and returned to her room to dress not knowing where Jeff would take her today. She thought about yesterday as she dressed in a blouse and shorts.

34

Jeff was sitting in the sun on the back porch of the house waiting for the time to arrive to leave for Melody's. Mary saw him enjoying the rare early morning heat and stepped outside to join him. He had propped himself in a chair up against the easterly facing wall with the radiance of the sun directly on him as he soaked the warmth to the very marrow of his bones. The air was cool still, but the sun's rays felt nice, he wanted to stand and turn his back to the sun to warm his spine, but he was too comfortable in the chair to move.

"Jeff, I hope you didn't feel embarrassed at the beach the

other day." his mother said, "We have enjoyed that life style many times and would hope you feel fine about it."

"It was fine Mom." was his reply.

"You really like Melody, don't you Jeff?" his mother inquired.

"Yah, she's special Mom."

"I really enjoyed taking the two of you on your little date last month. She looked so pretty."

"Thanks Mom" he said.

The conversation was a bit stilted. It wasn't that Jeff and his mom weren't close, she just has her own world. She usually worked or spent her time at the bar either with her friend Nancy or with Bill. She often met Bill in Eureka and they did who knew what. Jeff did not feel imprinted to his mother. When he was young and she desired a hug from her little boy, he would back off because he really did not want to be hugged by his mother. Gabe and Stan were both closer to her. When he thought about it now he realized that it was funny that he wanted nothing like that from his mother but would like nothing more than to get a hug from Melody as much as possible.

"Maybe sometime she would like to go with us." Mary said referring to Melody.

"What was that Mom?" Jeff was confused about the remark.

"To a Nudist beach"

"I...don't think so Mom," Jeff replied.

"Your a good boy Jeff, I hope you have fun today with her. Where you going?"

"The Zoo."

"Don't forget your trunks, you might want to go swimming."

Jeff decided not to wear them because he had not told Mel where they were going so she would not have a suit anyway.

Jeff left a little earlier this Thursday. He could not believe he only had four more days with her in San Francisco before they would be apart again. He was beginning to want to return home, but he wanted her to be there and realized he would be alone at first.

Jeff's arrival was similar to the day before. This time;

however, Carlos was gone and Melody was home alone.

"Come on up Jeff." Melody called after the door opened.

He walked up slowly and at the top of the stairs was surprised when Melody grabbed him and kissed him. Their tongues had now become a permanent part of their variety of kisses. She held him for a long time hugging his body up to hers. She was wearing shorts which was also something new to him.

"No ones home. Grandma's gone shopping. Come with me." she ordered grabbing his hand and leading him through a bedroom door.

"This is my room." she said hesitantly, "I wanted you to see it."

The bedroom was simple. The bed had a pink bedspread and two stuffed animals set on each of the pillows. She had a dresser with a mirror and several bottles of perfume, eye make up, and other toiletry items. What surprised him most was that on one wall were a couple of dozen assorted newspaper and magazine pictures of Bobby Vinton.

"I didn't know you were a Bobby Vinton fan."

"Yah, he's cute," she said embarrassed. "but not as cute as you." she lied.

Melody then shocked him even more by grabbing him and kissing him passionately. They started to fall toward the bed and he stopped the fall. Melody broke away from the passion and sat down ever so slightly on the bed. Tapping it next to her, she invited him to sit.

Jeff sat timidly next to her.

"I have never had a boy in my room before." she told him. "Kiss me again."

Jeff pulled her toward him and kissed her and they fell back lying together on the bed with his feet dangling down toward the floor. Her leg curled up and pressed against his legs as she kissed him aggressively.

Just as suddenly, she broke the kiss and jumped up and said: "Let's go before my grandma gets here."

Jeff felt a bit used as he rose. Before leaving the room,

Hidden Shore

Melody grabbed some pants that were draped over the chair. She slipped them on almost as if she had wanted to be bare legged for the obviously planned tryst on the bed.

They took the 14 Mission to town where, as Mike had instructed, they caught an L Taravel streetcar at the East Bay Terminal. This street car took them through downtown, through the stinky tunnel, through the Avenues. and to the Zoo.

They held hand the whole distance and talked and watched the other people come on the bus and disembark at their various stops.

At the Zoo, they walked arm in arm or hand in hand for a couple of hours. Jeff liked watching them feed the lions. Melody preferred watching the antics of the monkeys on Monkey Island. They each had a soft drink and hot dog at a stand that also sold stuffed Zoo animals.

"Can I buy one for your bed?" Jeff asked.

"Would you?" Melody rejoined answering a question with a question. She wanted a Teddy Bear but they had none so she settled for a gorilla. She hugged it to herself the rest of the day.

"Let's go swimming!" Melody suddenly blurted jumping up and down on her toes.

"We don't have any suits." he cautiously responded.

"They rent them at the pool. Let's go!"

"Okay, if you wish." Jeff said knowing he would grant any wish he possibly could at this point in their relationship.

They walked to the pool and rented the suits. Jeff's fit fine but Melody's was slightly tight. Hers was a one piece blue suit with a little white ruffled skirt stitched around the waist. "Kind of old fashioned wouldn't you say?" she asked as they met outside of the dressing room.

Jeff was enthralled seeing her in her suit. He had never seen her in a bathing suit. In Hidden Shore, no one wore suits except the little kids and the tourists. This was not a little girl's body, even though it was a suit meant for little girls.

"I forgot how these rental's looked, I was a lot younger when I came here before." Melody confessed.

Hidden Shore

Jeff could not take his eyes off of her. This was the girl who seemed interested in sharing herself in may ways with him. This was the girl who loved him. Although he had not even tried to touch this beautiful body that he could see before him, he knew that someday he would.

Jeff and Melody were too young to even think thoughts of marriage yet, but each had considered that there was a possibility that what was developing was the first steps toward such a possibility.

Melody was equally proud of the young man she had found. Though thin, she held on to him closely as they sat by the pool proud to let the other girls know that he was hers.

They swan and sunned until it was time to redress and return home. As they walked toward the changing rooms, Jeff followed behind her as she tweaked one of her ears with her finger trying to clear the water out of it. She turned a little sideways and the leg of her suit moved slightly toward the cleft of her backside. After the day on the beach, somehow this seemed even sexier because it was such a mystery. He would almost have her remain a mystery; if he could.

The ride home was difficult. They knew they would part again. In Hidden Shore they would stay together until late in the night because she often only had to go next door to Stevie's. They spoke little but sat in each other's arms.

When they arrived Jeff did his duty again and reported up stairs to her mother.

"See what we got at the Zoo?" she asked her mom holding the stuffed gorilla in front of her.

"Nice Mel." Mrs. Sanchez said obviously unimpressed.

Melody walked Jeff to his bus stop. They wanted to kiss and when Jeff ever so slightly leaned for one she put her index finger to his lips and whispered: "Tomorrow?"

"Oh Yeah!" he suddenly remembered. "Gabe and Stevie suggested spending the day with us. Gabe can drive and we can all do something together."

"Great." Melody said obviously excited to spend some time

with Stevie.

"They want us to go to dinner with them to a Chinese restaurant that my Aunt likes. Can you go?"

"I don't know Jeff." Melody contemplated for a minute. "Let me ask my mom. Call me tonight and I'll let you know. She might if it's early"

"I'll call you at six"

"See ya," is all she said as she turned and ran a block then walked the second. she had to hurry though; she felt the dampness and cramps that meant her "time of the month" was arriving.

That night as the cramps surged through her she laid remembering the stolen moment on that same bed with Jeff. Except for her brother, Jeff was the only boy to ever sit on that bed as long as it had been hers. His presence purified it for her. She quietly whispered: "I love you Jeff" as she hugged her gorilla and fell asleep comforted by her new found temporary surrogate.

35

Friday morning and still exceptional weather for San Francisco. Much discussion had gone on concerning what to do that day. Gabe and Stevie had gone to Melody's house the evening before to meet her mother and to assure her that they would supervise Melody and Jeff if she would allow them to all have dinner together that night. Stevie spent much of her time there with Melody discussing her cramps and offering solutions. Melody realized that Stevie had become the older sister that she had never had. They hugged before they returned to the living room were Gabe had sat to watch Red Skelton with Mama and Grandma. Grandma laughed even though she could not hear Red because his antics were just as enjoyable in silence. He was her favorite.

Hidden Shore

Mike and Stan and Sophia were going to join them during the day, but it would be a double date for dinner, just with Gabe and Stevie. Mike suggested that they all go to San Jose, which was about a one hour drive, to see the Winchester Mystery House. He also suggested that for dinner the two couples should go to the Sampan Restaurant on Ocean Avenue. "That's my Mom's favorite Chinese Restaurant." he clued them in.

They all piled in the station wagon. The station wagon was one of those long Chevy's with a bench seat in front, one in the back and one that faced backward that folded down then lifted up to expose the seat in the back. Stevie sat with Gabe in the front. Mike, Sophia and Stan sat in the middle. Melody squeezed down with Jeff in the back. The ride was pleasant because Melody and Jeff could squeeze together and hug and they did kiss quite a bit along with teasing from the others.

Melody had not met Mike or Sophia before. but they both liked her a lot. At one point during the walk around the Mystery House, Sophia sidled over to Jeff and told him how lucky he was to have her, and how unlucky she felt not having Ken with her.

The Winchester Mystery House was built in 1884 by a wealthy woman named Sarah L. Winchester who began construction of such magnitude that it was to occupy the lives of carpenters and craftsmen until her death thirty-eight years later. The Victorian mansion, designed and built by the Winchester Rifle heiress, was filled with so many unexplained additions, that it came to be known as the Winchester Mystery House. Sarah Winchester built a home that was an architectural marvel to appease the spirits of those whom her husband's rifles had killed; or so it was rumored. Unlike most homes of its era, this 160-room mansion had modern heating and sewer system, gas lighting that operated by pressing a button, three working elevators, and 47 fireplaces. From rambling roofs and exquisite hand inlaid parquet floors to the gold and silver chandeliers and Tiffany art glass windows, the group were impressed by the staggering amount of creativity and by stairways that led to nowhere and doors that opened to nothing. Sarah Winchester would build one room after another without

Hidden Shore

consideration of these items in her rush to appease the spirits.

On the way home they stopped at the Crystal Springs Water Temple where you could see the water from the Hetch Hetchy Dam in the Sierra course though a water channel.. This was the water that supplied fresh drinking water to the people of San Francisco.

After this they piled back into the car. Jeff noticed as Melody leaned closely to him that he could not see the chain of her heart pendant. Rather than just letting it go and asking her if she had it, he reached into his shirt and selfishly asked her to pull her chain out so they could match the hearts. Melody hesitated a moment and with difficulty admitted that she had left it home.

"I thought we were going to wear these all the time?" Jeff asked irritated. "In fact, now that I think of it, you weren't wearing it yesterday because I would have seen it with your swim suit on."

"Jeff, I can't wear it all the time here. Melody confessed. "It's obviously a love charm and if my mom saw it she would come unglued at the seams."

"But you could have it at least with you." He pleaded.

"Jeff, it would ruin everything if Mom knew I had it."

The discussion had begun in whispers and quickly escalated to the first argument between Jeff and Melody. The three in the middle sat uncomfortably trying to ignore the argument. Stevie called out once: "come on you two, cut that out." Gabe finally had heard enough and pulled the car in at the parking lot at Thornton's Beach.

"Out, out, out." Gabe ordered. As he walked back and opened the rear door to the station wagon.

"You just don't understand my situation." Melody said near tears as she climbed out of the car and ran with Jeff running hurriedly behind her.

He caught up with her and she stopped running. Gabe and the others stood in the parking lot pretending that they were doing other things rather than worrying about the troubled couple.

After a few more minutes of heated discussion that amounted to nothing Melody finally said to Jeff: "It's almost like the necklace is more important to you than I am. When I get home I'll just give it back to you and you can keep it and I'll just stay here and you'll never have to see me again I just have had about as much as I can take with everything that is going on at my house and having to hide this thing we have and with my Mom wanting me to stay here and not go back and me not wanting to stay and now you make it even harder for me and I'm not sleeping because all I can think of is you I just, I just, I just."

The diatribe ended with Melody in complete tears and Jeff hugging her as Gabe and Stevie stepped close to them.

"I'm so sorry, Melody." Jeff pleaded grabbing her against her struggle and hugging her as he began to cry himself. "I guess sometimes I just set my priorities wrong." This was the first time he had seen her cry.

"Come on you two, what's wrong." Stevie asked as they approached.

"My Mom wants me to stay," Melody cried, "and all Jeff can think about is his damn pendent."

It was out. Among all she had said Jeff had still not caught on that there was much more than the charm involved in what was going on around Melody.

"My God Melody, we're just going to have to make sure that doesn't happen." Stevie teased. "If your Mom makes you stay we'll just have to come up and kidnap you. We'll build you a cabin in the hills and feed you mussels and crab and anything else Jeff can catch from the river. Gabe will sneak you..."

Everyone broke out in a fit of laughter that quickly extinguished the situation.

"I'm so sorry, Melody. I love you so much." Jeff declared before his first witnesses.

"Okay you two, lets see you kiss and make up."

Jeff kissed Melody. Their first kiss in front of anyone.

"We now pronounce you steady and steadier." Stevie proclaimed. "You guys walk a while. We'll wait."

Gabe and Stevie returned to the car knowing that Melody and Jeffrey would have another first: They would discover the passion that kissing and making up meant.

Hidden Shore

The two lovers walked to a slight rise and sat and kissed and kissed and kissed. And Jeff ran his hand over Melody's side and legs and had he tried to touch her breasts he would have been permitted to do so because Melody wanted him at that moment like she had never wanted anyone before.

There was no way at all that Jeff could begin to have anticipated what Melody had said. He knew that her mother was strict, but he had no concept that there were other things even deeper than that which were troubling her. Melody had many things that she knew she should talk to him about but she could not even begin to tell him about them. She feared that revelations of this magnitude would cause her to loose him. She feared no one would want her if she revealed what had happened. On the way back she knew that Jeff was receiving the brunt of her problems. She knew she had been hard on him, but she also knew that he would need to be completely understanding of her if she were to ever reveal all the things that were troubling her.

Gabe deposited the three others and Stevie and Melody went to allow Stevie to clean up for their dinner date while Jeff and Gabe did the same. Melody and Stevie began to talk, and Melody revealed to the first person ever everything that had happened. Stevie was a little shocked but she assured Melody that Jeff would be more understanding than she had any notion of. She told her that she needed to do everything she could to return North because Melody needed her and Gabe and Jeff and everyone else there to be her friends.

"If I can do anything at all to help, please don't hesitate to ask." she assured Melody. "Mel, I love you too. I have enjoyed having you as a sleep over, even though your reasons are questionable, but I hope you will continue. She kissed Melody gently on the lips and said: "Big sisters can do that."

The two couples went to Melody's so she could freshen up with new clothes. Mrs. Sanchez seemed eager to help her. She fussed over her and helped her pick her favorite dress for the night out. She even let her use mascara which had always been a taboo.

"Sometimes, I guess I won't let you grow up. You are such

a beautiful girl. Don't grow up too quickly Melodita." She said calling her a name she had not used for Melody since her return home.

The Sampan was an a darkly lit restaurant with wooden tables highly varnished in wooden booths equally high varnished. The walls were painted dark green. Against the wood and with the low lighting, the place had the feel of stepping back in time about fifty years. Combined with the periodic rumble of the passage of streetcars outside, the place had a different atmosphere than any of the them had ever experienced. There was a counter in the far corner where when they entered a stocky built older Chinese man was sitting who rose to greet them.

"Fo peepo?" he asked rhetorically in his broken English, bowing slightly at the waist as he retrieved four menus from a holder at the entrance. He wore a white waiters jacket with a menu book stuffed into a side pocket. He had thick glasses that distorted his eyes and made them look twice as large as they were.

"Yes, that's right." Gabe assured him.

"Forrow me prease." he directed.

He placed the menus in front of each of them as Gabe and Stevie sat on one side of the booth and Melody and Jeff sat across from them.

They perused the menus and made their selections setting their menus down they talked quietly for just a couple of minutes.

"Are you ready." the waiter asked returning to the table with his book in hand.

"I'd like the Chicken Chow Mein." ordered Stephanie.

"Ah, Chicken Chow Mein one Chicken Chow Mein" he said as he held the menu book closely to his face and wrote the order down."

"I'd like the Pork Fried Rice." Melody requested.

"Ah, Poke Flied Lice." he repeated quickly. He spoke very quickly to each order.

"This Tomato and Beef Chow Mein sounds good. Can I have that with Pork instead of Beef." Jeff requested.

"Ah? Tomato and Poke not Beef? Ah, Okay, not so good but

Hidden Shore

you like I do."

Gabe ordered the Mongolian Beef. "Extra Hot" he requested.

"Oh! Mongolian Beef. Mo Hot. Good Good. Drinks."

Everyone ordered a Coke except Stevie who ordered a 7-up.

"He is so cute." said Stevie as he walked away. "Kind of what you would expect some writer to invent for a dime novel he seems so much in character."

After the waiter left the table Melody reached down and placed her hand on Jeff's lap. He thought of reaching down and grabbing her hand but decided he wanted her to do as she wished and she rubbed up and down his leg ever so gently. The reassurance of her touch was so nice he did not want her to stop. He looked at her and smiled. She raised her hand from his lap and placed it to the rear of his neck teasing the back of his neck and his hair line which tickled. He placed his hand on her lap and began to reciprocate and for the first time with Melody, he felt a stirring down below as they played touch and tickle together.

The dinner was delivered and remembering the lunch in Sausalito, Jeff ate slowly, this time savoring the chunks of onion, bell pepper, pork, and the noodles as he ran his tongue around each item so to appreciate the flavor longer and feeling an oral stimulation in conjunction with the rhythmic performance that was being performed by the lovers under the table.

After the meal Gabe knew he had to get Melody home but he wanted to take her and Jeff somewhere. Each night since they had arrived, Gabe had taken Stevie to the top of Twin Peaks to watch the sun set. When they stepped from the restaurant they were greeted with a chill that made them turn their coat collars up and wrap their arms around each other.

"It's foggy and early so we probably wont be able to see anything from up there now, but I thought you two might like to see where people park in this town." Gabe told them.

They drove up the crooked road to the top of Twin Peaks and parked in the lot which overlooked the city. They could see nothing but there were other cars parked there also looking at nothing.

"What could they be looking at?" Stevie teasingly wondered.

"I don't have any idea," said Gabe. "but I think Jeff and Mel do." he said glancing into the rear view mirror at Melody and Jeff who were now kissing passionately. Melody glanced up at them and they all laughed. "I guess we'll just have to watch the submarines race for now." Stevie kidded.

After a while, when everyone had regained their composure and with the windows steamed over, Gabe suggested that he had another idea. The road to the top circled the twin peaks almost like a brassier strap and directly behind them was one of these peaks. It'd only take just a couple of minutes to climb to the top, so he suggested that they should climb up.

They all liked the idea and got out and climbed. They were mesmerized by the fact that the climb took them above the fog. Looking below they could see the sun setting in the west. All around them was a sea of fog and the only other thing rising above the fog in majestic splendor were the red towers of the Golden Gate Bridge.

36

Saturday morning July 14th, Stevie found Jeff preparing himself for the day.

"When you're ready, let me know. Gabe and I are goin to take you to Melody's, but I want to stop and get something for her on the way." she instructed him.

Gabe drove Stevie and Jeff to Kay's Jewelers on Mission Street and the boys waited in the car while Stevie went inside. Emerging about fifteen minutes later she showed Jeff a gift wrapped long, thin, flat box.

"This is for Melody, I want to go in when we get to her house and give it to her."

When they arrived Stevie and Melody went into Melody's bedroom while Jeff and Gabe waited in the living room. Carlos and

Grandma were eating breakfast in the kitchen. Carlos came in later and he and Gabe began to talk. Carlos was considering going into the Army and the subject came up about Gabe's having enlisted. They had a nice discussion concerning it. Jeff thought it was nice to see Carlos' real personality; he had been so quiet before.

A little later Stevie and Melody emerged.

"Where you guys going today?" asked Stevie.

"I'd like to take Mel to the Fisherman's Wharf today." answered Jeff.

"We'll take you." Stevie said as Gabe looked over at her as if he felt he should be asked first.

"Don't worry," she continued, "We'll just drop you off. I know this is the last day you guys get to be together here, I'm not gonna let nothing disturb you guys today."

"What was so secretive?" Jeff asked concerning the box.

"Well..." Melody began.

"She'll tell you later." Stevie interrupted. "Let's go."

They all said goodbye to Carlos and Grandma and piled into the station wagon. Gabe took a circuitous route driving down Lombard Street, "the crookedest street in the world," through Chinatown, up to the foot of Coit Tower, and along the Waterfront. dropping them off at Ghirardelli Square right near the Wharf.

Ghirardelli Square had been a chocolate factory built of brick many years before and had just recently been turned into a shopping mall. Melody and Jeff first walked around there. They wandered into a music box store that had music box works with a myriad of different songs.

Jeff asked: "Do you have 'I Love How You Love Me?'" Checking the list the clerk told him: "No." She had him write his home address and told him they would contact him if one ever came in.

They did, however, have the theme from <u>Days of Wine and Roses</u> which was the movie they had seen together for their first date, so Jeff purchased one and when he spent the next week alone without her in Hidden Shore he built a wooden box to accommodate the song and burnt Eureka Inn and the date June-9-1962 on the top.

Hidden Shore

Across from the Square was a Maritime Museum which they toured and then walked along a beach that was behind the museum. The beach led to a long pier from which there were many fishermen and boys throwing crab pots in the water trying to catch crab.

Near the end of the pier, Jeff and Melody found a secluded spot and sat on a bench.

"Jeff, I want to show you what Stevie got for me but you have to kiss me first."

Jeff willingly stood up and wrapped his arms around her as she reciprocated. They kissed and while they did Melody removed her arms from around Jeff and brought her hands to the clasp on her pants. When she did, Jeff was curious of what she was doing as she began to move her hand, but since she was shorter the back of her hand was gently pressed against his penis but what she did was to undo the clasp on her pants and slowly lower the zipper enough to open her fly. She broke the kiss and said to Jeff: "You can look, Jeff."

She backed her mid body just slightly to give him room to see and when he glanced downward he could see the top of her panties through the opened zipper. She then slightly lowered the top of her panties just enough below her belly button to reveal his charm attached to a much longer gold chain that circled her hips.

"This way, I can wear it and Mom would never see it there. The only time I need to take it off is when I take a bath in case she comes in and sees me."

The first glance down without knowing what Melody was doing was actually embarrassing for Jeff. He was not sure what he was supposed to do with her pants open that way. It was a relief when he found out her intention.

Melody pressed against him again and returned her pants to their proper condition. "When I return to Weston, I'll put it back on your chain." she assured him.

They walked a little way back and about mid-pier Melody began to giggle.

"Jeff?" she said sexily. "Give me your chain."

Melody held out her hand. Jeff raised his hands and

unclasped the chain. Handing it to Mel, she re-clasped the clasp, put her left arm around him pulling him close. She pulled the tails of his shirt out from the front of Jeff's jeans and tucked three fingers in over his belt buckle and down into his shorts just slightly.

"Tuck in your stomach." she ordered, "hold up your shirt."

Jeff obeyed and she glanced quickly into the top of his shorts. Seeing little but a few whisps of hair, she teasingly winked at him and dropped the pendent and chain down into the warm confines of his male guts. She started to turn her other hand and tap at his crotch from the outside of his pants, stopped, thinking better about it, and quickly rose her hand over her head and said: "Keep it there until we can kiss back home again.

Jeff suddenly remembered what she had told him the day before that she might not return. This made him sad but he hugged her and they walked to the Wharf together arm in arm as he began to feel the chain and the heart begin to fall around his penis and dangle on both sides tickling his testicles and then finally falling over the head and settling below the front of it. The sensation had been titillating considering Melody had caused it.

At the Wharf they each bought a little paper cup with crab that was sold by the merchants at cookers in front of the shops. Each one came with small round saltine crackers and a smaller paper cup of cocktail sauce.

While eating Jeff looked up at Coit Tower, remembering the night with Sophia. He decided he needed to right a wrong and told Melody: "I know we drove up to that tower before, but there is a stairway that leads from here and then I'd like to take you to the top so you can see the city from up there. Feel like a climb?"

"Sure." she said.

The two repeated the climb that Jeff and Sophia had made a week earlier. For them though it turned into a game. When they started she ran up a couple of dozen steps and then sat down to wait for him to reach her. He then bolted up a couple of dozen more, and then sat and waited for her. This process was repeated for over an hour. Each time they would meet they would kiss on the shared stair allowing the next to run after the kiss. The game seemed to come naturally. No one had devised the rules, they just seemed to like the game. Near the top and just before the tower, they gaily began to run hard hand in hand to the foot of the Coit Tower.

After climbing the tower, Melody expressed fascination with the view; much like Jeff had that Wednesday evening with Sophia. Just like Sophia, he wrapped his arms around her, not to warm her as Sophia had but because he loved her.

"I wish you could see this at night." he said.

"How can I have lived most of my life here and never seen so much of what you have shown me." she asked, "If we ever get married, we'll have to come here on our honeymoon.

This came so quickly to Jeff that he did not know how to respond. He chose not to respond.

They kissed instead. This was romance, not just a visit like it had been with Sophia.

"Please don't stay." Jeff said. "You've gotta come home."

Melody knew what he meant. The walk and the bus trip home were sadly performed. They held each other tightly. Just before Melody's bus stop, she instructed Jeff, who was to leave the next afternoon, to be at her house at 8:30 the next day to go to church. She did not really want him to go but she wanted even more to see him one last time. "We'll then go to the cemetery and Mom said you can't go. We wont be able to talk or touch again until I get back to Weston. And Jeff...I will somehow." she said kissing him. "You stay on the bus and go home, I'll see you tomorrow. I can walk home on my own. I'll tell my Mom you had to be home right away."

Jeff wanted to walk her, but he obediently followed her directive and remained on the bus. After stepping off, Melody kissed her hand and blew a kiss to him from the sidewalk from outside his window.

As they had a couple of other evenings, Jeff and the family went to the Granada Theater and watched a movie. Afterwards, he sat thinking about recent occurrences. He had always assumed being in love would be simple. He thought one fell in love, all was wonderful, marriage, children, work, grew old, and that was it; very simple. But he was discovering the intensity that came with love. He thought it should all be happy, but right now he felt intense sadness. How different than he thought it was supposed to be. He reached his hand into his shorts and pulled the chain out. "She was the last to touch this before it went in." he thought. He kissed the heart feeling his feminine self come out. He thought of Melody and lowered his hand to his member as it began to rise. Then he stopped. He vowed that the next time he had an orgasm it would be shared with Mel. No matter how long he waited. He was sure it would happen some day and decided to remain chaste until the time came.

37

On Sunday morning, he dressed in his cousin Mike's only suit and walked and bused to Melody's. The others were going to the nude beach again and he felt happy that he was not. He did not want any one to see him again until Melody did. Being a virgin, he felt purer with his commitment.

He rang Melody's doorbell and again the mysterious door opened and Melody again invited him up. He heard Mrs. Sanchez yell to Melody to "get your dress on" as he could hear her footsteps run to her room.

"Hello, Jeffrey." Mrs. Sanchez greeted him as he reached the top of the stairs. "Would you like a cup of coffee?"

"No, thank you." he responded politely.

"Hot chocolate maybe." she persisted.

"Sure." he gave in.

He followed Mel's Mother into the kitchen where Grandma was drinking a cup of coffee at the table. Both ladies were dressed in their Sunday best outfits and the smell of their combined perfumes wafted past his nostrils turning his stomach.

"Mama!" Mrs. Sanchez yelled. "fix Jeff a cup of chocolate."

She then headed into the room she felt Jeff had no idea was. About ten minutes later, after the chocolate had been served,

Melody and her Mother emerged. Melody was wearing a little girl baby blue dress with a bow around the waist and an Easter hat on her head.

"I'm so embarrassed, I thought she would let me wear a normal dress since you were coming." Melody exclaimed.

"Oh shush." said Mrs. Sanchez as she grabbed a brush and began combing Melody's hair, "You look beautiful."

She had a pair of Dorothy Gale type shoes short white socks. Her legs were mature and looked strangely odd sticking below the knee length dress. There was a petticoat that flared the dress and looking at Melody it was shocking to Jeff that this was the same young woman who had showed him her panties the day before.

The Church was about ten blocks away. The four walked to church in an orderly manner with Jeff and Melody in the lead and the ladies following closely behind like chaperones. Mrs. Sanchez talked about her inability to get Carlos to join them telling Jeff how out of control Carlos was.

Jeff had never been to church before. He sat uncomfortable with Grandma and Mrs. Sanchez between him and Melody.

Melody had become the same stilted person she was on the first day he saw her at her house in San Francisco. After the church service, the four walked in the same orderly fashion to catch a 14 Mission bus. They all got on the bus together and rode outbound until Jeff disembarked in the Excelsior. The ladies would ride to the end of the line and call a cab to take them the three miles further to the grave of Melody's father in the small town of Colma.

Jeff felt so empty as he walked the few blocks back. He thought maybe it would have been better not to go that day, but he was able to see what Melody was put through on every Sunday with her Mother.

38

The ride home to Hidden Shore was equally as frustrating

for Jeff. As miles began to increase between the two it was almost as if he could not feel her presence in his heart as well. He felt lonely; discontented. Like part of him was missing; and what if she never returned? Jeff tried to put that possibility out of his mind.

As bad as Jeff felt, Melody felt worse. There is no way to express how miserable she felt.

The taxi cab took the three ladies to the cemetery and deposited them at the grave marked: Cpl. James H. Pruite. This was a girl who pranced nude in the foothills of California but now sat in her little girl dress while her mother placed flowers, trimmed grass, and wiped the stone at her father's grave. Mrs. Sanchez did not want anything to change. She had first dressed her daughter in this fashion the first time she came to the cemetery and she refused to have her "meet" her father in any other way. For Melody to look any different would be a desecration of the holy spot where her father was buried.

Melody felt the chain that encircled her waist as she sat on the grass with her skirt flailing around her, her hat properly positioned on her head. She thought about the last week, of how she loved Jeff and how she was almost willing to give herself willingly to Jeff if he would but take her. Her Mother made her feel like a sacrificial lamb, she would have willingly been one for Jeff. She knew she was not the innocent little girl that her Mother tried to portray at the cemetery. She knew her Mother knew that she was not the innocent little girl that her Mother tried to portray at the cemetery. She knew her Mother was in denial about her daughter. She felt that Jeff was more innocent than she was.

The next week would seem like an eternity especially since she planned to be picked up by her Aunt and Uncle the following Sunday but she had no idea if her Mother would actually let that happen. The next Sunday seemed so far away.

She did very little except to write a letter to Jeff on Monday and surreptitiously mailed it to him.

39

Tuesday the only thing that happened was that her Mother yelled at her because Carlos came into her room to ask her something.

"No one comes into your room but me and your Grandma and maybe a girlfriend. No boys and especially not your brother." her Mother yelled.

40

On Wednesday she went for a walk around the neighborhood wearing her knee socks and pleated skirt with a simple blouse like she wore most of the time. She had a copy of Tom Sawyer and was trying to read it when she realized someone was standing over her. It was Bob again.

"Hi." she said holding her hand up to block the sun from her eyes.

"Hey, what's new!" he greeted her.

"Not much. It was nice to see you the other day." she lied.

"Yah." he said as he sat down. "Who was that guy you were with?"

"My boyfriend." she replied without hesitation.

"Yah, I got one now...a girlfriend I mean; named Gloria."

Melody was happy to hear this. Bob was her boyfriend when she left San Francisco, but now this made it easier to talk to him and explained why he had not written to her after she left.

They talked over an hour until he had to be back in summer school.

"I gotta go." he told her.

During the whole discussion he looked nervous and uncomfortable as he looked side to side as if he was watching for someone. What she did not know was that he was watching for his girlfriend Gloria. Gloria was a good girlfriend to him but she was extremely jealous so he did not want her to see him with Melody not knowing what she would do. The first time that he had been sexual with Gloria he admitted he had sex before but he would not tell her who it was with; So Gloria wrongly assumed it had been with his last girlfriend: Melody.

41

On Thursday, Melody was at the park when Bob approached her again. They were not together long when he had to return so she picked up and began to walk home.

Suddenly, she heard a girl yell at her:

"Hey bitch, that's my boyfriend. Stay away from him."

Melody was in shock. She turned and looked and there was a girl standing a ways behind her. She was tough, obviously street wise. Melody just looked away and continued heading home.

"I mean it bitch." the girl yelled again as Melody walked away.

The next day she returned to the Park again. Again Bob approached her and they sat and gabbed. Mel did not mention the incident the day before, she did not think it was important, but suddenly three girls approached Bob and Mel. The lead one was Gloria.

"Hi, Sweety." Gloria said to Bob. "Who's this?"

"This is Mel." he replied. "You know her."

"I don't think so." she said angrily.

"She's just an old friend." Bob replied downplaying their former relationship. "Mel, this is Gloria."

"I gotta go, nice meeting you" Melody interrupted as she stood and walked away. Bob and Gloria began to talk for a moment then a friend of Bob's walked up and asked: "Isn't that your old girlfriend?"

"I thought you were just friends." Gloria shot back.

"Yah, we're friends, she was kind of an old girlfriend."

Bob tried to comfort Gloria, "It's cool, don't worry 'bout it.'

"Well I'm gonna leave" Gloria announced.

"Okay, see you later." Bob said as he headed back to the school.

Melody was heading home and was nearing the edge of the park thinking about Jeff and about starting to pack for her possible departure home to Weston. All of the sudden from her right she saw Gloria and the two girls approaching.

"Hey, bitch, I know you and Bob are exes, If you're smart stay away from my man." Gloria demanded.

"I wasn't doing anything, he's a friend of mine."

"You're not listening to me; stay away from my man."

"I'm not doing anything." Melody said excitedly as he realized that this was about to become very volatile. "I can have friends too."

"You stay away from my man or I'll beat your ass." Gloria threatened.

Melody turned toward her and said: "I don't care what you want." She then turned her back to Gloria and started walking quickly away.

"Well, you will in a minute you stupid tramp." Gloria yelled.

Gloria grabbed Mel by the shoulder and spun her around toward her bringing the two girls face to face. She reached up and smacked her hard, bitch slapping her cheek. Melody pulled back in disbelief and Gloria reached out and grabbed Melody's blouse from the shoulder popping all the buttons and after ripping the blouse from her shoulder threw it to the ground next to Melody. Mel bent down to pick it up and Gloria kicked her in the butt knocking her over then began to kick Melody in the ribs and side, the friends joined in and all begin to put the boots to Melody stomping and kicking as she tried to rise as the girls pushed her skirt up and kicked her wearing only her bra trying to humiliate her any way they could.

All of a sudden from a distance she heard someone yell: "You loco bitch, you pendeja, get off my sister."

"You can have her, we're through with her now." Gloria said as Carlos ran toward her. The girls walked away as Carlos helped

Mel up and taking off his own jacket wrapped it around his humiliated and painfully wracked sister.

Carlos walked her home and tended to her as best as he could. When Mrs. Sanchez arrived they had to tell her what had happened. Later Melody saw Carlos in his room and walked in to thank him for helping her out. In pain with bruised body she hugged her brother just as her Mother walked by the bedroom. Her Mother came unglued, yelled and screamed at Melody who ran crying to her room feeling completely destroyed.

42

On Friday July 20, the same day of Melody's fight and about the same time, Jeff walked to the mailbox to see if, by any chance, he had received a letter from Melody. He was very excited when he discovered there was one waiting for him. He tore it open and began reading before he even got into the house.

Dear Jeffrey   Mon.
July 16, 1962

I have been trying to get some thoughts down to you for most of the day. I'll begin a letter then tare it up not wanting to say nothing that might upset or   scare you.

I love you Jeff, I love you, I love you. I couldn't say it enough times to   make it appropriate.

I was so embarrassed yesterday. I wanted you to take me away tare off my dress and dress me like a princess and then ride away with me on your faithful steed because you are my night in shining armor. I love having your charm around my   waist   it makes me think of you every time I move and I feel it tickle my tummy.

I still don't know if mom will let me come home to you. I am so lonely. If

I don't please don't forget me. Please be my friend. I won't expect you to keep me as a girlfriend you would need someone closer to you.

I got to go

Mel   XXXXXX

PS I love how you love me

The letter was both encouraging and discouraging. She was always a good speller but there were many misspellings in it. It seemed disjointed and out of place for Melody. Jeff tucked it in his pocket and walked alone to the only place that gave him solitude: North Beach.

When he arrived he sat and thought, and sat and thought, and thought. At one point he thought he saw Greg down by the tide pool with a dark haired girl, but he knew that Greg would not ever avoid him and Greg didn't have a girlfriend.

43

At 5 PM the next Sunday, two days after he read the letter, Jeff's phone rang and Stan handed the phone to him.

"It's Mel" Stan casually announced.

Jeff's heart leaped almost out of his chest.

"Jeff, Jeff, I'm here, I'm here." Melody blurted before he even said anything on the phone.

"Where?" he asked.

"Weston, you dummy." she kidded.

"To stay?"

"Are we gonna talk or are you going to come and get me?" she demanded to know.

"I'm coming, I'm coming." he yelled hanging up the phone.

Hidden Shore

Melody was left with a dead phone in her hand. She shook her head and went into her room to dress for Jeff's arrival. She decided the heart belonged at her breast so she slipped it back onto his chain and placed it over her head and into her cleavage. She studied the bruises still evident on her side and breast from the beating two days before. They were all where Jeff would not see them unless the reunion became more passionate than she expected. She decided not to tell Jeff about the fight because she knew it would just upset him for no reason. She considered how much different it was here rather than in San Francisco. In San Francisco she had to perform like she was a little girl, she could not even enter her brother's room without getting in trouble. With so many things to do in San Francisco, she could do no more than walk a few blocks from her home. She had no boyfriend there. Her Mother would put a stop to that if she tried to have one. Here, she could be a girl, a woman. She could walk around the house naked and not get any criticism, in fact it was encouraged. She could go wherever she wished; and most of all she had a boyfriend that loved her and she could love back without restraint. She was old enough to make adult decisions there, not like in San Francisco where she could not even be a teenager.

Jeff madly dashed around the house vowing that he needed to get his own transportation. He found Gabe at Stevie's and the three of them drove to Weston to pick Melody up.

Melody was waiting on the front porch with her suitcase still packed for her return to Weston.

"I thought I could use some clothes if I can stay with you for a couple of days." Melody asked Stevie.

"You bet." Stevie assured her. She then walked into Melody's house to assure her Aunt and Uncle that she would take good care of her.

Gabe dropped Jeff and Melody at South Beach and left them alone. Jeff kissed her and hugged her close. He noticed the chain around her neck and asked: "You have our Chain?"

"I always do." she responded sitting down with him on the sand. "Where's yours?"

Hidden Shore

About the same place you put it." he informed her.

"Different shorts I hope.' Melody joked.

She looked at the fly of his pants and said: "We're home. It doesn't have to be there any longer."

Jeff looked down and considered the situation.

"Do I have to get it?" she asked.

"No, that's okay...unless you want."

"I think you can handle that." she reassured him.

Jeff turned slightly sideways and began to undo his pants.

"Let me watch." she asked.

"Watch me get the charm?"

"Please."

Jeff unsnapped his pants and lowered the zipper. He lifted the band of his shorts and reached his hand into them finding what had become a partially erect penis. Reaching lower he stared at Melody as he watched her concentration on his hunt for the charm. She could make out the size of his penis as he reached behind it pushing it forward to locate the charm. She knew it was no longer flaccid and knew that she was the cause of his present state. She placed her hand on his leg and teased his penis into full erection as she ran it up and down his inner leg. Jeff pulled the charm from his shorts and forced his member back down within his pants and laboriously tried and finally succeeded in zipping the pants back up. He rolled over attempting to make it shift into a less conspicuous position; finally reaching his hand down and to press against it to push the head down his pant leg; much to Melody's amusement. With a chuckle from Melody, he rolled over toward her as she placed the charm around his neck, and kissed her and found her legs with the palm of his hand at her knee and through the kiss he guided his palm up the inside of her leg within the skirt, feeling the softness of her inner thighs. Melody reached down to his hand and considered raising it higher but instead raised it off from her leg and guided the palm of his hand to her left breast. Jeff softly felt the outline of her bra and caressed her breast softly. Before the situation got out of hand, Melody then took his hand from her breast and said: "Be responsible with me, I trust you." Things had happened so rapidly in the development of their relationship while they were in San Francisco. Now things would settle down as they slowed the development and just enjoyed each other at the point they had achieved. Melody and Jeff had both grown much older in the last six months. Neither of them were little any more, they were making adult decisions and living with the consequences.

"What happened that changed everything? I've been so worried since I got your letter." Jeff asked.

"You got it. When things changed I hoped that maybe it would get lost so you wouldn't worry. Mom just changed her mind. Maybe she'll want me to come back some day but for now I'm here and that is all that matters."

What Melody was not telling Jeff was that after the beating and after her Mother yelled at her for being in Carlos' room, she decided it would be best for Melody to be away from San Francisco and Carlos still. Carlos was considering joining the Army. When he went, Mommy would have her come home. She hopped Carlos would take a long time before he joined.

The next day, Jeff presented Melody with the box he had built that last week. Melody placed it on her dresser with the gorilla on her bed, she was beginning to surround her bedroom with memories of Jeff.

44

The rest of the summer was spent being kids at summertime. Until school started Jeff and Melody were habitually together. They would walk on the beaches and play among the tide pools. Jeff walked with her up Dead Man Creek showing her their favorite swimming hole. He even admitted to her that as kids they had often skinny dipped; at first he did not mention the girls but Melody pried that information out of him.

"So you mean that a lot of these girls have seen you and I haven't?" she teased him.

There were other dates. They went to the soda shop in Weston frequently and visited with Greg or Stevie. who was lonely with Gabe in the service, or Clint even had a new girlfriend from school who lived in Fairbury named Tanya. Everyone called her Tawnie.

Their relationship was limited to kisses, and once in a while, Jeff would boldly caress Mel's breasts but he never tried more than that. He was satisfied with that one indiscretion for now. Sometimes the kisses and touch would lead to the passionate encounters called "making out" by the kids. Their breathing would become heavy as the testosterone level would rise. Jeff found it uncomfortable as his passion would lead to the often present bulge in his jeans. But on the most part, the summer was one of fun and games, and being with friends.

One day in early September, just before school began, Jeff and Melody were walking along Dead Man Creek when they noticed that some kids had left their swing rope tied over the swimming hole. Jeff suggested: "Let's go swimming." Melody hesitated but said: "Okay but we don't have swimming suits."

"We got our underwear." Jeff countered.

"Which becomes see through when wet." she argued, but began undressing. "Keep your distance and we can."

So Jeff and Melody stood away from each other and Jeff stripped to his T-shirt and shorts, Melody to her bra and panties. Jeff swung in on the rope and Melody ran and swung in right after almost falling on top of him. They swam and talked but kept their distance. At one point Jeff crossed over to hug Melody and she stopped him.

"Don't touch me while I'm undressed like this." she said. "Don't come any closer."

This scared Jeff as he backed off. Her anxiety had shocked him. She acted like he meant to rape her. Melody was not ready to have someone touch her in that state.

Suddenly they heard another couple approach the swimming hole. Melody crossed her arms over her brassier and sat low enough so that her arms were under water as did Jeff.

Standing above them were Clint and Tanya.

"Hey, you guys, can we join you?" Clint called out.

"Uh." Jeff said looking over to Melody.

Melody gave him a worried look but did not object which would not have made any difference because Clint and Tanya began stripping all their clothes off. They stripped completely.

"It's my rope you know." Clint said as he swung naked landing in the pool.

"You guys will have wet underwear walking..." he said after rising out of the water and was cut off by Tawnie's dive into the pool.

Melody sat nervous for a while as Clint and Tawnie swam.

They finally settled together on the opposite side of the swimming hole from Mel and Jeff. Melody smiled at Jeff and shyly swam next to him and he put his arm around her.

"What's up with you guys? You've skinny dipped enough times." said Clint.

Jeff and Melody looked at each other.

"Melody and I..." Jeff began to say but was cut off by an elbow in his side from Melody.

"It's okay." she said and unsnapped her bra and reached below the water pulling off her wet panties and tossed them up to the bank. Jeff watched this in total disbelief. He had hoped to see Melody like this some day, but this was completely unexpected and there she was stark naked standing not only before him, but also before Clint and Tawnie. Jeff hesitatingly followed suit.

The two couples relaxed and swam and Melody felt as comfortable as she did at the camp with her other friends. Jeff was pleased to see Melody for the first time; AND NO BONER.

This was a real ice breaker. Not as much timidity between the two after that day.

45

Hidden Shore

The next Monday school began. Jeff became a junior; Melody a freshman. They had been assigned different buses so even though his bus picked up kids in Weston, he and Melody could not ride together.

The second week of school, Jeff started his first "real" job. Mitchell's hardware in Weston hired him three afternoons a week cleaning their store. Melody and Jeff would meet on the same days which were the same days they met the last year at the Library. He would walk her home and then he had to be to work just before they closed at six to clean for two hours and then he would walk home to Hidden Shore.

The swim at the Creek had not changed anything about their relationship. They never discussed it but they each had revealed themselves to each other. Jeff now knew the outline of Melody's pubic hair and knew the size of her aureoles, which did not match perfectly, and now when he saw her he could make out her shape in his mind. He did like her small full behind. He so much wanted to smack her on it when she bent over but he controlled himself.

One day Jeff and Greg were sitting at lunch in the Library studying and reading and Jeff almost got in the first school fight of his life. At the table was a boy named Leonard who was obviously a freshman. Jeff was talking about Melody to Greg and telling him how much he loved her and other intimate details that boys will sometimes talk about with their best friends. He was unaware that he was being overheard. The boy interrupted him looking up from his own book and said without any warning:

"Hey if you love this girl so much and you don't want to fuck her, why don't you just finger fuck her?"

Jeff went crazy and began to charge at the boy, but Greg and a couple of other boys held him back and Jeff got nothing more than a trip to the Dean's office again. This time for disturbance in the Library. What Jeff did not know was that this was the same Leonard who was Melody's short lived boyfriend from Weston School.

Jeffrey respected Melody completely. Though their relationship was developing a sexual aspect, he still considered it as love not just sex. To even think what this boy had said to him destroyed the tenor of the relationship and made it unholy in nature. Many people would judge their relationship already as unholy, but Jeff loved Melody and anything between them was because of his love for her, not because he simply wanted an object for his sexual gratification.

46

Saturday September 29th, Melody and Jeff did something that they often did not do; they wandered north on the coast. The northern beach was not as attractive to people as the South or the North beach south of town.

They were looking for agates which are a hard semiprecious stone found on beaches in the area which come in a variety of stripped or clouded coloring. They almost look like glass. Those that find glass that has been churned up in the ocean and worn round often mistake glass pebbles for agate.

They found a few and sat and talked about their find and compared agates and as can be expected they soon began to kiss. There was a very hard cold south wind blowing that day but Melody had an idea.

"Come with me." she instructed as she grabbed Jeff's hand and led him to the small sand dunes just inland from the beach. She found just what she was looking for; a spot perfect which dipped with walls of sand all around to protect them from the wind and where the sun beat warm. So they laid in the their newly discovered hovel and began to kiss again. Their loving became passionate. Jeff's hands began to wander as he brushed his palm over her breasts and a button on her blouse came undone. She looked down at her cleavage as if to say "you may." Jeff gently ran his left hand index finger along the top of her bra, slowly back and forth around the whole top edge of it, playing with the lace that bordered it. He drew his fingers together and slowly and deliberately inched his four fingers into the right cup of her brassier slightly separating two fingers just enough to allow her nipple to slip between the space. He gently toyed with the nipple and curling his index finger he swirled it over her now erect soft nipple.

Melody laid as her breathing stop-gapped each time he tweaked the nipple. She slowly ran her own right hand into the bottom of his shirt and passed this T-shirt opening her palm to the softness of his stomach. She knew the time to cross the line had come. She unhooked Jeff's belt buckle and unsnapped the snap of his jeans and cupped his now engorged penis in the palm of her hand. Softly running her hand up and down along it's length and squeezed ever so gently. She then wrapped her hand a little harder around his softly beating member. She felt the flare of the head and fingered the edge as she toyed with the flap eventually running her finger gently over the tip of the head finding the small hollow that was the opening. She swirled her finger over it with Jeff's member quietly undulating to the beat of his heart as Jeff shivered from the sensation.

Jeff removed his hand from her bra and unbuttoned the second then the third button proceeding all the way to her waist. Melody removed her hand and reciprocated by unbuttoning his shirt. He pulled back and removed first his shirt, then his T-shirt as she countered by removing her own. Jeff shifted to the other side of Mel as they laid back down. Mel began to reach back to unsnap her bra when Jeff stopped her and softly told her he preferred to do it himself. Melody shifted to the front of him and lowered her face into his lap at his still opened jeans and he unhooked her bra. As it fell forward, Melody sat up and pulled it off. Jeff gave a soft whistle and told her she was beautiful. Placing both of his hands on each breast kneading them as they faced each other. Melody reached her hand to the back of his pants and raising himself off the sand slightly, she slipped his pants from under his back and playfully kicked backward away from his touch finding the bottom of the leg of his jeans and pulled his pants off.

Melody looked down at Jeff's shorts with his sensual pole rising heavenward and raised herself enough to jump on top of Jeff forcing him backward into the sand. She kissed him pressing hard her chest against his then her middle against his as she felt his penis wedge between her legs and against her own pant covered treasure.

Jeff reached down as she raised with her knees dug into the sand on both sides of him and unclasped her pants. She reached down and unzipped the fly. He reached to both sides of her trousers and pushed them down as she rocked forward allowing Jeff enough room to push them down. She fell on him with her pants pulled down her legs and with one of her breasts at his face. He kissed one nipple and she rolled over, circled around and offered her feet to him. He pulled her pants off and tossed them on top of his own. Again they rolled into each others embrace. Melody could feel Jeff's manhood play against her panty clad body as they rolled in ecstasy. She lowered her hand again down to his waist and into his shorts this time. She watched her hand as did Jeff as she felt the curls of his hair. With three fingers she gently massaged the hair and slowly lowered them to the haft and down with the fingers to the length of his shaft and to the flair of the knob and finally reaching the now unencumbered opening. Jeff reached behind himself and pulled his shorts off over his feet as she held tightly to her lovers protrusion. They kissed and Jeff rubbed His palm over one of Melody's breasts and then the other he slowly lowered his hand down past her belly to the warm confines of her womanhood, feeling the aperture of her womanly channel through the soft pink panties protecting her. Melody breathing uncontrollably, gripped his limb and wrapping her hand around it tightly as she pistoned up and down the length of it as his fingers quickened the pace of their ruffling of her precious volvo cleft. Jeff lowered his face to Mel's breast and gently kissed and nipped at the nipple finally drawing one in with a kiss and softly suckling it he touched the tip of it with the end of his tongue circling it around the soft button. Melody continued to work his member until abruptly Jeff sucked in a great amount of air, proclaimed his imminent intention and falling back performed what Melody had intended to happen.

Melody had not seen such a development before. He spasmed and spewed, his face distorted as his upper body shivered and he gasped for air. She cried and said she loved him and through his gasps he told her he loved her too.

Jeff laid back and let the spasms subside as his breathing began to return to normal. Melody rose on her elbow and studied the cream colored liquid that he had deposited all over his belly and into his belly button. She ran her left index finger into it and watched her finger play as it swirled around and into the dark patch of hair and the flaccid penis below his belly.

"I'm sorry I didn't wait for you." Jeff apologized.

"You did." she assured him.

They laid in the warm sun together and discussed the beauty of the promenade they had just performed. Melody suddenly yelled: "Let's get wet." She pulled her panties off and grabbed Jeff's hand and together nude, they headed for the ocean and played in the surf and washed the sweat from their bodies occasionally kissing but generally having a good time.

47

By the fifth of October, between his job, other extra yard work and what he already had in savings as well as selling his 1956 Stan Musial baseball card, Jeff had enough money to purchase his much desired Yamaha 80 motorcycle.

The bike was beat with a torn seat and a bent gas tank but it would suffice for his first vehicle. Since Gabe had gone into the Army, he had completely lost his transportation.

He arrived at Old Man Higgins' house and proudly handed his one hundred dollars over. He followed Mr. Higgins to his garage where the old man explained all the intricate details of the simple two cycle bike.

Mr. Higgins mounted the bike and tried over and over again to kick it over. Since it was such a small bike the engine kicked quite easily.

Hidden Shore

"Damn thing started right up last time I took it out." Mr. Higgins said frustrated.

"How long ago was that?" Jeff asked.

Oh, three years I guess, but it's a two cycle enjun just needs a little adjustment I guess."

So Mr. Higgins pulled the side off and adjusted the gap and turned the magneto and primed the carburetor and finally it popped out the carburetor and sputtered and popped out the tail pipe and finally started up.

"Damn thing was 180 degrees off. I got it now. I better ride it to your house for you since you don't have a license yet."

Mr. Higgins lived a whole two blocks from Jeff and with all the cops in Hidden Shore, Jeff kindly allowed Mr. Higgins to drive it.

"Jump on back. Here." Mr. Higgins said as he handed Jeff a helmet which was an old football helmet from the 1920s or 30s, Jeff wasn't sure.

Jeff straddled the bike behind Mr. Higgins who squeezed the clutch with his left foot and the bike lurched forward and died.

"Stay there, it just died." Mr. Higgins assured Jeff. He proceeded to squeeze the clutch handle again. "Hold on," ordered the old man as Jeff grabbed the sides of Mr. Higgins' body. With that he popped the clutch and the bike kicked again and died.

"We'll get it kid." Mr. Higgins said trying to encourage Jeff. This time the bike jumped forward and down the street as the pair went wobbling on the over loaded bike.

Jeff had a friend at school who had a nice bike that he told Jeff he would teach him to ride on. So Jeff took the bus to Eureka after school one day and got his learners permit. The particularly patient friend spent hours with Jeff teaching him how to ride. When all was done, his friend took him to the Department of Motor Vehicles again and Jeff took and passed the driving test on his friends bike. Jeff was now licensed to drive.

Of course the first place Jeff went was to drive the bike to Melody's. The ride was exhilarating as he drove the four miles to her home.

Melody was waiting out on the porch when he arrived.

"Come on, jump on." he called to her.

"I can't." she said helplessly.

"Why? What's the matter?" Jeff demanded to know as he turned the bike off and leaned it on the kick stand.

Melody approached him and appealed for his understanding.

"Jeff, my Uncle won't let me. He had a friend killed on one of those once."

"Oh, Man" he said.

"Jeff, my Aunt and Uncle are very lenient and don't put many restrictions on me. I'm not going to go against this one."

"Okay." Jeff said dejected.

Melody would not ride on the motorcycle. Jeff kept it at work during the day and rode it home and then back in the mornings. He would catch his bus in Weston. This way he could visit with Melody until one of their buses arrived.

48

One morning he missed meeting Melody who worried about him all day since he did not go to school at all that day.

Every time he started the bike it would backfire and then he would kick it again and it would start. A few times it would backfire through the carburetor which did not have an air filter on it. After having the bike for two weeks, on October 19th, Jeff walked his bike as he always did to the front of his driveway. Usually, he would kick it over and wait for a few minutes for it to warm as it ran. This time, when he kicked it he heard a pop in the carburetor and then sat and put on his helmet before kicking it again. Suddenly, flames were shooting from between his legs. His carburetor had caught fire. He leaned the bike on its stand and ran around not knowing what to do as the fire grew. Finally, he pushed the bike to the middle of the street as flames began to shoot over 50 feet in the air. Black smoke billowed out like a house on fire. One of his neighbors called the Volunteer Fire Department who contacted the Weston Fire Department when they saw the smoke. The fire crews arrived and they dowsed it and chopped at it using their axes, much to Jeff's chagrin, chopped the tires and spokes and the rest of the bike assuring themselves that the fire was out. After all was out Jeff pried a metal blob from the pavement of the street which had once been his carburetor. One of he hooks for the gas float stuck up above the flat melted metal and Jeff always kept that nailed to his wall as a remembrance of the fire.

Jeff was devastated. His well earned motorcycle was now a burnt out hulk. When his Mother and Bill arrived home that afternoon, he cried. Bill suggested that he rewire and rebuild it with used parts. He offered to help Jeff find them in Eureka.

"Like the Phoenix rising from the ashes, you'll have that running again if you really want it to." Bill encouraged.

Jeff doubted it but he would try.

That evening, he walked to Melody's after work and she comforted him. Melody was going to the camp with her Aunt and Uncle so she could not spend the weekend with Jeff.

Jeff spent the whole weekend stripping all the burnt out parts off of the bike including the wire harness, leaving his bike frame and the engine block as the only parts completely salvageable. He sanded and primed and painted the frame knowing that if the bike ever ran again he would gain a lot of knowledge about working on vehicles.

Jeff could have prevented the fire if he had done only one of three things. If he had turned the fuel cock off the gas tank would have stopped feeding the fire. If he had tried to kick the bike over again the compression of the engine would have snuffed the fire out. Finally, if he had the air filter on the bike, it would not have had air to feed the fire.

49

Hidden Shore

Just before November 25th, Melody told Jeff that she was going to the camp with her Aunt and Uncle that weekend. Jeff was bothered because he could not understand why Melody always went off with them and never invited him along.

"It's a private recreational club, you have to be a member to go there." she explained to him.

"Why don't I just join." he asked.

"Because you have to be recommended and it's very expensive."

She did not want to tell him yet about the camp. She really wanted to go that weekend. During the winter, activities moved in doors. They swam and competed at the indoor pool, did body painting contests, and celebrated holidays in the large gymnasium. This was the weekend for Thanksgiving activities and there would be a big dance. She wanted to be home with Jeff for Christmas and New Year so she knew to be with her friends at the camp for at least one of the holidays, she would have to be there for Thanksgiving. She enjoyed the Halloween party just a few weeks earlier. Everyone painted their bodies in Halloween designs. She came in second among the teenage girls with black arms and black sides and back and with orange all over her face and down the middle front to form a vee at the spot between her legs. She also wore a cape. This was her version of a Dracula costume.

Jeff , though upset, worked on his motorcycle for the weekend. He had replaced a new wiring harness purchased a new battery and seat. He was putting in a new magneto when Greg found him and came into the garage.

"What's up?" Jeff asked.

"Not much." Greg looked in a thoughtful mood at Jeff.

"Let me get this thing in and I'll be with you." Jeff worried as he continued wiring the magneto in. He knew Greg got quiet sometimes but this was different. Greg looked like he had just lost his best friend. Of course, being his best friend he knew it was something else.

"Can you help me a minute?" he asked Greg.

He handed Greg a pry bar which he placed within the

magneto to keep it from turning while he tightened the center bolt with a torque wrench to bring it to it's proper torque.

Jeff finished this and asked: "You got something bothering you?"

"Yah, but not much." Greg answered slowly.

"Let's go inside and talk."

They went in the house and Jeff got himself and Greg a coke from the refrigerator and jumped on the sofa.

"Now, what's up, buddy?" Jeff asked.

"I need to talk to you about something that's been going on. I've been wanting to tell you for a long time but until yesterday I couldn't. Now she says I can because I need to tell someone."

"She?....I knew you had a girlfriend." Jeff blurted.

"You did? How did you know?" Greg responded.

"Well, I haven't seen much of you lately and it hasn't been because I have not been around and I thought I saw you with this chick a while ago, who is she?"

"Mary Woo." Greg admitted.

"Mary?...Mary?... I didn't even notice that she was Chinese when I saw you!! Mary?...My God" Jeff went on.

"Jeff don't tell me you are going to be like everyone else just 'couse she's Chinese?"

"No! Of course not, I just didn't have any idea. She's cute...but...Mary?"

"Jeff, you know how you feel about Mel! Mary and I have the same feelings."

After the first day with Mary, Greg began to position himself at locations so that he would "bump" into her "accidentally." They began to meet in secret at the tide pools and other places, but they made sure they avoided people at school or in town. Their feeling for each other blossomed. But Mary would not even let a hint of their feelings for each other get to her parents. She knew they would cut it off immediately.

The day before Greg showed up at Jeff's garage, Mary had invited Greg into her home. Her parents went to San Francisco to purchase some items for the restaurant so she was left home alone.

Hidden Shore

Greg had to walk along the river bank to her house which fronted the river with the restaurant further in from it. Mary did not want anyone to see him walk up to her house and a kid on the river would not look suspicious. When he reached the house he bolted into it as Mary waited at the back door. She shut the door quickly and encircled her arms around him hugging him. This was the first time they had ever shown any affection away from the bluffs or the beach and a couple of times when they secretly met in the bunkers.

Mary's house was neat, very neat. The living room looked like every other living room with a TV, a sofa, two soft chairs and a fireplace. Between the fireplace and the television sat a large gold Buddha. Jeff had seen pictures of Buddha's before but never one up close like this.

"I wanted you to see my house, Jeff" Mary exclaimed. "I'll let you see my bedroom but don't go in. It would be disrespectful to my parents for you to enter it." she said as she took Greg by the hand and led him to her room stopping at the door. She knew even letting Greg in the house would be viewed by her parents as disrespect, but she weighed the differences of the levels of disrespect.

The bedroom was also very neat; as he envisioned any other girl's room. Very similar to his older sisters' rooms. He did not know what he had expected to be different about it, but he had pictured it as dark or something.

They left the house separately and he headed to the river, she out the front door. They met on the beach and went to the bunkers to be alone together. This was the day they first made love. All the hiding, all the frustration, all the building anxiety led to the encounter. Now they wanted some people to know. Some people they could trust who would not let it get to her parents. Greg knew his parents would disapprove also.

So Greg went to Jeff's house that day hoping that Jeff could help him out of the dark. He told him how hard it had been not to share the secret with Jeff. He told him how the mystery of their requited love had added to the passion of their meetings. He told him that they both wanted to have friends to be with together such as him and Melody.

Jeff assured him that he would help. They stood and Jeff put his arm around Greg and gave him a hug; two friends who now had another secret to keep.

Jeff told him he understood, explaining how he and Melody had done the same thing in San Francisco; but at least Melody's mother knew he and Melody were together.

When Melody returned from the camp, Jeff filled her in and at lunch the next day Melody and Jeff talked to Mary Woo and assured her that she would be invited to activities as Melody's friend, and Greg would go as Jeff's and when the four were alone, her and Greg could be warm as Jeff and Melody would be.

The four began regular double dates and this was good for Melody and Jeff. They were not as passionate with Greg and Mary around so it helped to slow the speed of their developing relationship.

50

Clint and Tanya were the other important couple in the life of Jeff and Melody. The difference between this couple and Greg and Mary was like the difference between night and day.

Clint and Tanya had a love/hate relationship. It was as if for their relationship to work Clint and Tanya (or Tawnie) needed to argue.

Clint met Tanya in high school and she lived in Fairbury. When they were together, neither of them could flirt with any body else but apart each became lecherous.

Clint met Tawnie when she was dating a college boy who lived in Fairbury. She lost her virginity to an Alpha Beta Chi fraternity boy at the Midway Drive-in Theater between Eureka and the home of Humbolt State: Arcata. She then lost it again to the fraternity house leader and then to two of the Basketball players. Funny how her virginity could be taken by so many boys all who would become pillars of their communities and married the sorority girls that they dated while relieving Tanya of her virginity; each one proud of the fact that each one deflowered two virgins. It was always "I can do anything but that" but that is all she ever did.

Clint took her virginity when he and she were Sophomores the year before. Now as long as each were where they should be when the other one wanted them to be, they got along fine. However, they were seldom where they should be when they should be.

She had a name for Clint's manly aperture, she called it just what she called it the first time she saw it: "Big little guy!" She also used to tease Clint incessantly which no one else could get away with. Though they both strayed from the normal commitments of a relationship, each provided for the other a stability that neither had any other way. When times got tough, they had each other even though sometimes it took a while to find the other but when they did there was no one else more comforting.

Their love-making was passionate but rough. Everything possible was tried. Some was even kinky. Clint, considering his past, tried every way to get Tawnie to let him have her back side. After much persuasive pressure and finger play, Tawnie finally relented and decided she did not mind it so much. She liked water sports and eventually neither could use a bathroom without the other wanting to watch or play. It grossed Clint out at first but a frolic in the bathtub one day and he was converted.

On double dates with Jeff and Mel, the constant bickering was a stark contrast to the cooperation of Jeff and Mel. The mind games played were watched by the two and they vowed not to do the same. But without discussing it, Melody felt sorry for Clint and the way Tawnie treated him, Jeff felt sorry for Tawnie and wished Clint would be kinder.

Except for the time at the Creek, little sexual connected play occurred among the four except the time they parked and "made out" in Clint's father's car, Clint and Tawnie in the front seat and Jeff and Mel in the back, after going to the theater in Eureka to see Dr. No. Clint teasingly suggested switching partners but none of the others took him serious.

Once in school, Clint actually made what Melody considered a pass at her, but Melody quickly put him in his place and the indiscretion was forgotten.

Jeff and Clint's relationship had cooled over the last couple of years. Since the incident at the Creek, though Jeff had assured Clint that all was forgiven, Jeff still maintained a friendly but distant relationship with his former best friend. Since Clint's father was the Chief of Police in Weston, Clint always had use of a vehicle which left Jeff, who's parents did not provide him with a vehicle, as somewhat inferior. Clint did nothing to dispel Jeff's feelings that he could not compete with Clint and depended on him for transportation for dates.

Through most of the school year until spring, most of Jeff and Mel's dates were double dates. It was a good time. Jeff and Greg grew much closer as did Melody and Mary. Though they sometimes doubled with Clint and Tawnie, they enjoyed their doubles with Greg and Mary better.

One weekend in December, Mary spent a night at Melody's while her Aunt and Uncle were gone to the camp. Jeff and Greg went over on Sunday morning and Mel and Mary decided they wanted to go to the store. Greg walked them there leaving Jeff alone at Melody's. Jeff was sitting at the kitchen table taking in the atmosphere of Melody's home when he stood up and walked into this second bedroom of hers. There was a damp towel setting on her unmade bed and taking in Melody's essence he lifter the towel to his face feeling the dampness of the towel and breathed in. Through his mind raced visions of her having caressed her body with the towel after her bath. The feeling was intoxicating and made him feel warm and even more love for her. He then surreptitiously kicked off his shoes and laid in her bed taking the covers and pulling them over him. He laid with his head spinning thinking of how this was the bed in which she slept and he could feel her presence. Rolling on his side, he saw a soiled bra and panties lying by the bed. He raised the panties to his face, as he had the towel, and smelled the slight perfume of her femininity in the panties. He laid there content with his life and held the panties and touched them with the tip of his tongue.

Not wanting to be caught and not knowing how Melody would react, he rose from the bed and was sitting in the kitchen again when the other three returned. He approached Melody and wrapping his arms around her and with Greg and Mary standing there, he said to Melody: "I don't think you know because I don't tell you enough but I think you are the most wonderful person in the whole world and I love you with all my being. I know you can't now but I really intend to marry you some day."

Melody hugged him for the thought and melted into his arms to the applause of Greg and Mary. The four caught up in the romance of the moment slipped into the game room and "made out" at the same time at opposite sides of the room. This was the first time that they shared a passionate moment with anyone else. Both girls were stripped of their top clothing by their boy friends and at one point during the encounter Melody looked across at Mary who at the same time looked across at her and they laughed.

51

About mid December a problem began to arise in Jeff and Melody's relationship: Stone Aches. Jeff would meet Melody after school and they would go to the park or library or swings and most of the time these encounters would end with passionate kissing and heavy petting. Jeff would become excited and without the possibility of relief, by the time he arrived at work he would be suffering from stone aches. Stone aches are caused from muscular strain within the testicles. If a man (or boy in this case) is able to ejaculate, the pains subside. Since Jeff had vowed not to masturbate and doing it at the hardware store would be very inappropriate, Jeff just suffered the pain. So Jeff explained the situation to Melody who found it quite amusing and they agreed to keep the play to a minimum before he had to go to work. Her only stipulation was that he had to behave at all times or she would punish him by exciting him and making his two hours at work a painful drudge.

1962 would be the first year that Melody and Jeff would be able to spend a Christmas together. Mrs. Sanchez had called and wanted Melody to come home for Christmas and tried to reason with her that she needed to be "home" for Christmas. Melody argued that with school term papers and tests and other commitments it would be impossible for her to be home. Her Mother finally gave in and Melody and Jeff spent Christmas 1962 together.

The weather was truly frightful as storms pounded the northern coast. Jeff wanted to get Melody something real special for Christmas. He thought about it, asked her for hints and walked around every store in Weston and Hidden Shore as well as many in Fairbury trying to find the perfect gift. He even called Mike in San Francisco and asked him to make sure their song had not been made into a music box works for him.. Mike called back and told him it had not. Finally, he found in a record store an old 45RPM of I Love How You Love Me. This was the best but the record only cost a dollar so he knew he needed something else. He found a small plastic record player. So for Christmas that is what Melody got. A record player and a slightly played, because Jeff played it to himself over and over after purchasing it, recording of their song.

Melody had a much more perplexing problem. Not only did she have to decided on what to get Jeff for Christmas, she also realized that his birthday on January 19th would follow shortly after Christmas. She decided to only worry about Christmas and then get something that would compliment the Christmas gift in January.

Melody figured out what she thought would be the perfect gift. With all the cold rainy weather she knitted him a scarf. She knew that he would appreciate the love that she poured into it as she worked on it. She also knitted him something to give him as a birthday gift. Both appreciated the love that the other put into their gifts. Christmas 1962 was a good Christmas.

The weather eased between Christmas and New Year 1963. The sun came out and it was actually quite warm on Saturday, December 29th. Melody asked Jeff to take her someplace where they could be completely alone. Jeff decided that Dead Man Creek would work because almost no one went up there in the winter.

This was going to be an important day. The day after Christmas Melody spent the whole day composing a letter to Jeff which she hoped would express to him how much she truly loved him and to finally come clean about everything about her life.

They walked up the creek path with a picnic basket and a blanket which Jeff slung over his shoulder. They arrived at the clearing by the swimming hole which, as Jeff knew it would be, was completely deserted; not even a swing rope. They laid the blanket out on the damp ground and Melody sat in front of Jeff and took his hand.

"Jeff, I have written a letter to you and I want you to read it right now." she told him.

She handed him several pages folded neatly which he accepted cautiously and bent to kiss her. She stopped his advance and asked him to read pointing at the papers and then leaned back against a tree to watch him read. He would glance up and smile periodically at Melody who sat stern faced but curious about his feelings.

My Dearest Jeffrey,

This is probably the most difficult letter I have ever or will ever write. I assume it will be a long letter because I have much to say and I hope you will be understanding of how hard this is to write.

Jeff glanced at Melody for the first time. His fear was either that this was a Dear John letter or that she was returning to San Francisco which would be the same. The letter continued:

First of all I want you to know I am writing this because I love you and I want you to know some things that you may be angry with me about. I know you have this vision that I am innocent and that you are the first boy I have ever been intimate with. In my mind you are. But Jeffrey, I am not a virgin. I have been afraid to tell you this because I don't want to lose you and I know you are a virgin and I know you want a virgin to marry but that is something I cannot give you.

Let me explain to you some things about myself. As you know my mother is a very strict and exacting person. She has rules that even a hint that they might be broken can lead her into angry yelling spells. She was so strict to me as a little girl that I could never even say such words as pregnant in front of her without getting my mouth washed out with soap. Don't take me wrong, I love my mom, but she made it hard sometimes. She never talked to me about intimate female things because that was something just not discussed. When I had my first period I thought I was going to bleed to death seeing the blood in the toilet after going to the bathroom one day. I was so scared. Carlos was the one to explain to me about feminine napkins and mom just thought I figured them out on my own when she began buying them for me. Mom still thinks I am a little girl. That is why I was dressed the way I was that Sunday in San Francisco. She won't listen to me. She dresses me like that every Sunday and has all my life and then takes me to my father's grave who I never knew and expects me to cry over him which I never do.

The first time I ever saw a man without clothes, meaning I saw his, well you know, was when a friend of mine was at my house and Uncle Jim was visiting. We peeked at him in the bathroom. Before I had no idea what a man looked like or how different they were.

The reason I moved to Weston is because I did something that I am ashamed of and because of this mom sent me here. One day I was at home and looking for a rubber band to tie my hair up with. I went into Carlos' room and he was lying on his bed with his you know what in his hand and it was hard as he was masturbating looking at a dirty magazine. Instead of running away I stopped and stared. He seemed upset at first but covered himself with his hands and told me not to worry. He then stood up and asked me if I had ever seen a boys thing before. I said no because I was curious, it did not look like Uncle Jim's whose was soft. Jeff, I was only just 13 years old. Carlos asked me if I wanted to touch it and I said yes so he walked up to me and I reached out and touched it as he held it in front of me. He then asked me if he could see my thing. I really didn't want to but since he had let me touch his I thought I should let him see mine. He's my older brother after all. I didn't know it would be wrong. Well Jeff, I'm writing this because I think you need to know how it happened. Anyway, I sat on his bed and laid back and Carlos sat next to me and he pulled my skirt up and pulled my panties down. Carlos then put his hand on me and rubbed me a little playing with me down there and it tickled. I giggled and he told me that boys put their thing in there on girls. Jeff, I didn't understand this but he stuck his finger in and it hurt a little but I wanted to see what this was all about. Finally he rolled on top of me and stuck his penis right into me which really hurt that time and I slightly screamed. It was only for a second but I know he broke me. Then suddenly my Grandma opened the door to Carlos' room and she began to scream and picked up Carlos' baseball bat and started hitting us with it. My mother came running and they yelled at us and never let us be anything like alone again. This was about a year before I moved here and mom treated me like I was a bad girl for a long time but then she began to treat me like her little girl again. Any time Carlos and I get at all close she screams. Finally she decided one of us had to go away. She felt she could not find anyone to take Carlos so she sent me to Uncle Jim's.

Uncle Jim and Aunt Peggy are opposites of my mom. They have been wonderful to me but when I first arrived I felt I was the only one being punished for what happened.

I had a boyfriend when I left but we were just being friends. You met him that day at the park, remember? the boy named Bob? Well, Bob never wrote or called me after I left so I never heard from him until that day in the park. I found out later he now has a girlfriend but that's another story I'll leave alone now.

When I first arrived here I felt unloved and unwanted. I hated my new school. It was so uncomfortable starting at a new school mid-semester. My first day in each class I had to be introduced and then I had to make sure I didn't sit in someone else's seat. No one was nice to me. It took me a long time to even get to know a couple of kids. I finally met this boy named Leonard and we became boyfriend and girlfriend for only about a week but all he wanted to do was touch my breasts and kiss me and treat me bad and try to touch me where I didn't want to be touched while we walked home from school. I finally dropped him. Not long after that I met you and then things got better for me immediately.

The other thing is that I need to tell you the truth about the camp I go to with Uncle Jim and Aunt Peggy. Its a nudist camp. Jim and Peggy are nudists and they go to this camp. I go with them. The first time I went it was very uncomfortable just walking out without any clothes on. Here I was a girl who could not even say the word pregnant to my mom and now there I was naked in front of hundreds of people. But it wasn't so bad. I'm gonna tell you this now but no one has said anything to you because I didn't want them to. I saw your mom and dad there once not long before the trip to San Francisco and they promised not to tell you because they said you didn't know they were nudists and I was not sure we were close enough to do that kind of thing together. But they said that when I was ready I could tell you. Now if you would like to I wouldn't mind having you come with us sometime.

Jeff, I'm afraid you won't be very happy with me after reading this. Please understand and don't leave me but if you must I'll understand. There's so much more I want to say I'm sure I haven't said it all. All I can say now is that I love you and I do hope we will get married some day. I want to give you children some day. I think we would be good parents but that is still a long, long way away.

I love how you love me,
Melody

Jeff looked up at Melody with tears in his eyes and crawled over to her and kissed her. They held each other close then Jeff began to tell her about himself. He told her about Clint and that he was not as pure as she thought. He told her he felt that the time with

Clint was very similar to what happened to with her brother. He told her about the day at the beach in San Francisco and calculated that it was after she had seen his mother at the camp. They realized that his mother had said nothing that day because of her vow to Melody. Jeff more dearly understood his mother's comment on the back porch about Melody joining them at the nude beach some day.

Melody felt a rush of relief. It was anesthetizing for her as she became giggly and relaxed. They made love similar to the way they did on the beach that day. This time though Jeff wandered from her lips planting kisses down her neck and then her chest nibbling the soft points of her nipples. He then proceeded down her tummy pausing to insert his tongue into her belly button. She cooperated by stooping him and they both removed all their clothing and Melody pointed to her tummy and said; "I think you were about there." Jeff continued his trip over her hip and down her leg eventually to lick her toes. He turned upward softly kissing the inside of her legs burying his face in her inner thighs. He proceeded up to the lips that he gently kissed and separated studying their shape and structure. He swung himself into a position aligning his penis with Melody's willing and waiting mouth. He traced his finger over the soft lips of her womanhood as she took him into her mouth and swirled her tongue around the head of his ready member softly inserting the very tip of her tongue into the tip of it. The sensations brought both lovers to an ultimate ecstasy after which they laid in each others arms to warm themselves against the December chill.

52

Melody was 15 and Jeff was 16 when 1962 came to an end. The school held a special dance which lasted until just after midnight so that everyone had a safe place to celebrate the New Year. They could not drive and the school bused them in. For a theme, they chose Out With The Old, In With The New. It was a costume party where each student was to dress either as old or baby. Jeff and Melody decided he would dress old and she would dress baby. Jeff wore an old double breasted pin-stripped suit that Bill had which had once been his father's. He wore a gray beard. Melody wore a very big diaper and one of Jeff's T-shirts with a bib and she fashioned a hat like a baby's hat. Mary Woo dressed the same with Melody's help and they went as twins while Greg wore a long trench-coat and carried a gleaning stick that he cut of wood and used a broomstick for a handle.

All had a great time at the dance. Clint and Tanya both wore baby clothes. And the six of them gathered around at the stroke of midnight to count the remaining seconds. The kids had been told not to kiss more that one quick kiss at midnight and there were plenty of chaperones to make sure that rule was adhered to. Jeff and Melody's kiss probably lasted too long except that many other kids' lasted longer. The three couples jumped from one another, Jeff kissing Tanya and then Mary, Greg kissing Mel and then Tanya, Clint kissing Mary and then Mel.

Melody was very uncomfortable because when Clint kissed her he opened his mouth and forced his tongue in her mouth and as he did this he reached his palm to her rear end and squeezed it. She did not like that at all; however, she did not tell Jeff but she asked Mary if he did the same to her. Mary said he did not. Melody decided to let it go.

53

January 19, 1963 was Jeff's 17ty birthday. From the young boy that played in the hills and on the beaches or up Dead Man Creek had grown a tall handsome though gangly young man. Strong but not muscular in build, he could attract the eyes of new girls. But his eyes went in only one direction and that was toward Melody.

Being a Saturday there was no school and the night before he and Melody went to the theater in Weston and then to the soda fountain to eat hamburgers and French fries. Jeff still did not have transportation which was a consistent frustration for him, but Gabe was home visiting having been transferred to a base close enough for him to come home most weekends. He and Stevie met them at the fountain and suggested bowling. Jeff and Melody had never bowled before so they jumped at the opportunity and the four of them went to Fairbury and bowled. Jeff broke 100 which he considered pretty good for his first time. Melody bowled 112. Afterwards, they all drove home and Melody stayed at Stevie's again.

At 7:30AM, a knock came on the door to his bedroom.

"Hey sleepyhead, you gonna sleep all day?" it was Melody.

"I'd like to;" looking at his watch, "at least sleep until morning.

"Not with my plans for the day birthday boy." Melody insisted that he get up. Jeff groaned and rolled over. Melody walked over beside him and tickled him and they wrestled and they kissed but Jeff got up.

"Okay, were we going?" Jeff demanded to know.

"I'm cooking breakfast for all of you boys today." Melody responded. "Now get dressed and come out and get your breakfast."

She left and Jeff showered and dressed. When he walked into the kitchen, Gabe, Stevie, and Stan were already sitting at the table talking.

"Happy Birthday." they all shouted at the same time.

Melody surprised Jeff with one of the best breakfasts he had ever had. This was the first time she had ever cooked anything for him. After breakfast, he thanked her and said it was the best birthday gift she could have given him.

"Oh! That's not all, we're going with Gabe and Stevie. We got plans." she informed him.

They spent the day north of Eureka in Crescent City and then along the Oregon Coast. There were many great beaches and the four walked a lot and had a generally good time. On the way back to Hidden Shore, Melody gave him a little gift wrapped box that she had hidden in the glove box of Gabe's car.

Hidden Shore

"This is to go with your Christmas gift." she announced.

Melody had warned Stevie and Gabe that her gift was different and she reminded   them about the scarf she had given him for Christmas.

Jeff unwrapped and opened it. He pulled it from the box and held it embarrassingly in the air. It was a knitted cock and balls warmer. It was the same color as the scarf. It had the shape of a penis with two pouches for the balls. All four laughed and had a great time teasing about it. Stevie yelled for him to try it on for size, but Jeff was embarrassed. Melody whispered to Jeff that she had one more gift for him when they got home.

When they arrived back at Hidden Shore, Gabe announced that he and Stevie were going to Eureka and taking Stan with them. Bill and Mary were gone for the weekend so Jeff and Melody would have the house to themselves.

After everyone left, Jeff said to Melody that this was nice. It was almost as if they were married and home for the evening like any other husband and wife.

"That's what I want to tell you." Melody said.

"Tell me?" Jeff asked.

"Kiss me Jeff; please kiss me."

Jeff kissed her and she pulled away and looked deeply into his eyes.

Jeff, I have made a decision. I want to make love with you tonight. I've decided it is time."

"Are you sure?" Jeff asked.

"I don't think I have ever been more sure of anything else but this in my whole life. I love you Jeff and I want it now if you do."

Jeff approached her again. "If you're ready, I think I am."

Melody took Jeff by the hand and led him into his bedroom.

"I want it to be here so when you go to bed at night you can remember that it happened here."

Jeff started to unbutton his shirt but Melody stopped him.

"Me first, I want you to watch me and then I'd like to watch you." Melody insisted.

Hidden Shore

She led him to sit on the edge of his bed. Melody was wearing her familiar pleated skirt and simple blouse with the knee socks. She first placed her left foot on the side of the bed and unstraped the shoe strap. She pulled the shoe off and did the same with the other shoe. She then placed her left foot again next to Jeff and motioned for him to roll the knee socks down. He did then pulled it off. She repeated the procedure with the other sock. Then she turned and offered the button on the back of her skirt to Jeff who unbuttoned it and zipped the zipper down. She let the brown skirt fall to the ground and stepped out from amongst it. She had on white panties. She slowly and sexily unbuttoned her blouse and pulled it from her setting it with her skirt.

Jeff reached up and unfastened her brassier. She allowed it to fall from her breasts. Her nipples were hard in anticipation about what was to happen as she sat and looked at Jeff.

"Your turn." She announced stopping with her panties still on.

Jeff unbuttoned his shirt and pulled it off. He then removed his T-shirt as Melody helped him. She undid the belt of his pants, unzipped the zipper and pulled the pants from him. She laid him back down and pulled his socks off one at a time. She took his hand and had him stand and hugged him close and kissed him.

"Jeff, the timing is right for this. I'm afraid you might not like something, so if you would rather not we can just do everything else." Melody worriedly told him.

"What do you mean?" he asked.

"I'm having my period. I know it's a little messy but I don't want to get pregnant. This way, there's no way I will.

"Melody, I love you and I'd take you any way you come."

"Stevie said it's sometimes better for the girl at this time because their more sensitive. Also she said that it might help my cramps."

"Melody, it makes no difference to me." Jeff assured her.

Melody placed her hands on Jeff's hips and pushed his shorts down as his manhood jumped into view. Jeff pushed Melody's panties down and saw the string from her feminine napkin. Melody picked up some tissue from the side of Jeff's bed and as Jeff watched she pulled the napkin out. She assured him it was not as bad as she thought. She looked at him as they sat on the bed.

"I'm ready."

With that simple phrase, Melody reached to Jeff's lap and leaned over placing his tender post into her willing mouth. She raised her head up and down as he entered and exited her oral bounds. Jeff pulled Melody away and kissed her and wrapped his arms around her. She fell back on the bed and he laid atop her. He positioned himself between her legs and began to rise and lower himself with her legs closely locked together without entering her. She felt the anticipation of his entrance as he slid up and down against her soft lips but he did not enter her. Slowly he rose and lowered his hips. Melody reacted by lowering her hands down to him. She found his manhood and spread her legs slowly. She felt for her opening and guided him into her. First the head and then the flange and then the shaft. He buried it tightly against her learning that this was how it felt. Melody gasped for air. Slowly he raised and lowered. Again Melody spread her legs wider and tucked her feet below him as he rose and lowered at first slowly and then began to increase the speed of penetration. Up and down, in and out. More furious more force. She began to moan. He began to breath heavily. Again and again. He suddenly felt the impending knowledge of inevitability. He announced his intention to Melody. She called to him to stay in. "It's okay, stay in." He pumped in, out, in, and out and one last time collapsing on her and gasping. He groaned and she wrapped her arms and legs around him and held him tightly as he writhed and bucked she told him she loved him. They fell to the bed exhausted and expired. She relaxed her hold as Jeff held tighter. He collapsed on her panting for air. Melody giggled adoringly telling him: "I love you so much.'

They laid long together cuddling until they felt it was time that they should get ready because the others would return.

"I have never felt such contentment." Jeff told her. "I wish we could just lay here together all night."

"Some day Jeff, someday."

Hidden Shore

54

On February 23rd 1963 Amanda arrived in Hidden Shore. She had graduated from high school in Springfield Massachusetts and rode the bus clear across the country. Her mother was Mary's sister Edith who left Hidden Shore shortly after Mary and Abner's marriage. Amanda was a strong willed, independent sort who left home just for the adventure. She knew her mother was from California and wanted to see it badly. Her money was gone now though and she needed someplace to stay.

"Well, one more around here won't make much nevermind to me." Mary said on her arrival.

Amanda took over Gabe's old room and became a member of the family. One day sitting around with Gabe who was visiting and bunked with Stan, Amanda told Gabe a little about her life:

"Boston's big, nothing like around here. I grew up on James Avenue, not too far from Boston Common. It was pretty rough growing up there, you get a real education about the streets. I used to hang out with some pretty tough kids when I was little. We even mugged this drunk once near the Public Garden. I always felt bad about that, but that's life on the street. You either get tough or get going. Then we moved when I was about thirteen to Cambridge and when I was fifteen to Springfield. I guess that started my westward movement but that's where I got in real trouble. I started drinking and hanging out with the wrong kind of kids again. That's the reason I came here; to see the country and get away from all that back there."

Amanda and Stevie became fast friends and she liked Melody a lot. Stevie liked having someone to do things with whenever Gabe was away. Gabe only came home on weekends about every three or four weeks which left Stevie alone and she missed him. Once her and Amanda even took the bus to Gabe's base and stayed at a motel. Gabe spent the night with them and while Amanda graciously went to the movies, he made love to Stevie.

"You know," said Stevie after their time together, 'sometimes I wonder how it would be with a girl. I get these feelings every once in a while and it's kind of confusing."

Gabe found this interesting at best.

"You don't mean like Amanda?" he asked.

"Well, I just wonder. She really is nice and seems pretty wild, but I couldn't do that."

"She's told me about her past, but I think she's a guy's girl. She's pretty tough though."

"I know. Just forget it, I just thought I'd tell you how I felt that's all." she ended the discussion by getting up from the bed they were in and heading into the bathroom.

Amanda returned back with a bottle of vodka and some orange juice and the three drank screwdrivers until they all fell asleep on the same bed. Nothing happened.

55

The telephone rang at Melody's house and she answered it.

"Hi Mel," it was Jeff. " Clint called and said that they're going to the drive in and wanted to know if we wanted to go."

"Sure, I can't wait I've been working on homework all day, You gonna come and meet me."

"Clint said he'd come and get me and he'd come and pick you up on the way, Is that okay?"

"Sure, how's your bike coming?"

"Pretty good." I'm just about to the point to start it up. I could do it now but I want the whole thing done before I do. Clint said he'd pick you up at 7 o'clock, okay?"

"See ya, love ya" Melody hung up and finished crossing all

the Ts and doting all the Is on her history term paper. She wanted to go to the camp the following weekend because it was Linda's birthday so she wanted to get the paper done. Her school grades looked like they were going to be better than they ever had.

At 6:45, the bell rang and Clint was early.

"Where's Tawnie? asked Melody.

"We'll pick her up on the way to Eureka after we pick up Jeff." Clint responded.

"Give me another five minutes and I'll be ready."

"Okay."

Melody went into her bedroom and finished dressing and was looking for her coat and when she turned around Clint was standing at her bedroom door.

"My God, you startled me." Melody told him.

"It was getting boring in your kitchen and I need to use your bathroom, where is it?"

"It's on the other side of the kitchen." she responded disturbed that she had not known he was standing there.

"I'll find it." Clint headed toward the bathroom.

Melody hurriedly threw her jacket on and walked to the kitchen. The bathroom door was wide open and she could hear Clint urinating. This also disturbed her.

When Clint finished Melody said she was ready and the two headed out the door. They picked up Jeff and turned around and headed out the back way to Fairbury to meet Tawnie.

Tawnie was not ready when they arrived and Clint went in to hurry her along leaving Jeff and Melody sitting in the back seat. She told Jeff how strange Clint had acted and asked Jeff not to ever send Clint after her again.

"He does things different sometimes. He's okay though." Jeff defended Clint.

Melody did not appreciate Jeff's defense of Clint so they said little about it after that and were a little distant when Clint and Tawnie arrived. It was obvious immediately that Clint was mad at Tawnie for not being ready and the two were also distant, but that was nothing different for those two.

Hidden Shore

They arrived at the Midway drive-in north of Eureka. Jeff and Clint got a Tombstone Pizza at the concession stand and sodas and with Jeff and Melody in the back and Clint and Tawnie in the front, they watched the movie. About half way through Clint and Tawnie had obviously forgotten their disagreement and began to "make-out" pretty feverishly. This was uncomfortable for Jeff and Melody, not just because they were not feeling very romantic themselves, but because the other lovers were sitting in front in full view. At one point Clint rolled over on top of Tawnie and appeared to be mounting her when he glared at Jeff and Melody and winked.

"Hey, if you guys are going to do that, why don't we switch places." Melody suggested.

"Why don't we just jump back there and make it a foursome." Clint suggested after which Tawnie elbowed him in the ribs.

"I'll tell you what," Jeff suggested, " I have to go to the restroom, why don't you guys switch while I'm gone and he got out and headed for the concession stand. A couple of steps away from the car he heard the door open and shut and Tawnie ran saying: "I gotta pee too, wait up." Tawnie said to Jeff's embarrassment.

This left Clint alone in the car with Melody. He raised above the front seat and plopped in next to Melody. Melody started to open the door to get out and move up front when Clint grabbed her arm and told her: "They'll be a little while, why don't we just get comfortable while their gone?" Clint wrapped his other arm across her chest and pulled her up on his lap. "Get your hands off me Clint, you got a girlfriend and I got Jeff."

"So I won't tell if you won't" he said trying to and then succeeding in kissing her on the neck."

"I will tell Clint." she yelled as Clint suddenly became all hands.

Melody started hitting him and kicking him and then succeeded in jumping away from him and opening the door jumped out. She ran away leaving Clint lying in the back seat. She found Jeff and Tawnie and told Jeff she wanted to go home.

"What's the matter?" Jeff asked.

"I'll tell you later." she did not want to say anything in front of Tanya.

They went back to the car and Clint was sitting in the front seat again.

"My car, my front seat you guys, you're just going to have to put up with us." he selfishly told them.

"Don't be such a bastard Clint." Tawnie scolded him.

"Clint, Melody's not feeling too well, she'd like to go home." Jeff asked.

"But the first movie isn't even over yet." Clint reasoned.

"Yah and you've been watching the movie?" Tanya burst in. "I don't know why we come to the drive-in, You never want to watch the movie. I don't think we have ever seen a drive-in movie. We could just save the money and park somewhere with all the good one of these are."

"SHUT THE FUCK UP." Clint yelled at Tawnie.

Clint and Tawnie began to fight and Jeff and Melody just sat not on the best terms themselves. Clint finally agreed that staying was no longer an option and started up the engine and drove rapidly out of the theater. He did not say a word the whole drive home. He took Mel and Jeff to Hidden Shore and they got out and he left spinning his wheels to take Tawnie home.

"So what was that all about?' Jeff asked.

"Never mind. I'm going over to Stevie's" she said as she walked away.

Jeff angrily went into his garage and started tinkering with the motorcycle.

Melody found Stevie at home watching The Jackie Gleason show with her mother. She walked in and asked Stevie if she could talk to her.

"Sure, let's go for a walk." she suggested.

The two girls walked strait for one block and then turned left then right and then right again following no pattern just trying to make the walk last as Melody cried and opened her heart to Stevie.

"How could I say anything about what happened after he wouldn't understand how I felt about the way Clint acted at my house? or he might go after Clint and I don't want that, nothing really happened."

"Mel, little sister, you got to sit down and tell him what happened tonight. Don't let things like this fester or they can hurt the really good thing you two have going. Let's go get Jeff and sit him down, I'll be the referee."

They went back to the house and Jeff was now in the living room worried about Melody."

"Are you okay?" he asked.

"See, he cares." Stevie assured Melody. "Jeff, sit down and shut up, Melody has to tell you something and I want you to listen and be understanding."

Melody began slowly and told him again what happened at the house.

"I really think he left the door opened on purpose Jeff. He wanted me to either see or hear him. He's so strange sometimes. Then when you and Tanya went to the restroom, Clint jumped in the back and attacked me. I didn't let him get away with anything but he practically tried to rape me while you were gone." Melody was crying at this point.

Stevie looked over at Jeff. "You really need to be here for her right now."

Jeff leaped to Melody's side and held her close. "I'm sorry Mel, I just..., you also need to understand that Clint is my oldest friend. I know he has problems, including sexual problems, but it's tough. But he went too far this time. No more double dates with them, we either go out alone or with Greg and Mary. I'm so sorry!!!"

"Well, I think you guys need to be alone for a while, your mom should be home soon but I think you have a little while." Stevie said heading for the door. "Come on over as soon as you have, well whatever you do to kiss and make up."

Jeff and Melody knew how to make up. And they did it splendidly.

Jeff had a tougher time though. He loved Melody, but he had lost his best friend. He thought of the times that Greg had said he envied Clint because they were best friends and he was just his other best friend. Now Jeff was going to have to make Melody and Greg know that they were his closest people.

Jeff never said anything to Clint. Clint knew he had done wrong but he felt he had enough friends and if Jeff did not understand then "fuck him."

56

Wednesday March 27, 1963. It had now been a year since that first day that Jeff saw Melody during the school visitation of her junior high class. Since that day they had dated and made love and experienced so much. That year seemed to pack more firsts than the previous 16 years had for Jeff. When Jeff rode his bike to meet Melody and leave it at the hardware store, he had that to celebrate too.

The Saturday before he finally reached that point where he was ready to start his motorcycle up. He invited his Mom and Bill to be there because Bill had almost challenged him to do it that afternoon after the bike first burnt. Melody had gone with her folks to the camp and Jeff had wanted to be there, but he could not. This was still a source of frustration for him. Here was his girlfriend running around nude with all these other people and he was not with her. He almost wished he still did not know about it. But she had promised to let him come if his Mother and Bill came too for the first time and coordinating that was not proving to be easy.

Mary and Bill, Stan, Greg, Stevie and her mother and even Gabe was there to. Jeff pushed the bike to the exact spot from which he last kicked the bike over before the fire. He straddled it. Clamped on to the throttle. Turned it twice and kicked the kick starter once. Nothing. What he had hoped did not happen: he wanted it to start first kick. He opened the choke. Still nothing the second time. "Dummy," he hit himself on the side of his head as he realized that he forgot to turn on the fuel cock. He noted in his brain that not turning it off had contributed to the fire, now he forgot to turn it on. He needed to be more conscious of the position of the fuel cock.

He turned the cock on and choked the carburetor again. He then kicked it and the bike started and purred like it had never done. Everyone applauded and he took off down the street returning to give each and every one of them a ride all the way to the end of the block and back.

Now that the bike was running, he rode it to Weston through the fog on that special Wednesday. He walked to Melody's and she greeted him with a big hug. They walked to the bus hand in hand almost as if it was like the first time they ever did.

For a gift he knew he now possessed the best. The telephone call came just after the incident at the drive-in and he was so excited because he knew that they would be celebrating their anniversary and he had had no idea of what to get for her. He called Mike in San Francisco and asked him to go to Ghirardelli Square and purchase the now arrived copy of I Love How You Love Me on a music box works. In addition he had seen some small jewelry boxes with the Golden Gate Bridge on them and he asked Mike to pick up one of them and send it to him. Jeff waited nervously for quite a few days until the package arrive just Monday, two days before their anniversary. He cut and screwed and had the box perfectly made so that the song came on when the lid was opened. Now with the box wrapped and securely tucked into his pocket he arrived in Weston and met Melody.

They walked to the bus together and after a couple of blocks he first indicated the day to her.

"Melody, did you know this is the first anniversary of the day we met?"

"Really?" She said.

"I have a gift for ya." he said handing the prized box to her.

Melody stopped and took the box which Jeff handed to her with a broad smile on his red streaked fog chilled face. They both were chilled as Melody could feel the chill climb up her legs, but the joy of the moment warmed her. She slowly opened the package and finding the box opened it. Tears flowed from her eyes. She kissed his chilled cheek which warmed him. "I gotta go." Melody called out as she ran back in the other direction.

"If I'm late just go on without me." she continued to call out.

Jeff was left stunned watching her quickly disappear with her skirt back bobbing up and down as he had become accustomed to observing whenever she ran away. He continued his walk toward the bus stop and arriving he waited for her return. Just as the bus was filling and began to pull out he saw, from the window of his own bus, her arrive and catch her bus in the nick of time.

Jeff did not see her until lunch time and all he could wonder about through his early classes was why she had run back home. He tried to meet her at her locker between one class because he knew she often went there between that class period, but she did not arrive so he went on to class.

Finally at lunch time he returned to the locker and found Melody waiting there.

"You are so strange sometimes."

"Jeff I am so sorry, I didn't even know this was our special day. I will never again let this day pass without making it the most important day for us. I'm so sorry."

"I should have made a point to let you know it was coming." Jeff countered.

"I didn't want anything to happen to the box so I took it home and put it with your other box. Then I remembered that I had thought of a gift I wanted to give to you whenever something special happened and this seemed like just the right special day. Take this gift, she handed him an envelope and a tiny jeweler's ring box. These are for you, I made them myself but don't look at them until after class and," handing him a note, "read this letter and it will explain about these things, but don't let anyone ever see this letter it is very P-E-R-S-O-N-A-L personal."

Jeff could not wait and he begged and cajoled and pried and Melody finally relented. He opened the note.

Hidden Shore

Dear Jeff,   March 27, 1963

I am so sorry that I did not realize it was now a year since I first met you. I guess I was awfully young back then not to pay attention to the date. I love you Jeff and I want you to have something that is part of me that you can have forever so that whenever you are away, you will always have a bit of me with you.

The envelope contains a lock of my hair. I hope it didn't put too much of a gouge in my hairdo to get it but I wanted you to hold it tightly in your hand.

The box contains some clippings from my special place. these are for you to know that I reserve that place for you and will never let anyone near that place.

I love you Jeff and I am the happiest person to know that you and I are one. Thank you for taking the time to come and make contact with me at the Library which started all this. I know you had never been there when I was before. I knew it from the beginning because I always knew who was in the Library before. Please always remain the giving person that you are.

I love you more than life itself.

I love how you love me,   Melody

Jeff opened the envelope and looked at the lock of hair. He pulled the lock out and fingered the hair.
"I want to see this when I get home." he showed the box to her.
"Jeff, I wanted to put that into a heart shaped locket for you to wear around your neck next to our half heart, but I was not prepared for that yet."

Jeff smiled. "We'll get one."

57

Not long after this the whole group were at Jeff's house and looking for something to do, they decided to play a game. No one really knew who made the first suggestion to play the game. The six of them were sitting around in the living room just talking about the things that teenagers talked about on a Saturday afternoon.

They finally decided to play strip poker. So the rules were clearly laid out. The first rule: Nine items of clothing were to be the limit for each and each person would be required to identify the nine articles of clothing which constituted their wardrobe, but when they were done they all were required to be totally naked after the nine items were discarded.

Jeff went to his room and got the deck of cards that had the naked models printed on them while the others calculated what they would count as articles. For the guys it was pretty simple: Shirts, Ts, shorts, pants, 2 socks, 2 shoes and Jeff included his knife, Greg had on a baseball cap, and Gabe wore his army cap. For the girls it was tougher. Mel wore a pink cotton blouse, skirt, brassier, panties, 2 knee socks, 2 tennis shoes, and Jeff's ring. Stevie had the same except for petal pushers instead of a skirt but she also had her sun glasses tucked inside the cleft of her blouse. With Amanda it was a little more difficult. She was only wearing her one piece bathing suit, Levi's, and 2 thongs. The boys thought that should be fine; it would guarantee a quick peek at Amanda. The girls though had fun determining things to add to Amanda's wardrobe. Stevie ran next door and got her mother's wig, that would make it five items she borrowed Greg's Dog tags for six, borrowed Stevie's bracelet for seven. Jeff lent her his bandanna which she wrapped around her forehead making eight items. One more item and the wardrobe would be complete. Amanda asked Jeff to let her go to his room for a moment and she knew what she would do and it would be a secret.

Hidden Shore

So she slipped the final item onto her body and returned to the party.

The second rule: Each player had to become naked at some point. So the rule was made that each player would eventually remove all nine items. When all nine items were removed, on the final loss or end game, the winner, whether male or female could give the loser, whether male or female, a special instruction and the loser must follow the instruction of the winner no matter what it was. When an item was to be removed by the loser, the winner was able to determine which item to remove. The second worst hand could remove the item them self. In the event of a tie, each player would be considered as one, requiring them to do the same thing together.

Mel, Stevie and Greg had their doubts about the end game rule but agreed to follow the rules as long as no one was required to do anything they did not want to do.

Five cards were to be dealt to each person. The winner was the one with the most points: Kings were 13, Queens 12, Jacks 11, and so forth. The two jokers, one of whom Gabe thought was the best woman in the naked deck, were worth 20 points.

The game began. The playing order was Jeff, Melody, Amanda, Gabe, Stevie and Greg completed the circle.

The cards were dealt by Jeff first, only because they were his cards.

On hand #1 Melody was extremely nervous and impatiently watched the cards being dealt. To calm her nerves and to let Jeff know she was nervous she reached over and placed her hand on Jeff's penis on the outside of his pants. He looked at her and smiled even more excited feeling his penis begin to rise at the anticipation that this was a new experience for the two of them. Although Melody was used to being naked in front of people, this was different. Instead of just undressing in private and stepping out amongst a large group of other nude people who did not seem to know they were nude and was already nude herself, she found it a bit uncomfortable to have to undress with others watching, especially since most of them were not nudists, just kids either with a lot of testosterone or just plain horny.

Hidden Shore

Melody's nervousness quickly lessened when she saw her points equaled 51 which pretty much meant she was safe on the first round.

Already Jeff and Amanda were the first losers, each having 31 points, so they were both to stand on the table and remove an item of the winner's choice. The second least points were 41 which was Stevie so she could remove her own choice. The winner was Mel with her 51 points. Stevie opted to remove her sunglasses beginning a pile which would soon be quite stacked with article of clothing. Jeff and Amanda climbed on the table and Mel was kind, asking Jeff to remove his belt and knife and Amanda to take off "that gawdawful wig." Each item was placed in the pile.

The second round found Gabe the loser with only 25 points. The winner was a tie so a new rule had to be adapted. Each winner would be able to pick an item for Gabe to remove. The tie was between Amanda and Greg so Greg quickly told Gabe to remove his cap and passed the more difficult second item to Amanda. Amanda stood, put her finger to her cheek and gave every indication of being in thoughtful consideration of what to have Gabe remove. "Let's see now...Shirt." Everyone booed expecting her to be more daring. Gabe removed his shirt exposing the muscle tone under his green kaki A-shirt that his army training had developed. He climbed off the table while Amanda fanned herself and rolled her eyes as if what she had just seen made her hot. The second least points were Jeff's so he quietly removed his shirt and was sitting in his T-shirt while everyone was watching Gabe. Mel leaned over and kissed him affectionately. Amanda looked over and cried "That's not fair." when she realized he had removed it without anyone noticing.

The game proceeded to round 3. Mel was feeling even more comfortable as the third round began. She actually was looking forward to losing once, just to see what it would be like. The others had made her feel more comfortable because they seemed to be enjoying themselves just like the kids at the camp during their games. She again reached over to squeeze Jeff's penis, who whispered, "I'm not really sure you should be doing that, remember I'll have to take my pants off at some point and I'm not sure you want me to be pointing." Mel laughed.

The loser of round three knew it immediately. Stevie had only 18 points, the worst hand so far. She was a bit apprehensive because she knew she had already lost her sunglasses so she hoped one of the girls would win because she knew the boys would ask her to remove something more daring. This was the unsaid rule decided through exchanged glances among the girls. The second loser was Greg who immediately removed his baseball hat, tossing it in the pile. The winner was Gabe.

"A shoe honey." Stevie exclaimed kissing her honey full on the lips "Please, please, just a shoe." Repeatedly she kissed him. Her tongue finding the loosely pressed lips and entering his mouth beyond them.

Gabe pushed her off, paused, and exclaimed, "Shoe."

Stevie applauded. Removed her shoe as sexy as removing a shoe could be done in appreciation for Gabe's gallantry.

Suddenly to everyone's surprise, Jeff and Gabe's now 15-year-old youngest brother Stan arrived home. "What the heck are you guys doing?" he said.

Amanda walked over to him, "Playing strip-poker big boy, wanna join?" She said rubbing up against him.

"You gotta be kidding me! Really?" Stan called out. "Can I just watch?"

"No, you gotta play. No lookey" said Amanda

"How far you gonna go?"

"All right you can watch, but you must sit next to me" Amanda instructed. " You can be the judge"

So it was settled. Stan sat next to Amanda and for the rest of the game he was a perfect gentleman, assisting the girls up and down from the table and shouting encouragement.

Now it was time for round 4. Mel still sat with all her belongings. This time things changed. Mel came in second to last with 30 points. She surprised Jeff by standing up and removing her blouse. You would have thought Jeff was going to fall right out of his chair.

"I'm so nervous that I thought that would make me feel

better," she said as she stood there with only her brassier between her breasts and everyone's eyes.

Everyone applauded and she sat back down clamping her hand on Jeff's member even harder. This made him go to full erection so he remained in his seat happy that he did not lose that round.

The loser was Gabe again with only 26 and the winner was Stevie.

"Turnabout is fair play," Gabe yelled mockingly.

"Shoe." was all Stevie said.

Gabe removed his...left shoe.

By round five it became obvious that 9 items were entirely too many so by a democratic vote the players agreed unanimously that shoes and socks should be seen as one item together making it only 7 items total. So Stevie and Gabe each willingly removed their other shoes. This now gave Amanda another item because she only had thongs and no socks so she quickly removed her Levi's leaving her sitting in her blue one piece bathing suit thongs bracelet bandanna and then of course her secret item.

Melody was nervous when the cards were dealt for round five. She had voluntarily become the only girl to be sitting in her bra. Now as she counted her points she discovered to her chagrin that she only had 31. So far that would not have been a losing hand, but in fact it was even one point higher than her last second least score. Still it would make her feel better now if one of the other girls would loose her top.

She lost. "Oh my God, not the brassier," she thought as she closed her eyes and waited to hear who the winner was. The second loser was Jeff at 32 and he removed his shoes.

The winner was Amanda with 43 points.

"Hi Mel"

"Hi Amanda," said Melody nervously.

"I think you made a big mistake last hand," said Amanda, "I think you need to remove... your ring."

Melody sighed with relief. Just the ring.

"Thank you Amanda"

Hidden Shore

The real fun part of the game was the interplay between the players. They all pretended they did not want to expose something; however, they all knew that by the rules each one would have to be standing on the table completely naked at some point. But most of the fun was not letting on that there was an exhibitionist inside each one of them. Amanda was different, she still pretended nervousness about undressing but no one was really fooled, it was obvious she cared less and wanted everyone else embarrassed. In her choice to have Melody remove only the ring, she actually wanted to be the first one to show anything of significance. She probably hoped to remove the swimming suit in one fell swoop for the thrill of it and be the only one standing naked in front of everyone.

Round 6 began with a new dealer. Each player had taken turns to shuffle and deal the cards. When it became Greg's turn, he passed them to Stan and told him this would give him something to do instead of just ogling the girls.

Stan dealt. Mel knew she was safe this time. In fact, she knew she would win this time because she had 51 points. Amanda knew the same thing because she had 52 points so Mel was disappointed to hear she lost the choice for the next loser was Jeff so now even though her score was high it would be Amanda telling her boyfriend to remove something. Each one had received a Joker. With only 27 points Jeff lost to Greg's 28 points, Greg removed his shoes.

Amanda looked at Jeff.

"No shoes. No shirt. Just your socks, pants, tee, and well we all know what else."

"I think those pants can come off since your shoes are gone." she blurted, "Lets see what else."

Jeff looked over at Melody. His penis was still semi-erect but he hoped it would not be too obvious. He undid the snap on his Levi's, lowered his pants, sat down, and offered the leg of his pants to Amanda and Melody to pull off. They both grabbed a leg, pulled, and Jeff jumped to his feet resplendent in his socks, BVDs and T-shirt. He bent over pointing his hind end at Amanda and shook it. Amanda reached out, whacked him on the butt and he returned to his seat fighting off Melody's grope for his private.

Round 7. There was now developing a difference between players.

Jeff was losing with only three items left. His older brother Gabe now had four, Greg, Melody, Amanda, Stevie each had five left. The ones most exposed were Jeff and Melody. Jeff sat in his underwear, Melody with her brassier exposed. The rest still looked little different than on a picnic. Amanda in her bathing suit, Gabe in his mussel shirt, and Stevie and Greg looked just about the way they did when the game began.

Jeff won round 7 with 48 points. The loser was Amanda at 26 and Greg again came in second from last.

Greg threw his socks in the pile. Jeff looked over at Amanda. Amanda smiled. all the guys, including Stanley yelled "The suit", "The suit."

"Give me my bandanna back," Jeff exclaimed as he reached for it.

No major changes in the game.

Round 8:

A new rule was made that when someone got naked, then did their end game point requirement, they had to wait out of the game until all the others were naked and completed their end game requirement.

This game began having elements of community. Democracy, agreement, discussion, change. Give a little, take a little. Bribery, coercion, extortion.

On to round eight.

Gabe lost again with only 21 points. Stevie won again with Gabe's loss having 46 points. Stevie eyeballed him and laughed clasping to Gabe's arm instructed him to take off his socks.

Gabe offered his feet to Stevie so she could pull off his socks.

Jeff had unconsciously set a precedent during the last couple of rounds, by offering his pants to the winner in round 6 and taking his bandanna off of Amanda in round 7. It now became a rule by tradition, or common law, for the loser to have items removed by the winner.

Jeff had only 29 points so with only 3 items remaining, he voluntarily removed his socks leaving him in his shorts and tee shirt.

Round Nine.

Jeff again got 29 points probably assuring him the loss of one of his remaining two items. But when the tally was made, both him and Greg were tied with 29 so they both climbed to the table top. The second loser was Gabe so he removed his mussel shirt leaving him with his pants and shorts.

The winner was Melody. Jeff felt safer now. Greg knew he had little to fear. Melody decided to be kind. She instructed Greg to bend over and unbuttoned his shirt and she removed it. Then she told Jeff to bend over. She placed her hands on both sides of his waist, pretended to grab and pull down his shorts, then quickly pulled his tee-shirt up and off. Jeff really felt the bulge in his groin grow as he stepped down from the table into Melody's arms. He was shore she was going to expose him and was ready, but the anticipation had worked against him as the swelling grew.

"I'm Hungry", Stevie called out, "Let's eat."

Everyone else agreed.

Jeff began to grab his pants and put them on but was stopped by Amanda and Stevie who informed him that everyone had to remain in their present state through lunch. Jeff did not think this was too good of an idea because he was afraid his mother might suddenly show up for lunch and sitting around in his underwear would be harder to explain than simply playing strip-poker.

It was not as uncomfortable as Jeff thought. As the lunch and conversation progressed it seemed that maybe the game had come to an end and maybe they would not get around to finishing. Everyone appeared more relaxed and the testosterone levels seemed to have abated. As Jeff sat with Melody the immediate urge to "make out" with her occurred to him so he grabbed her by the hand they tried to slip into his bedroom but on the way their path was blocked by Amanda.

"Hey you guys," she yelled, "Hey everybody, before these two love birds decide to screw things up, lets get on with the game.

No nookie until the game is over!!!" she yelled even louder.

So all returned to their respective places and the game continued.

Round Ten.

Post lunch Jeff began to feel a little more comfortable as did Melody. Everyone seemed more relaxed, the break seemed to calm some of the sexual energy that was generated prior to lunch and the banter between the participants was more casual than before.

This time Gabe got his favorite Joker girl. He stood up and rubbed his crotch much to the chagrin of Stevie who hit him on the arm and told him to behave.

The loss went to Amanda. with her suit tongs and bracelet she waited for the winner Gabe to announced what he wanted. The second loser was Greg with 28 points and he this time removed his T-shirt. Gabe kissed Stevie who whispered in his ear and he said: "Stevie says I should get her bracelet back; the bracelet will be fine."

Round Eleven proved very interesting. Gabe and Stevie each had 43 points which proved to be the most. This meant That they would each be able to choose an article to be removed. Jeff only had his BVD's left. If he lost, one of them would be able to choose the first end game challenge. Greg had only his pants and shorts to make him the first naked person. Amanda would have to remove her suit and tongs if she lost thus revealing her secret item. The second loser was Greg who removed his pants, tying him with Jeff. Amanda lost.

So was this to be the revealing moment? Stevie opted for the tongs taking them from Amanda. Gabe smiled. "Yah, stand straight." He climbed up on the table next to Amanda, stood behind her, lowered each strap from the side and slowly with a deliberate attempt to make it sexy slipped the suit from her ample bosoms bringing Jeff back to attention again as well as Stan who had never seen a woman's breasts before. Laughter broke out among everyone as Gabe lowered the suit the rest of the way to reveal Amanda's secret item: On Gabe lowering the suit from her waist she inserted her hands inside her suit to keep a pair of Fruit-of-the-loom under shorts that she had found in one of Jeff's bedroom drawers from being pulled down. She had obviously spent time inspecting each of his under shorts because the ones she chose were very raggedy with a hole on the right butt area and fraying at the elastic.

Knowing she was in the exact same shape as Jeff and Greg, and in mockery of Jeff's dance on the table earlier, she bent over in front of Jeff who followed the established tradition and smacked her right on the hole in the shorts.

Jeff had now been joined by Greg and Amanda remaining with only one item. What also remained was to find out who would be the first to reveal their pubic area. Melody now felt very secure that the first would not be her. She had lost very few times and still had her brassier, pants, shoes and socks. Stevie was in even better shape having lost only her shoes. Gabe remained in his pants.

Round Twelve had the potential of being a major round. The deck was shuffled and dealt by a nervous Stan who now sat next to a topless Amanda and tried not to look like he was staring at her breasts.

Jeff had 41, as did Melody, both felt relatively safe. Amanda also totaled 41 so this appeared to be very interesting, especially if their scores were the top. But the top score went to Greg with 44. Gabe had 36 points, and Stevie had 37. That meant that the two older ones would loose something. Stevie chose to remove her socks, still leaving her fully dressed.

Gabe said: "I suppose you get my pants"

"Go ahead you can take them off," responded Greg.

"No," said Amanda and Stevie, " you got to take them off Greg."

So Gabe stepped up on the table and Greg, with much embarrassment, unhooked his belt, undid the pant snap, and with shaking hand reached for the zipper hook. He slowly zipped the zipper opened and pulled Gabe's pants down trying not to give any indication that Gabe's crotch which stood at his eye level was of any interest to him.

Round Finished.
Round Thirteen.

Gabe had now joined Jeff, Greg and Amanda in the same shape. The boys were disappointed because they seemed not to be getting anywhere with Melody or Stevie. At least Melody had removed her blouse so that made her more of a contributor. This was the importance of the rule that no one went without going naked. No one would be able to be a "party-pooper" and quit after seeing the others.

In round thirteen with four people with only one item, it appeared that at least one would loose their shorts. The law of average dictated that. With at least two losers in each round, the chance of Mel and Stevie being the two losers appeared very low. The real drama was if it would happen to two at once, or if only one, would that be the one on the table with the winner removing the item or the one not on the table who would be allowed to remove his or her shorts while seated at the table; thus, out of sight.

Melody, only had seventeen points. This was the lowest hand yet so she immediately knew she would lose and stepped up on the table without even revealing her cards. Jeff grabbed the down turned cards and laughed revealing them to the others.

Gabe had 61 points, the highest number of points yet. So Gabe stood and walked up to Melody deciding weather he wanted to remove her shoes, skirt, or bra. Meanwhile, it was revealed that the law of averages had failed. Stevie was the other loser. She had a pullover blouse on so she crossed her arms to both sides of her blouse and lifted it over her head while Gabe stood smiling at her in front of Melody.

"Kneel down." said Gabe.

"No! not that." retorted Melody offering her shoe to him.

"Kneel down."

Melody obediently kneeled upon which Gabe fingered the bottom of her brassier and slowly popped the bottom up over her breasts. Lifting the bra, he raised it over her head which was difficult since Melody was now cupping each breast in a hand in embarrassment.

"This is a little harder than I thought it would be," Melody exclaimed as she dropped her hands.

Hidden Shore

"We can tell, they're hard" said Amanda.

This embarrassed Melody who then crossed her arms over her breasts and sat down next to Jeff. Again Jeff could feel the rise between his legs.

The four still had their shorts, Melody was topless with skirt, shoes and knee socks and Stevie was now down to her brassier and peddle-pushers.

Round 14

Melody prayed silently that if she lost it would either be second place or won by one of the girls. She leaned her back into Jeff's chest who brought his arm across and over her breasts.

"Cut that out you two," said Amanda, "you don't see me hiding do you? You want to put your arm across my chest Stan?"

Stan was embarrassed but really wished she had meant it. He had never touched a breast before.

Round 14.

Jeff's first two cards were aces which made him nervous until he saw the other three were higher cards giving him 37 points. Amanda won with 48 points. Gabe was the looser. Amanda could now remove Gabe's shorts. He stood before her on the table and smiled. Amanda stared at the bulge in the shorts for a couple of minutes. "Up! Up!" She commanded.

Stevie yelled: "Just get on with it."

Amanda held her breath, hooked her thumbs on each side of his shorts and Gabe spread his legs slightly allowing room for them to come down to the applause of the other girls as Gabe's member sprang free almost hitting Amanda on the chin.

"Hey, its the game." Amanda said sitting back down with a big grin on her face. "By the way, you were second Greg it's your turn."

"I already did it." said Greg as he leaned back revealing his naked crotch with his penis tucked neatly between his legs.

Round 15 found three losers. Jeff, Amanda and Stevie each had 31 points. So all three paraded to the top of the table and the winner Gabe with 47 points stood up. Both Greg and Melody had 42 points; so Melody removed her shoes. Greg argued that he did not have to do the end game challenge because it was supposed to be the losers, whoever had the least amount of points. It was agreed that they would follow that rule, so Greg was put in wait until sometime when he had the least amount of points. In the mean time he remained sitting with his penis securely tucked between his legs.

Gabe pointed to his brother Jeff first.

"Let's get you out of the way." he said.

He instructed Jeff to face Melody.

"Ready Melody?" he asked rhetorically.

"I guess so." She said shyly

"This whole game has been a turn on, hasn't it Jeff?" said Gabe, "We can all tell because the soldiers at attention."

"Just get on with it Gabe." said Jeff

And Gabe pulled Jeff's shorts popping them down as his penis jumped up in front of Melody. Not wanting to make a big deal about it, Melody just stood up and helped Jeff down into a hug, pressing against his engorged member.

"Stevie?" Gabe played.

Stevie obediently stepped up to Gabe

"It's time for the pants."

He pulled the pedal-pushers down and leaving his girl friend in her panties and bra.

"Thank you honey." he said.

"Well, is she not a sight guys?"

The boys and the girls all applauded.

"Amanda." teased Gabe.

"Amanda!."

Amanda walked up to him in her holy fruit of the looms and sat down on her heals with her knees spread wide.

"What have we here?" he asked opening the fly to the shorts.

Amanda just chortled: "Hum, I guess your going to be the first to see."

Gabe reached back and pulled at her shorts down over her butt.

Her butt was pointed toward Jeff and Melody.

"How's that you guys?" he asked teasingly.

Hidden Shore

"Not bad" said Jeff.

Melody looked away embarrassed.

Amanda went to her knees and Gabe pulled the shorts down to her knees with a soft wolf whistle exclaiming, "Wow."

Amanda rolled down on her left buttock, pulled the shorts over her ankles, and tossed them to Jeff".

"Throw these away, why do guys hold on to shorts this disgusting? Are they the ones you lost your virginity in so your keeping them for old times sake? Huh Melody?"

Melody glared at Amanda for that.

"Just kidding Melody."

"Next round you guys." Gabe interrupted. "We should have an end game loss person this time. Get ready kids, I'm not going to be kind about that."

So round sixteen began. It seemed amazing that with six players 4 would be naked without having an end game challenge yet. Melody was sitting in her knee socks and skirt, and Stevie was in her brassier and panties. Really only five items left between the last two players.

Amanda, Jeff, Greg and Gabe all waited to see who might be the first challenge. To have a challenge this round, of course, one of them had to be last in points in their hand. Any of them who was not last would wait for the next hand without changes. That last person, after completing his or her challenge from the winner would then also wait until everyone had completed their own challenge; however, that person would not be dealt a hand.

Jeff revealed that he had 44 points. Melody revealed only half that at 22. Amanda had 29, Gabe 46, Stevie 32, and finally Greg had 41.

Melody lost. Gabe won again.

After walking up to the table, Gabe reached up, apologized jokingly, undid the three buttons on her pleated skirt and drooped it to the table top exposing Melody in her panties and knee socks.

"You know it could have been the socks, Gabe." she said. She then sat down next to Jeff again a bit more timid. Since Jeff had lost everything, she avoided him all together not groping as she had before. There even seemed to be a kind of space moving between them. It was almost as if the more they were exposed, the less they felt close to one another. Their relationship had always been private, that seemed to make a difference now that everything was coming out in front of everyone else.

The second loser on this round was Amanda but since hers was not the lowest score, no challenge would happen on this round.

Round 17.

"There's a lot of naked people in this room." said Amanda, let's make it unanimous this time. Come on girls, I don't like being the only girl with all her stuff for the world to see."

" You know, I think that each of us should write a challenge on a piece of paper that would work for any one of us and put it in an envelope." she continued.

"You know, that's a great idea," said Gabe, "that way nobody feels picked on and then if you make one too challenging you might get it yourself."

So Gabriel organized the mid-loser's challenge. He handed a piece of paper, envelope and pencil to each player. He then put a number on the outside of each envelope which was 1 for Jeff, 2 for Melody, 3 for Amanda, 4 for himself, 5 for Stevie and 6 for Greg. Then he went into the game drawer by the table and removed a pair of dice.

"When a person loses he or she must roll a die. That number is the number envelope to use."

A great deal of consideration went into each person's decision before they wrote on their paper; until finally, all the envelopes were sealed and handed to Stan.

"If anyone absolutely refuses to do what the paper instructs, then Stan gets to announce a punishment after talking it over with each of us." Gabe said.

All agreed. They also agreed that they would do what was on the list no matter what it was but just this once.

Round number 17.

Each player sat and collected their cards as they were dealt very nervous of the outcome.

Hidden Shore

Jeff got both jokers for a total of 62 points breaking the old record, that meant he would definitely not have to meet a challenge and would be the winner. And the shocker was that Amanda, Stevie and Greg all had 32 points. That made them all lowest. The second lowest turned out to be Gabe with 41 so since he was already done, he was passed.

Stevie still had her bra and panties so Jeff instructed her to turn around and he undid the snap on her bra and pushed the bra forward exposing her breasts. Stevie stood up and shook her breasts for everyone and then sat down with just her panties remaining.

"Okay'" said Gabe, "as winner you get to pick the first person and then open the envelope and read it to either one."

"Amanda, you go first" instructed Jeff.

Amanda stood up and picked up the die and placed it in a cup. She shook and scattered the die on the table when the number 2 appeared.

Jeff got the envelope from Stan and opened it saying: "Okay Mel, lets see what you wrote.

Jeff read: "Play hide and seek with all 5 players. The last one you find you get to kiss but you must kiss with everyone watching.

"All right you guys, hide well or you might get kissed." announced Gabe.

"What about Stan?" asked Amanda, " he should be able to play this one."

"Yeah, why not? asked Stan.

"I don't know," said Gabe, Mom might get pissed if we involve Stan too much and she finds out."

"Shit," said Amanda, "he's a big boy, you won't say anything will you Stanley?"

"Nah, I want to do this. Come on, quite treating me like a little kid."

They decided it would be okay after all.

So Amanda was instructed to go to one of the corners and to "keep your ass pointed outward" while she counted to 50.

They all scattered.

"One, two, three, four," all the way to 50 Amanda behaved herself and counted without looking. At 50 she called "All the All the ox are free, ready or not here I come."

She began searching. The first person she found was Stevie in her panties.

"Gotcha." she called. "I got Stephanie, here I come."

Then she found Melody in her panties and knee socks.

"Hey, I got the girls. Looks like I get to kiss a guy, and you are all naked.

She continued her search finding Stan next, then Greg. That left Jeffrey and his brother Gabriel. It took some time with these two: after all, this was their house and they had played hide-and-seek many times in there as kids.

It really became frustrating until she heard the slightest sound and found Gabe.

"You win Jeff, come out, come out wherever you are." Amanda yelled.

Jeff suddenly emerged from a space above the fire place from where he had been watching "all the naked people running all over the place."

"I get to kiss you Jeffrey. Up on the table." Amanda commanded.

Jeff jumped up and Amanda said, "I get to kiss him wherever I want. I want to kiss the head of your penis." she announced.

"Oh, my God." everyone said.

"Hey, what do you think this game is all about?"

Jeff looked over to Melody and she said: "No way." at the same time that Jeff did also.

"Just kidding," reassured Amanda.

"Now kneel down and spread your legs." Amanda demanded as she brought herself between his knees and with his member pressed against her breasts she kissed Jeff full on the mouth using her tongue in conjunction."

Jeff pulled away putting his hand between his leg and rolling on his side hoping that Melody would not see his state.

Amanda smiled, and then laughed and sat down, again

Hidden Shore

fanning herself. "If that is what you call a loser then I would like to lose every time." she said. "Now get your butt back up Jeff, remember there was another loser."

An amazing thing about Amanda was her ability to break the ice. Since she had done that part without shying away, the rest of the others now felt like they could participate without too much problem.

Jeff stood up on the table again and instructed Greg to come forward.

"Roll the dice Greg." he instructed.

Greg rolled the die and it came out 6 which was his own.

Jeff received the envelope from Stan.

He read: "Go into the closet with two of the opposite sex not to include a boyfriend or girlfriend for 5 minutes."

"Okay Gregg, since none of the girls are your girlfriend then you can pick any two, according to your own instructions."

Gregg announced that he would like it to be Amanda and Melody,

The three of them went into the closet and no one really knows what happened in the closet except for the three of them; but while they were in there the others could hear a lot of laughter, kissing sounds, and playful screams.

After 5 minutes they were ordered out of the closet from which they emerged disheveled and laughing. It must have been a good time. Greg was smiling.

This finished round 17. Amanda and Greg were now finished except to redress. In the mean time all they could do was wait unless they were the winner at a deal, then they could either remove one of the three remaining pieces of clothes from Melody with two or Stevie with one. Any one of the four remaining players could be last even if Amanda of Greg scored lower.

Round 18: As it was Greg scored the lowest with 25, but that did not count. Amanda scored the highest, that did count. The lowest of the four remaining was both Gabe and Stevie with 41 points. This meant that Stevie was to loose her last remaining article of clothes.

Amanda said: "Lets get this out of the way first. Stevie, up on the table."

"You saw how I made Gabe do it!"

Stephanie obeyed. Amanda approached her just as she had Gabe. Stevie stood in front of Amanda, but this time Amanda told her to turn away from her toward the others and just as with Gabe, she hooked her thumbs in the elastic on both sides of Stevie's panties from the back side. "Come on spread them a little so they can come down" demanded Amanda. Stevie obeyed and Amanda pulled them down. She then leaned forward and kissed Stevie right on her back side left cheek. Amanda quickly withdrew. Stevie turned and looked down at her then kneeled down and kissed Amanda full on the lips and said: "That's okay, this is the game."

Now it was Gabe's turn. Amanda handed Gabe the die and he shook it in the cup and spilled it forward. It came out No.1.

Amanda asked Stan for the envelope and handed it to Gabe. As she did she whispered into his ear: "She's hot Gabe, so are you honey," and stepped away much to Gabriel's shock.

Gabe read the letter which was his brother's: Run outside hitting each corner of the back yard and return to the game.

"Easy, I can handle that," Gabe announced.

Gabe not only proceeded to run the corners of the back yard while all watched from his mother's bedroom window, he then proceeded to run back into the house and out the front door with his penis swinging violently from side to side. When he ran back in, he said: "You know, if the Army found out about that, they would probably kick my ass out."

That finished round 18.

The only person with any clothes left was Melody. The only ones left to fill challenges were her, Jeff and Stevie.

The winner was Greg. The loser was another tie. Both Jeff and Gabe had received 32 points. Gabe was not qualified. The second loser was Melody with 39 points. This meant Melody could remove one item by herself. She still had her knee socks and her panties. She rolled her knee socks down and removed them both herself according to the rules.

Hidden Shore

"Wow, I guess I was lucky." she said.

Now it was time for Jeff's challenge.

Greg handed Jeff the die. Jeff served: 4

This meant that he had chosen his brothers.

"This better not be bad Gabe." he said with Gabe laughing hysterically.

The instructions read: "Kiss the a private part of each of the opposite sex."

"Aw come on." said Jeffrey.

"Hey, we did our challenge, it could have gone to any one else including Melody, if you don't do it we'll vote that Melody has to and by our agreement she will have to." said Amanda.

"Who could ask for a better thing to do." proposed Gabe.

"Come on girls, sit in a line on the edge of the table and spread them for Jeff." Gabe ordered. "Sorry honey," he said to Stephanie.

"Hey this isn't fair to Jeff or Melody" she retorted.

"Anyone who doesn't want to do it will get a worse challenge."

"What does private part mean Gabe?" asked Stevie. The others just sat in confused silence.

"What ever Jeff picks, so it's up to him." Gabe responded.

"Okay Jeff, we're trusting you now." Stevie gave in.

So Melody, Amanda and Stevie sat in a line. Jeff approached Melody first.

"Hi Mel."

"Hi Jeff."

"I want to kiss you between there." Jeff said pointing to her panty clad womanhood.

Shocked but willing Melody timidly spread her legs and Jeff bent to kiss her.

"Wait, pull those things aside, or he's not really kissing her on a private part." Demanded Amanda. Melody was still wearing the last remaining article of clothing amongst all the players. She was swimming amongst a swell of nudity. Jeff had picked this spot with Melody especially because she was still wearing her panties and he knew it would make the other girls nervous that he might pick the same spot with them and they had no panties on. It was obvious now though that Amanda might not mind.

"No!" said Gabe, "I agree, this is where she is and by the instructions that is where she remains until she loses them. Make her do it and Stevie will not go along with this challenge."

"Okay" snapped Amanda.

Jeff slowly lowered his face into what had now become very familiar territory for him. He kissed her baby white panties and then hugged her placing his hand on her breast.

Melody cautiously pulled his hand away.

"Hey, that's not part of the agreement," said Gabe, "do that to Steph without approval and I'll kick your ass."

Jeff then turned to Stevie who was very nervous about this one as she shot a glance at Gabe. This was a particularly uncomfortable situation for Jeff. He could now place his face in the crotch of what he assumed would some day be his sister-in-law since she and Gabe were engaged. He placed his hands on her knees and quickly leaned over and placed a kiss on the nipple of her left breast as Melody slapped his back side

"Thank you Stevie." he said.

"Why your very welcome young man?" she smilingly returned.

Now it was time for him to kiss Amanda. This was not too difficult. Jeff was curious what it would be like with her but he loved Melody too much to mess up his relationship with her and after all, she was his cousin.

Jeff stepped in front of Amanda and she laughed. "Chickened out with Stevie huh?" She spread her legs just wide enough to admit his head. He thought this was strangely timid of her. Jeff glanced over toward Melody who gave him a whatever you want look. He again started to feel the blood rush to his penis and quickly leaned his head between her thighs intending to slip his head up to her breast as he had with Stevie,; however, Amanda clamped her knees shut encasing his head between her thighs and forcing his face into her damp womanhood and screamed: "Take that young man." and then she released him. As Amanda laughed he stood back and embarrassingly wiped his mouth which seemed moist but then not so strange considering where it had just been.

To ease the tension, everyone applauded.

Melody did not look happy, but when he sat next to her she whispered "It's just a game but that might have been a little too far that time."

"I'm sorry." he responded.

"That's okay, I still love you.

It was now time for Round 20.

The only article of clothing left was Melody's panties. Jeff, Amanda, Gabe and Gregg were all eliminated waiting to re-dress.

This time Amanda was first. The loser was Gabe with 32 points, but again, he had been eliminated. So the next lowest person was a tie between Greg and Melody. There was no need to come up with a second lowest, because there was no one left. Greg had been eliminated so this meant Amanda could remove Melody's panties.

Amanda walked over to Melody and put out her hand. She helped Melody up to the table. Melody glared at her and said immediately "That was not that funny Amanda." Amanda shrugged. She instructed Melody to stand facing Jeff. She reached up and hooked her hands again into another pair of undershorts and pulled them down. Melody blushed and stepped into Jeff's awaiting arms.

Gabe then stood up and announced: "Since no one else has any clothes left, I think that Mel and Stevie should do the last two challenges so we can all get redressed and go to the movies; It's getting a little late and mom will definitely be home in about 45 minutes.

"We can skip it if you want." said Melody and Stevie at the same time.

But Melody and Stephanie walked up to the front of the table and hugged each other, feeling the press of each others breasts against themselves which felt quite comforting to each.

Stevie spun first. The notes from her and Amanda were still left.

Stevie spun a three which was Amanda's challenge.

The note read: "Let Stan touch your genital part and your chest for one minute each.

"Well, I thought Stan should be able to do something." Amanda argued.

"Wait a minute." Gabe again objected. "I went along with the hide-and-seek game but I don't know."

Stevie shocked everyone by exclaiming "You know honey, you let me and Jeff fulfill his challenge, I don't see any reason why since we have been doing what we have and he has seen it all, why not?" Stevie shot back. "Come here Stanley. Would you like to participate in this one as the challenge calls for?"

Stanley looked at his oldest brother's girl friend and meekly said: "I ain't no baby."

"Give me your hand Stanley," Stevie gently suggested.

"Have you ever touched a girl before?"

"No, I haven't. You know Sue, I kissed her enough but she always stopped me whenever I wanted to touch her."

"This is too much, I don't know." said Gabe.

"Shush Gabe, it's only between friends."

"Okay, I give up. Do what you want."

"Here," said Stevie as she placed Stan's hand on her left breast, feel my breast? That's it." She placed her hand over his while the others watched. Her nipple rose to a perfect pencil eraser point. Stan felt the nipple rise and felt with his finger around the aureola.

"Now, feel this." she said gently. Stan felt the softness of the down pubic hair and then explored feeling the lips of her vagina.

"That's enough." Stevie told him patting him on the cheek.

The experience was quite sensational for the observers. Stevie had introduced Stan to a new experience but did it with kindness and gentility.

The final challenge was Melody. The only one left was from Stevie and Melody felt that Stevie would not have done one very difficult.

It read: "Dance on the table top to "Rock Around The Clock."

Hidden Shore

Jeff felt good about this one. He knew Melody could dance well and he thought this would be very entertaining for all of them. He went over to the phonograph machine and found the Crickets hit.

Everyone sat up close to the table and the music began.

"One o'clock, Two o'clock, Three o'clock rock" the song blared. As always at first Melody was a bit shy. She danced in front of Jeff swaying and dipping. She then danced, one at a time, for Amanda, Stanley, Gabriel, Stephanie and Greg.

As she danced toward Greg, he noticed something on her he never knew about. She had a heart shaped birth mark on her leg just below her right buttock. He did not think much about it at the time, but it did seem appropriate that it was shaped like a heart; he knew how much Jeff loved her and he wondered if Jeff had ever noticed it.

By the time the song ended everyone had had a good time watching Melody dance as she slowly loosened up, and shook her small breasts and kicked her legs to the music.

And that is how the game went. Everyone enjoyed themselves; however, after it was all over, most of them were a little shocked at what they had done. A change in their attitudes had begun. Sex was a little more open but most knew they probably would never do it again.

By the end of the game they decided to go to the theater to see Mary Poppins, so they dressed and went to the theater together and tried to return to the same innocent fun that they had before, but it would never be the same again. Especially for Melody and Jeffrey.

Gabe caught the bus the next morning and returned to his base. Stephanie always felt like something was missing and each moment when he was away was taken up with thoughts of his return.

58

The next Friday evening after the game, Melody and Jeff

were trying to deciding what to do that evening. They pretty much determined to stay home and watch television until Melody had to go home. To their rescue, Stan walked through the door.

"What's up you guys?" he said.

"We can't figure out what to do tonight." answered Jeff.

"I want to go to the movie but Mom said that I can't walk there alone." countered Stan.

"What's playing?"

"The Birds", and they say it is going to be the last time it will go around the theaters, so I really wanted to see it again." answered Stan.

"Lets go." said Melody. "We can probably just make it if we leave right now. Should start in an hour."

So the three of them walked the three miles from Hidden Shore to Weston. It was just hitting dusk when they entered town.

The Loab Theater in Weston was not one of the large theater's found in large towns. Since Weston was a small town the seating capacity was only 300. There was one double door that entered the theater and to the left of it was the ticket booth. One of Jeff's classmates, Laura, worked in the booth. She sat on a bar stool with her knees secured on the edge of the counter in front of her. The high school boys always tried to catch a peek down her skirt between her legs. Invariably one of the boys would swear he "saw them" or "Damn, she wasn't wearing any tonight." She would collect the two dollar admission charge and hand them a ticket telling them: "Don't loose that now, you might win a dinner plate tonight." Every evening Mitchell's General Store to advertise, not that everybody in town did not already know about the store, awarded a plate which a customer would win when Laura pulled a duplicate ticket with a matching number from his or her ticket stub. If you got a set of six the Mitchell's assumed that you would want to come in and match it with a bowl set and maybe glasses and new silverware.

Stan, Melody and Jeff headed, like everyone else, strait to the line in front of concession stand and perused the options which were always the same: Cola, Popcorn and candy. The cola selection

Hidden Shore

was one: Coca Cola. Popcorn came Fresh Popped or Fresh Popped Buttered. The candy, on the other hand had a larger selection: JuJu Beans, Butterfingers, Neco Wafers, Junior Mints and others all aligned under a marquee lamp which had years earlier faded the display boxes. But everyone knew what each one was and everyone always studied the choices like they had never seen them before; The pungent smell of buttered popcorn permeating both nostrils.

The three of them made their choices, paid the outrageous price, gathered them up and headed into the door at the rear of the auditorium. Stan liked the middle, but as always Jeff and Melody began to head to the side row of seats. Since Stan was with them and they would not be alone anyway, they deferred to Stan's preference and sat mid theater with Stan and Jeff on both sides of Melody.

The movie began with laughter as everyone recognized Alfred Hitchcock leaving a pet store in the first scene; most who liked Alfred Hitchcock movies made it a challenge to spot Hitchcock in his ever present cameo role. The shape of his body and his unique walk always led to points and chuckles and "There he is!" whether one had seen the movie, and him, or not before.

One laughter that Melody recognized immediately caused her to stare to the rear of the theater and then lean over and tell Jeff: "Clint's in the Lodge seats."

"I Know. I heard him." said Jeff.

"He's with Tanya." she added.

"Good, now settle down and just enjoy the movie," Jeff said as he wrapped his left arm around Melody's back and tucked his hand below her arm pit caressing her left breast.

About the time the service station blew up in the movie, both Jeff and Melody were getting quite amorous and began kissing. Since their first passionate afternoon occurred in a theater, this had become a recurring situation for them. When they went with the rest of the "strip gang" just a week earlier to see "Mary Poppins" Melody and Jeff remembered non of it after "Supercalifragelisticexbialidotious," because they were so distracted.

Hidden Shore

"You know last weekend must have been exciting for Stan." whispered Melody, "Do you think he might try something more with Sue after what Stevie did with him? I hope not, that wouldn't be fair to Sue, it wasn't fair to her as it was."

"Ah, Stan's okay," Jeff chided, "He'll be all right."

"Hey," Jeff continued, "Put your hand on Stan's knee and tell me what he does, but don't let him know I know your doing it."

Melody glanced over at Stan's knee and slowly placed her hand over it.

Stan reached over with his hand and placed it on top of Melody's, squeezed it and Melody withdrew her hand.

After reporting this to Jeff, he told her to see how far Stan would let her wander in his lap, but "do the same thing to me that you do to him so I'll know what you are doing." he instructed.

Melody whispered: "Are you sure? He might get mad."

"No he won't, but if you don't want to, that's okay."

Melody thought about it for a few minutes, decided not to.

Then suddenly Melody changed her mind and sat strait up in her chair and placed her left hand again on Stanley's right knee. At the same time she placed her right hand on Jeff's left knee. Stan did not immediately cup her hand but after a minute his right hand clasped her left hand again.

Melody began to breath a little heavier as she thought a while about what to do next with each hand on each boy's knees. After a small hesitation she began to twitter her fingers a little, tickling the soft muscle pat at the fold of the inner knees of both Stan and her boyfriend. Stan squeezed Melody's hand a little harder a couple of times as if to say: "I like that."

Melody, with this gesture, decided to be a bit more daring. She straightened out the fingers of both her hands and began to ever so slowly pet the inside of each boys legs, just a inch further up the leg during each circular motion of her hand.

Upon feeling this Jeff began to again feel the familiar rising between his legs knowing that what felt so good to him, was also being done by his girlfriend to his young brother.

Melody continued the slow upward progress of her circles

until it got so far up Stanley's leg that he had to take his hand from hers because his elbow bumped against the small space between the seats. Melody slowly followed the stitch line that ran mid leg between both boys legs. Eventually she could feel the fold of pant material right at each of their crotches. She could feel the warmth and knew she was in the spot between each of their testicles and leg. She slowly enclosed her two smallest fingers in the almost muggy but warm and comfortable spot.

Jeff leaned over and whispered in her ear: "Are you in the same place on him?"

Melody slowly, not to be spotted by Stan, turned her head toward Jeff, gave him a small smile out her right side, winked and ever so slowly shook her head in the affirmative.

Something almost lecherous went through Jeff as he waited to see how daring Melody would be or how much Stan would let her do. He whispered: "If he does anything to stop you: do."

She slowly shook her head again and her thoughts returned to the task at hand as she slowly squeezed the muscle between each leg and let her hand raise away enough to press against each boys penis which she felt were both hard.

Stan then did something different. When he sat down, he had placed his jacket on the empty seat right next to him. He suddenly grabbed the coat and draped it over his lap hiding the illicit activity. Squeezing both legs tightly, Melody leaned over to Jeff's ear and whispered: "He just put his coat on his lap, I think he is expecting more."

"You wanna stop?" asked Jeff?

Melody shook her head: no.

Melody then twisted her thumb and forefinger around and began to gently pinch the hollow in which she had been playing. The next move was to work her knuckles forward and back against each genitalia pressing harder and harder and harder until both Stan and Jeff let out almost silent sighs and shifted in their seats simultaneously.

Without hesitation Melody simultaneously pointed both small fingers forward and snaked her hands forward, around and exactly snug over the boys' penis'.

For the first time, Stan glanced over at Melody and she winked at him. He had kept his eyes glued to the picture screen as if he were afraid that looking at Melody would make her aware that he knew what she was doing, but with her wink he smiled and she took her hand away from Jeff's crotch and pointed to the screen signaling to Stan that he should be watching the picture and making him feel that her left hand was the only one busy.

Melody slowly Kneaded the guys for a couple of minutes just to make Stan feel that this was going to be it. She then began to run her small fingers along the length of their zippers. Fumbling a little she worked her thumbs and forefingers up to the top of the zipper, grabbed the clasp and slowly worked both zippers down. This took some doing so that Stan would not hear that she was working Jeff's zipper at the same time.

Finally after a little persistence both zippers were all the way open. Melody teased running her fingers up and down the length of the open hollow of their pants. She inserted her small finger and petted the very tip of Stan and Jeff's penis'. She cupped them with the two small fingers and pulled the soon to be exposed members out slightly. With this Melody decided that the game had gone far enough, she lifted both hands away, bent over and kissed Stan on his right cheek, turned her head and kissed Jeff on his left. Both boys, when convenient, rezipped their zippers and again began to watch the birds attack the citizens of what they knew was Bodega Bay a town south of them.

The movie ended at 9:30 and since they had to walk home, they decided to hurry out.

On the way out, Clint jumped in front of them and asked how they were getting home. "Walking." Jeff said.

"Well I got my truck, want a ride?"

Stan immediately said yes. Melody said they could walk. Jeff shrugged his shoulders.

"Come on Mel, we don't mind going out there"

"Yah, come on Mel." Tonya interrupted Clint grabbing his arm.

"Up to you Mel." said Jeff.

"Okay, but we gotta get right home." she warned.

"Yah, Yah, for that you have to ride in back." Clint determined, "Wanna ride up front with Tawnie and me Stan?"

"Yah, Lets go."

"The love birds can cuddle up in the cold."

The ride home was a typical Clint operated ride. Too much gas, no break until the last moment, and exaggerated turns.

Jeff and Melody did cuddle in the back. Tanya had handed them a blanket because it was very foggy when they emerged from the theater.

Once home, Mary was there and reminded them that Gabe was returning the next morning and that Jeff needed to drive her car to Eureka and pick him up at the bus depot at 6:30 so they had ought to get to bed. Jeff looked at Stan and asked if he would like to play a game in his room with him and Mel.

"Sure." said Stan always agreeable

When they got to Jeff's room he asked Stan if he would like to play poker.

"Sure." Stan again said. "Where's the chips?"

"On the way over we talked about playing a quiet strip poker game since you couldn't play the other day."

"That's all you think about Jeff."

"Oh you didn't mind it so much when Mel was playing with you in the theater."

"She told you?" Stan said glaring at Melody, who felt very uncomfortable.

"You don't think that she would do something like that without my knowing about it. She was doing the same thing to me while she was doing it to you. We don't do anything unless the other knows about it."

With that, Stan furiously left the room with Melody calling out "Stan? Don't be angry."

"That was horrible, Jeff." Melody scolded.

"Oh Yah, it was okay as long as he felt he was getting away with something. As soon as he found out I would be involved he didn't want to have anything to do with you as long as I thought it was all right."

"Still, you can be a real ass hole sometimes." she blurted as she left to go next door.

59

Exactly six weeks after arriving in Hidden Shore, Amanda went to Eureka and met Jennifer.

Jennifer was a Notary Public and an office clerk for an Attorney in Eureka. Both appeared to hit it off as best friends the first day and Amanda spent the night at Jennifer's.

The next day, Jennifer drove Amanda home and she fell in love with the isolation of Hidden Shore. Seeing a sign in front of a house advertising it for rent just two blocks from Jeff's house, she rented it and Amanda and Jennifer moved in.

Jennifer was twenty three and Amanda was nineteen. They began setting up house. Amanda had very little money, still living on a little her Mother sent, but Jennifer wanted to live in Hidden Shore and having a friend like Amanda to come home to meant everything to her. The first few days they shared a bed but for appearance sake, Jennifer set Amanda up with her own room shortly thereafter.

By Friday, the house was complete and Amanda discussed with Jennifer the possibility of having a house warming party.

"I used to love sleep-overs when I was a little girl." Amanda told Jennifer. "Let's just have a slumber party and invite some of the girls over! This way you can meet them and they can see our house."

"That would be fun." Jennifer agreed.

So Amanda took Jennifer's car on Saturday morning and drove to Stevie's, and then to Melody's to invite them. Stevie thought it was a great idea.

"Gabe's not here this weekend and I'm so lonely, that would

be great." she told Amanda.

Melody jumped at the chance.

"Can I invite Mary too? Melody asked.

"Sure, the more the merrier," Amanda told her, "first we'll go to a movie in Weston and then we'll go to my house and we're supplying the beer and soda."

"Well, soda for me." Melody told her.

So all the plans were made. The boys were disinvited because this was to be the girls' night out."

The evening of the big sleep-over arrived. Stevie, who had just purchased her first car, picked up Melody and Mary and arrived at Amanda's in time to pile into Jennifer's car for the trip to Weston for the early show. Melody sat remembering her last trip to the movies with Jeff. The girls giggled to a new Jerry Lewis movie and went together to the soda fountain afterward. There were some Fairbury boys there who tried to separate Amanda and Melody from the rest of the group but their advances were spurned and the girls returned to Hidden Shore.

"That's why I love it here," Jennifer remarked, "it's so quiet here. You can get away from anything out here."

The girls watched Jackie Gleason. They all got up and danced along with the June Taylor dancers on the show and Amanda did a good impression of Crazy Guggenheim: "Hi, Ya Joe, Hellooooo Mr. Dungahe he he." and they all said: "And away we go!"

When the show ended the girls dressed in their nightys and talked about boys and other important things in a girl's life. Finally Amanda suggested playing Truth or Dare.

"Melody, how many boys have you kissed?"

"Two" she answered, "if you mean romantic kisses."

"What other kind are there?" kidded Jennifer.

"Okay, how many girls have you kissed?"

"That don't count," said Melody, "I already answered one."

"Okay," Amanda asked, "every one else answer my first question then you each can answer one."

"Mary."

"One." said Mary.

"Really?" asked Amanda, "you and Mel are just babes in the woods."

"Stevie." she turned to Stevie.

"Well there's Gabe and Patrick and the kid in the third grade. Then my cousin a couple of summers ago." Stevie thought. "Five, if you mean romantic."

"Five," Amanda calculated, "Gabe, someone named Patrick, the kid in the third grade and a cousin. Who's five?"

"I've already answered my question." Stevie argued.

"Okay, Jennifer?"

"Well, I'm a bit older; probably a dozen." she answered. "Let's see? One, two, three," she counted on her fingers, "four, oh Yah! the Halloween party, geeze! a couple of dozen. And that's not counting girls."

"Girls?" Stevie asked.

"Yah, that's my question. I liked Amanda's; how many girls."

"Wait." Melody cut in. "it doesn't count unless Amanda answers her own question."

Amanda answered ten and the game proceeded like this. Other questions were Jennifer's: "How many girls?" which Amanda answered three, Stevie, Melody and Mary all said none and Jennifer said "The same as with boys."

"Really, were you playing games?" Melody asked.

"Not necessarily." said Jennifer.

"What's it like?" asked Stevie.

"Like kissing boys but softer. Men are rougher always thinking they gotta twist and push just like their fucking you." she answered. Wanna try?"

"What?" said Melody.

"Well you can add four to your list of romantic kisses if we each kiss. Let's make it a Truth or Dare. If you don't want to answer a question, you need to kiss each of us."

"I have a tough one," she went on, "either kiss each of us or run naked around the block."

Hidden Shore

None of the girls felt like a cold romp alone on the streets of Hidden Shore.

"Okay, I'll go first." Jennifer bent over and kissed Amanda full on the mouth in front of the others.

"Stevie?" she called. Stevie bent over and for her first time she kissed another girl. Jennifer recognized her willing response and kissed her French style.

"Wow." Stevie said when they broke the kiss.

"Melody?" she called again. She bent over and respecting Melody's distress kissed her only a simple but lingering kiss.

"Mary? I've never kissed someone Chinese, boy or girl." she said as she bent over and kissed Mary. Mary's response was better than she had expected as Mary reached her hand up and rubbed it on Jennifer's side. Jennifer reciprocated with a lingering kiss and a little tongue.

"Okay, everyone else try every one else." she instructed and the girls proceeded to switch around. Melody kissed Stevie as good friends, as she did with Amanda; but she was shocked when Mary's kiss proved to be more passionate than she expected.

After the kiss, Stevie came up with a fun idea.

"Let's go see the boys. We'll go as ghosts. We'll wear what we have on and there is a spot in our fence at home that I use to cross over to Gabe's back yard. We'll try to scare Jeff and Stan."

The other girls thought it would be fun. They put their coats on and drove to Stevie's. They went into the back and through the opening and in their long and short nightgowns they Ooo'd and Whooshed and made all kinds of scary sounds until they saw Bill come to the back window and ran back to the car and back to Amanda's screaming and laughing.

When they returned, Amanda brought out the soda's and beer and the girls drank and played and listened to Leslie Gore records and danced.

Melody gave in and tried her first beer. She and the other girls got tipsy and all crashed in one bed or on the sofa in the living room.

The next morning, Sunday morning April 14th 1963,

Hidden Shore

Jennifer had to go in to work to type some legal papers so she left about 7AM which rousted Melody and Mary. Mary tried to raise Stevie and Amanda but both of them had had more beer the night before and they fought off Melody's efforts. Melody and Mary walked to Jeff's and called Greg to invite him over and they all spent the day on the beach together.

Amanda and Stevie were left alone at Amanda's. At about 10 o'clock with the spring sun filtering into Amanda's bedroom she awoke and found Stevie still lying next to her.

"Hey sleepyhead," Amanda said softly, "let's sleep the day away."

Stevie turned her head and stared at Amanda glancing down to her breasts which were visible through her nightgown.

"Sounds good." she uttered softly and rolled on her side facing Amanda.

Amanda pulled the blanket from her knees and turned facing Stevie and noticed that she could see Stevie's brassier through her night gown. Amanda extended her arm and ran it down Stevie's side and shifted closer to Stevie. She then wrapped her arm behind Stevie's back and cuddled closer interlocking her legs with Stevie's pressing her bent knee against Stevie's womanhood. "That feels nice." Stevie whispered encouragingly.

Amanda took Stevie's hand and placed it on her side. Stevie ran it up and down Amanda's side until Amanda rolled on her back. Stevie shifted closer and found Amanda's breasts with the palm of her hand through the night gown.

"Oh, that feels good." said Amanda. She pulled her night gown up offering the soft warmth of her breasts to Stevie. Stevie played with them for a few minutes just slightly running her hand palm back over Amanda's willing breasts.

Stevie ventured over closer to Amanda and the two pressed their lips together as Amanda reached behind Stevie. She lowered her hand to Stevie's panties on the back and then raised inside Stevie's night gown to the clasp of her bra. She unsnapped the clasp releasing Stevie's breasts from their confines. Amanda rolled over on top of Stevie, pushed her knees together and raised up lifting her night gown up and over her head. Stevie wiggled out of her gown also raising it over her prone body and discarding it with her brassier. Amanda scooted back and pulled Stevie's panties to and off of her feet. Stevie spread her legs allowing Amanda access to her womanly channel. Amanda played and tweaked Stevie's lips and then buried her face into the lips pinching them with her own facial lips.

Stevie groaned as Amanda raised her hands to Stevie's breasts. She moaned and enjoyed the oral play and sensations that ran up the length of her body. Her breathing became labored as she accepted Amanda's act of pleasure. Stevie motioned Amanda to lie next to her and she curled around finding the cleft between Amanda's legs as she again offered her own to Amanda. They finished and curled into each other's arms and fell asleep again.

Around noon they began again urged on by the warmth of the room. Amanda was again down softly licking the soft lips of Stevie's place when from the doorway come the words "Can I have some of that?" Stevie leaned back surprised and Amanda looked up at Jennifer who was standing at the door. "Do you mind?" Amanda placed her hand softly between Stevie's legs and asked her. All of this was new to Stevie and she hesitated a moment. "No, I don't mind if you don't?"

Jennifer slowly kneeled at the end of the bed and placed her face between Stevie's legs joining Amanda as they tongued her to orgasm intertwining their own tongues in a female play of sexual pleasure.

For Stevie, this whole morning was a new experience. She felt that if she ever experimented with a woman it would be to share with Gabe not the way this began with Amanda. While Amanda and Jennifer kissed and played, Stevie gave them pleasure moving from one to the other. The pungent odor was different but both were pleasant. She wondered if every woman had a different identifiable odor.

For Stevie this was an experiment. She missed Gabe and felt a need to hold someone. This did not seem like cheating. She felt more comfortable with a woman in keeping her commitments to

Hidden Shore

Gabe but still relieving penned up sexual feelings. She would do it one more time with Amanda only about a week later but she knew she was not a lesbian; she only tried it to experience and satisfy her curiosity. After the second time with Amanda, she told her she did not want to do it again. Amanda simply said "If you want."

Strictly defining a lesbian, Amanda was not one. She preferred to be with either partner sexually, male or female. Jennifer was convenient for her at the time. Jennifer supplied a partner every night if she wanted one. Jennifer would not get jealous over a man because she thought they were no threat to her. Women were different. If Amanda was with a woman's woman Jennifer would get jealous. Jennifer was a lesbian. The day that Jennifer found Amanda with Stevie, Jennifer did not care because she knew Stevie was a man's woman and was just experimenting so Jennifer saw Stevie as a play toy something to use and to share but to discard when used. To her Amanda was different. She knew Amanda liked men she also knew Amanda would leave with any sudden provocation. So she let Amanda do as she wished and hoped to play along as long as it lasted.

When Amanda first met Jennifer she was sitting at a Cafe in Eureka. The Cafe was full and seeing Amanda by herself asked her is she could join her. Amanda, always willing to help someone out and alone feeling sorry for herself, said "sure, have a seat."

They hit it off immediately, Jennifer had dated two male attorneys moving in with one and seeing the other on the side until the one on the side's wife found out and it was all over the law office. The first attorney kicked her out and she moved in with one of the female attorneys who introduced her to the lesbian world in Eureka.

The evening that Jennifer met Amanda, she took her to an apartment where she met two other women and the three introduced Amanda to the pleasures of women. Amanda took to other women like a duck to water as the four engaged in love-making at a feverish pace. From warm encounter to play with toys, Amanda learned that there was more to life than just boys.

With women, Amanda soon discovered, a quick fling was

not all there was. Even after going home with Jennifer, she found Jennifer to be still ready for more sexual play unlike with boys who ejaculated then wanted to ejaculate her right out of bed or were not interested in any more but to smoke or sleep.

This made Amanda and Jennifer compatible. They both had an insatiable appetite for sex but knew that with each other there was no fear of pregnancy or some sort of disease.

Amanda was never jealous of Jennifer. She did not seem to have the ability to be jealous. Throughout her life if some one she liked wandered elsewhere, she just said "oh Well" and went on to someone else.

One time Jennifer invited some friends to Hidden Shore for a lesbian party. Amanda was attracted to one who looked a lot like Melody. She kissed her and another dark well built woman jumped in and attacked Amanda. Jennifer came to her rescue and cooler minds prevailed and the four of them retired to the bedroom together; Amanda was able to do as she had originally wanted with the woman she desired.

60

On Saturday the 28th of April, Amanda was alone in Hidden Shore and went to Jeff's house hoping Gabe or Stevie or Jeff or Melody or any of them might be there.

Stevie was not home and Jeff was already gone with Melody but Stan was there by himself.

"Hi, Stan whatcha doin' kiddo?" she asked him.

"Not much just watchin' television." he responded.

"Can I come in and watch with you?" she asked.

Stan agreed and Amanda sat and watched Johnny Quest and Space Ghost with him. She began thinking about Stan's innocence at the Strip Poker party.

"Hey Stanley, you've never been with a girl before." she said to her young cousin.

"Not really." he replied.

She sat next to him and pulled off a sweat shirt she was wearing and brought Stan's hand to her bra.

"You can touch me." she encouraged.

Stan just rubbed her a little and did not move any closer.

Amanda stood and pulled her pants off and lowered her panties.

"Stanley, you can try me if you wish." she told him.

Stan leaned over and put his face to her chest. He glanced down at the thick down soft bush between her legs and put his hand on her down there.

Amanda laid back and offered herself to Stan.

Stan just stood there. She reached up and started to touch him between his leg reaching for his penis. Stan backed away.

"I don't want to do that Amanda." he told her.

"Are you sure?"

"I'm sure."

Amanda put her clothes back on.

"You wont tell anyone about this will you Stanley?" Amanda pleaded.

"Hey, I take it as a compliment but I want it to be with someone after I'm married. I won't tell anyone if you won't tell anyone I turned you down."

"You don't like boys do you?"

"Please...no." he responded and walked out the front door leaving Amanda frustratingly sitting alone on the couch.

61

There was a Laundromat in Weston and Amanda was there doing her laundry. She stepped next door to the Cafe to have a cup of coffee while her clothes were being washed. In walked Clint. Clint did not know Amanda and Amanda had only heard about

Clint. She was sitting at a booth slowly sipping her coffee and breathing in the smell of freshly cooked bacon and other breakfast items being prepared in the kitchen as well as considering what to play on the juke box. Clint sat at the counter and ordered a cup of coffee and a snail. He reached up, deposited his coin in the juke box selection box, and played a Country and Western song. Amanda deposited a coin and played a rock and roll song. It came on after Clint's. Clint put in a coin and played another country song. The game turned into dueling juke box songs.

"You like that Country stuff, huh Cowboy?" Amanda finally asked him.

"Well its better than that Elvis garbage you been playin'" he responded.

They set a while neither sure what to say next. Finally Clint grabbed his cup and moved to the booth with Amanda.

"Why don't you just take a seat Cowboy." she asked as he was sitting down uninvited.

"Don't mind if I do." he said. They laughed and Amanda introduced herself.

"I'm Amanda. What's your name or should I just continue to call you cowboy?'

"Clint, from Clinton but no one calls me Clinton."

"Clint the Cowboy." Amanda teased.

"No, Clint Johnson."

"Any relation to the head cop here?"

"Yah, that's my dad."

"Well, Clint the cowboy Johnson that's gotta be no fun having a cop as a Dad. I'll bet you don't get to have any fun."

"I do about whatever I want." he assured her.

"That's probably because if you get caught he gets you out."

"Fuck you , you bitch." Clint shot.

"Hey now, be a good boy or you can just wander back to your perch at the counter." she demanded that he behave.

"I'm sitting here because I choose to, not because I have any kind of permission from you."

"Are you Jeff Williams' friend?"

"Yah, you know Jeff?"

"I'm his cousin, I've heard a lot about you."

"Yah probably from that bitch girlfriend of his. Well, fuck her."

"That's about as much as I care to hear. I'm going now." Amanda picked up her purse, walked over to the counter, paid and tipped the waitress." I'm giving this to you. I don't trust that jerk over there." she pointed to her now vacant table. Clint had moved back to the counter.

"Get off my ass bitch." he said to her.

"Clint, behave yourself." the waitress scolded him.

"Thank you." said Amanda as she walked back to the Laundromat and finished her clothes.

When she saw Jeff later that evening she warned him.

"I certainly don't know how you ever could have a friend like that guy. That's the scariest person I've dealt with in a long time, and I have dealt with some pretty scary guys. I think he's got something loose upstairs. If I were you I'd keep my girlfriend far far away from him."

62

On Friday May 24th the day finally arrived when Jeff would accompany his Mother and Bill to the nudist camp. Gabe was home for the weekend and he and Stevie were going also. Melody had told her Aunt and Uncle that Jeff's parents were nudists also and she had introduced them at the camp when she bumped into them. Jeff wanted to ride with them but Melody told him she wanted them to go separately and meet at the camp. She had informed her friends at the camp about the situation and she wanted to prepare the way for his visit. Her friends were pleased that her boy friend was going to be one of them. Nudists (or Naturists) like to recruit or convert new people much like any religion does. "Cast off you deep seated puritanical beliefs and join us." was the essence of their message. Linda wanted to make things perfect. She proposed having Melody sit on a throne with cape and scepter to welcome Jeff officially. Melody liked the idea.

When Jeff arrived he had no idea what to expect. They were going to share Melody's folks' camper to dress or undress and join the crowd. Jeff undressed with his folks, Gabe and Stevie. They stepped out and were greeted in a way that was like walking through a veil into the light by Uncle Jim and Aunt Peggy. With them was Linda and two boy escorts who Jeff was introduced to. Linda was tall and thin and had extremely long hair knotted into a tail down her back.

"Jeffrey Williams we are your official welcoming committee, you must come with us." She led the way with the two boys on each side slightly behind her.

"Can we come too?" asked Stevie.

Linda paused and said: "You have permission to follow."

Jeff followed with Gabe and Stevie just behind him. He found it strange to march among naked people who parted to allow the procession to continue.

They entered a hallway where Melody was sitting on a throne (the one they usually used for Santa Claus at Christmas time) propped atop a pallet. She had on a purple cape and held a scepter also. There were many young people gathered as Jeff entered and walked down an aisle formed by the other nude kids. They proceeded up to the throne at which time Melody arose.

Jeff was quite impressed now knowing what Melody and her friends had cooked up for him. She stood there naked except for the open robe for all to see and he could tell she was not at all concerned about the other people.

"As Queen for the day," Melody began, "it is my honor and privilege to welcome you as an official member of the Evergreen Naturist Camp of California. If anyone among you know of any reason why this man and his brother and this woman can not join with us in holy natural right, let them speak now or forever hold their peace."

Melody waited an appropriate time for an objection. "Gabriel...Stephanie..." she smiled at Jeff. "Jeffrey, I now pronounce you three as one with us." she tapped on all six shoulders with her scepter.

The whole room erupted in laughter and applause as all the young people gathered around. It seemed so natural to Jeff. Everyone seemed to know everyone else. The ice was now broken. Melody threw off her cape and discarded her scepter and joined the three introducing them around.

When they returned, everyone was excited about having been there. Amanda wanted to go the next time. So did Greg but he only wanted to go if Mary could and he knew she would not be allowed to spend the night.

"Hey, I'll be here next weekend," Gabe proposed, "why don't you guys go with us and we'll bring you back Saturday evening.

The following weekend Jeff went with Gabe and Greg and the girls rode with Amanda and Jennifer. When they got there everyone had a good time. Jeff was sitting with Melody at the pool along with Greg and Mary.

"Can I ask you a question Mary" he asked.

"What's that?" Mary asked cautiously.

"You don't have a lot of hair down there. I once saw a girl shaved. Do you shave it some?"

Mary laughed which broke the ice because Greg and Melody thought it was an inappropriate question.

"I'm Oriental. We don't have as much as you Caucasian creeps." They all laughed.

"I was just thinking of something." Amanda cut in. "Do you realize that a strip poker game at a naturist camp would be a one hand game because you would have nothing to lose."

"You have to play Twister Amanda while your here. You would love it." Melody added. So they all ran to the picnic ground which had many twister games and all of them played twister entangling themselves among each other's bodies.

Mary and Greg and Stevie and Gabe left that evening. So did Amanda and Jennifer. Melody and Jeff stayed with both sets of parents.

The next morning was June 1st. Bill had a boat in the lake at the camp. Melody and Jeff wanted to go water-skiing. Bill took them out and they skied one at a time. The fresh air and the splashing water felt wonderful against their nude bodies. There was a small cabin on the boat and a little later Jeff and Melody began drinking beer and then when they ran out of beer they began drinking highballs. The two got extremely drunk, Jeff and Melody went below and made love while Bill brought the boat in. Jeff was almost paranoid making love to Melody with Bill on board.

"I can't believe we're doing this with him right there." Jeff confessed to her.

When Bill docked the boat, Jeff had to relieve himself badly so he left Melody on the boat and ran to the restroom.

When he returned, Melody was very disturbed about something.

"While you were gone, Bill came inside here and I was real nervous because he was acting funny so I pretended to be asleep," she began to cry. Bill was out tying up the boat and wrapping things for the walk back up to camp. Melody went on, "He came up to me and thinking I was asleep he pulled the covers down and began to say 'how beautiful,' 'just lovely' and things like that. He touched me up here" she pointed to her breasts, "and said 'how lovely" then he masturbated until he came bringing my hand over to his penis. He then pushed the blanket back over me and cleaned up then went outside. I was so scared."

"What do you want to do?" Jeff asked.

"He didn't hurt me but maybe we should report it," Melody suggested.

"That could be a mess. Damn, I better stop going to the bathroom," Jeff cursed.

"Let's just go home and we'll decide." Melody finally suggested.

"Bill, we gotta go home." said Jeff after stepping back out.

"What's the rush." Bill asked.

"Mel says something happened and she wants to get back."

"If she thinks something happened we need to talk about it."

"No that's okay Bill, she's just had too much to drink." Jeff did not want an incident there. He felt helpless. Bill had put him in a very difficult position. He did not want to cause trouble, but he also knew he needed to show some kind of strength in defending Melody's honor. He made the wrong choice. He chose to let the matter drop. The situation would fester inside Melody because she knew Jeff did nothing.

63

The Wednesday after the incident on the boat, Bill did something else improper. Amanda was at the house and Bill was there in the evening. Amanda did what Amanda does; she flirted. Bill being a grown up man responded.

"Let's go to dinner." Bill suggested.

"Let's go." Amanda agreed. Bill drove Amanda to Fairbury and they ate in a restaurant. He offered to buy a nice valuable coat of any kind she'd choose in exchange for Amanda to get a motel room with him. Amanda agreed but she wanted the coat first. It would not be that night.

Amanda had no intention of sleeping with Bill. She thought if she could get a coat out of him it would be worth the risk. He did not dare say anything if she did not go to bed with him. This happened on June 5th.

On June 14th, Bill failed to return home after work. He deserted Mary and set up an apartment with a woman who rode his bus every day.

64

On Wednesday June 12th 1963, a week after Amanda went to Fairbury with Bill and two days before he disappeared, Amanda was again at Jeff's house in the evening and found Jeff working on his motorcycle. Jeff was the only one home and Amanda talked to him until he finished the project he was working on.

"I've go to clean up," Jeff told Amanda, "wanna watch TV while I take a bath?"

"Sure, if you need anyone to scrub your back, just call." Amanda teased.

Jeff went into the bathroom and filled the tub. He slid in and began washing. The door opened. Jeff looked over and saw Amanda standing by the door. She had a wash cloth in her hand.

"I'm here to wash your back, Jeff."

Jeff sat up but did not cover up. He thought "what's the use" Amanda had seen him before. She walked over and kneeled by the tub and dipped the cloth in the water.

Amanda leaned across Jeff and pressed her breasts against his face as she grabbed the bar of soap from the soap tray. "OOPS! Sorry about that." she said as she dipped the cloth back in the water and soaped it between Jeff's legs. She glanced at his manhood and smiled slyly at Jeff.

"Lean forward dear." she cooed. "I can't wash your back in that position. She soaped and washed his back as he bent his knees and wrapped his arms around them. Then she worked the cloth down his leg and up the inside to the knee. Jeff leaned back and she dipped the cloth and raised it to his chest. She soaped and scrubbed his chest then worked toward his still greasy hands. She heavily soaped and wrapped her hand and cloth around each finger one at a time and pumped each finger and thumb individually. She cleaned his hands well and dumped them in the water. She then ran the cloth around his belly and finally worked it down to his now engorged penis. She soaped her hand and softly jacked his penis and then she rubbed it with the cloth.

"Turn around." she ordered. Jeff followed orders well.

She ran the cloth again over his back and when she reached the top of the breach of his behind she traced her finger down it finding the opening she inserted first her center finger which made Jeff rise a bit. She slowly inserted it to the knuckle and retracted it. She then retrieved the wash cloth and slowly inserted some of it where her finger had just been. Just a little at first then pushing as much of the cloth as he could take she then pulled the cloth from it's confinement and Jeff was rapt with ecstasy.

Jeff turned around again. Amanda held out her hand and bid Jeff to come with her. He stepped from the tub to a towel that Amanda was waiting with. She toweled him slowly and tenaciously giving particular attention to his penis. She stroked it and placed her tongue at the tip of it for a prolonged second. She then guided Jeff to the bedroom and kneeled down again before his manhood and brought her face again to it. She circled the knob with her tongue and allowed it to enter her mouth as she bit slightly paying particular attention to the flair as she lightly nibbled. Jeff's member grew to it's highest extent.

"Lay down big boy." she said. Jeff laid on the bed and placed his palm in the nape of his neck while he watched. Amanda put a song on his phonograph: Love Me Tender by Elvis Presley. She slowly and sexily began to unbutton her blouse as she whirled her hips slowly to the song. Jeff reached out and Amanda told him to wait. Jeff watched her remove her blouse. He saw the fullness of her bosoms as she removed her brassier. She undid her pants and turned her back to Jeff. bent over, and pulled them down with her behind just inches from Jeff. She then turned and slowly lowered her panties as Jeff saw first the top curls of her pubic mound and then the full dark patch came into view.

Amanda swung her knee over Jeff and sat on his belly with her vaginal lips pressed at his hair. She rubbed herself around to be tickled by his hairs as his penis slid up and down the fold or her behind. She leaned forward and kissed Jeff full on the lips, reached behind and took him in her hand set upon him driving him through to the hilt. She went up and down slowly rising and settling while he went in and out of her. She hugged him close and then they swung around with him on top he slowly rose and fell forcing himself in and out. Amanda reached and inserted her finger again into his backside. Jeff continued to pump and pump and it became furious as Amanda inserted and withdrew her finger to correspond with his own rhythm. Jeff screamed: "I'm cumming." Amanda pushed him up and out "Not inside me" and he pulled up from her laying his penis on her belly and depositing there. They laid together for a while. Amanda got up first. The phone rang. It was Melody. Jeff felt guilty as he spoke with her. He indicated that Amanda was there but implied they were watching television. The deed had been done.

65

Greg held a party on Saturday July 15th. He invited everyone. Even some of the kids that had moved from Hidden Shore to Eureka showed up. Jeff was to bring a load of Sodas which he had stored at his house. He went to Greg's and helped him decorate. Some of the kids arrived early. Two of the girls who used to play spin-the-bottle with them were there already. They were a couple of the younger ones, Alicia who was Sharon's little sister and Natalie Garcia. These girls had matured and were now quite the young ladies. They were both in Melody's class meaning they would be Sophomores next year in school.

"I could use some help bringing the cokes over if you don't mind." Jeff asked the two. Melody was being brought by her Uncle so she had not arrived yet.

The girls were willing so they went to Jeff's and loaded some on a little red wagon and went into the house to get more. The girls asked to see his room and he went in with them.

"You're really hooked on Melody aren't you." Alicia asked.

"Yah, she's special."

Jeff sat on his bed and the girls sat on each side of him.

"Remember when we swam naked in the Creek?" Monica asked.

"We sure were young then. You know we both had crushes on you." Alicia confessed. "You know we've grown up a lot since then." she bent over and kissed Jeff on the cheek.

"You ever had two girls at once?" Alicia asked sheepishly.

Jeff was shocked. These girls were trying to proposition him.

Alicia and Monica both took off their blouses and offered Jeff to touch them. Jeff did and the three began playing "touchy feely." They kissed his neck and took their bras off.

"A lot more than we had as kids wouldn't you say Jeffy?"

Jeff could not believe what was happening. They kissed a few more times and Jeff played with each of their breasts. That is as far as it went. They dressed and returned to the party.

On the way they told him that they knew he was Melody's, they just wanted a taste. Melody was there when he arrived and they all enjoyed the party. Jeff felt guilty throughout. He had been with Amanda and now the other two girls. For Jeff, life was getting very complicated.

66

June 20th 1963. Melody celebrated her sixteenth birthday to teasing of "sweet sixteen and never been kissed." Melody was now blossoming into a woman. She carried herself with pride and dignity, happy to be with Jeff and hoped that the next sixteen years would mean creating a world with him.

Jeff presented her with a heart shaped locket like the one she had mentioned at their anniversary. Inside he placed some clippings of his own pubic hair. and showed her that he had purchased one for himself to place her clippings in.

"These represent our commitment to each other and we hold a piece of what is ours next to both of our breasts." Jeff said upon presenting them. This was when he knew he was sorry. He had betrayed that trust. In his mind he knew he would never do anything like that again. He wanted Melody to be his only one forever, but he knew he had to tell her about Amanda or he could not live with himself.

The next day, June 21st, was a Friday. Jeff determined that he needed to confess to Melody. He was sure she would be unhappy. He arranged to repeat their first date even down to having his mother take them to Eureka. He picked her up and presented her with another flower knowing this time that it was his job to pin it on.

They went to dinner at the Eureka Inn again. Dinner was enjoyable but somehow it was not the same. They walked to the theater and watched the movie Lilies of the Field. After the movie, they returned to the Eureka Inn just as before and each had a sundae.

"Melody, I need to tell you something." Jeff began.

"Oh we sound serious," Melody responded, "what's up? gonna ask me to marry you or something?"

"Melody, I've been unfaithful to you."

Melody's heart fell to her feet. "What are you talking about, Jeff?"

"I was seduced by someone and I'm so sorry."

Melody sat back in her chair. She did not know what to say. Her world had just come crashing down around her.

"Who?" she asked.

"I'd rather not tell you. Does it make any difference?" Jeff answered.

"Yah, I want to know whose ass to kick. What do you think?" she blurted. "What were you thinking? I know we've played some games, but I never let anyone do anything without you there. Who was it? Not Mary I hope."

"No, not Mary."

"Jesus Jeff, I have no idea. Someone at the party last weekend?"

"No."

"Oh my God, not your cousin! Not Amanda! That's incest."

Jeff would not respond.

"My God! It is Amanda! That night I called and she was there! You fuckin' ass hole, that fuckin' bitch!"

Jeff had never heard Melody speak like that before. It shocked him but he was not surprised at her reaction.

Jeff's Mother arrived and Melody walked away from Jeff immediately.

"You sit in front with your Mommy Jeff, I've had about enough of you right now and I've got to think." she ordered Jeff.

The ride home was excruciating for Melody and Jeff. It wasn't too pleasant for Jeff's Mother either. Melody had her drop her off at her house, she did not even feel she could talk to Stevie at this point. When she arrived at her house she removed her pendant and locket and handed them to Jeff. "I'll consider whether I want them back or not." she informed Jeff.

Jeff was afraid to say anything as he watched her walk up to her door, turn around, and give him a look that was nothing less than pure hatred.

Jeff could not even discuss what happened with his Mom. When she pried, he told her he had made a big mistake; he admitted it was all his own fault.

He walked next door to Stevie's when he got home and fell apart as he told all the details to her. Stevie knew this was one she had very little idea of how to deal with.

For Melody and Jeff the next week was agonizing. Jeff tried to contact Melody and speak to her, she would have nothing to do with him.

On Wednesday, Jeff walked toward his locker and saw Greg and they began talking. Sharon joined in on the conversation. Suddenly, Jeff felt a crack at his jaw as his face slammed in the other direction against a locker. Not knowing what hit him, he fell forward and Greg caught him before he hit the ground. Turning and realizing he had been cold cocked he saw Melody walking away as Greg and Sharon in disbelief helped him regain his composure. Knowing he deserved nothing better, he decided to leave her alone for the moment.

Jeff's nights were miserable, so were Melody's. Both were

Hidden Shore

confused and agitated about the situation. Jeff continued to try calling Melody but her Aunt and Uncle would tell him she did not want to talk to him and she refused to answer the phone.

Jeff rode his bike to her house and tried to see her and was refused. Melody's Uncle Jim was sympathetic with Jeff but he protected Melody's wishes. He did not know what led to the disagreement but he surely had a good idea. Melody could see him sitting upon his bike outside and held to her own wish to make him suffer.

School let out for the summer that Friday. Stevie called Melody and invited her to her house.

"I don't think I want to be anywhere near Jeff." Melody told Stevie.

"Just come over and we'll have one of our nice sisterly talks," Stevie said, "If you don't want to see Jeff fine, I'll keep him away. This is just a time with you and me."

Melody had not cried as much as she would have thought she would have under the circumstances; her anger was uncontrollable though. She broke the music box from their first date, and punched her gorilla until it tore. Both were reparable, but she had vented her anger on them.

Stevie picked Melody up and they drove around hardly talking. When they arrived at Stevie's, Melody slipped into her house unobserved by anyone. Melody usually had use of their guest bedroom whenever she stayed at Stevie's, but this time Stevie invited her to sleep with her.

"I think you just need someone to hold you." Stevie said as she wrapped her arms around Melody who then cuddled into her side.

"It's so unfair. I'm willing to give anything to Jeff. I let him do anything he wished, all I ever expected was his loyalty to me." Melody told Stevie knowing that Stevie already knew what had happened. Melody broke into a fit of tears and cried as she laid her head on Stevie's breast.

"Now, now, you just let it out little sister." Stevie comforted her.

"You're so good to me," Melody cried, "I just want Jeff to love me, not anyone else."

Melody raised her head to Stevie's cheek and softly kissed her on that cheek. Stevie turned her head and kissed Melody sweetly on the mouth. Melody accepted the kiss and it became more passionate. Stevie softly kneaded Melody's small breasts and toyed with her equally small nipples as Melody reached over caressing Stevie's fuller breasts. The penned up frustration in Melody began to come out as she leaned over and eased her tongue into Stevie's willing mouth. The two began to run their hands around the fullness of each others bodies. Stevie placed her hand between Melody's leg and massaged and worked her clitoris. Melody moaned and pleaded with Stevie "Make me feel good. Please more." Stevie lowered herself down and found Melody's spot. Melody went wild with frenzy felt a feeling that was beyond anything Melody had ever experienced in her whole life. They slept the night in each other's arms.

"I love you Melody." Stevie told her as they fell asleep.

The next morning Stevie and Melody talked about what had happened.

"I've only been with one other woman before." Stevie told Melody deciding not to identify Amanda since Amanda had brought on the situation with Jeff.

"I've never been with anyone." Melody sighed.

"I know. And this does not mean you're a lesbian or anything like that. I probably should not have let that happen but since it did let's just remember how good it was for us to share. It can be just as good with a man if you and he want it to be." Stevie counseled Melody.

"What do I do next?" Melody asked.

"Let's get dressed and go find Jeff. You still want him don't you?"

"More than anything in the world." Melody responded.

"Jeff, Melody has something to say to you and you need to sit and listen." Stevie instructed Jeff after she and Melody found him at his house.

"I don't know why I'm even going to consider forgiving you Jeff. I guess it's because I love you too much to lose you but I can't believe you would take the special thing we had and ruin it like you have. I would never consider letting any other man do anything to me as long as we are committed to each other. What you did is an insult to me and an insult to yourself because you lowered yourself to the level of a slug slithering around sharing our special thing with someone else. I know she's your cousin but you need to promise that you'll have nothing ever again to do with her. If I ever begin to think that you are with someone else again, don't ever come and see me again."

Melody calmed and kneeled before Jeff. She put her hand on his chin and held it.

"Jeff, I say this because I love you and I will forgive this indiscretion because I do. Know this! You have my heart but break my heart again and I will equally search to find someone who wont. You may kiss me now."

Jeff wrapped his arms around Melody and they kissed. Stevie left them alone. They did not make love that day, they just sat and cuddled and toyed and regained what they almost lost.

67

Jeff's **M**other made it a little easier for Jeff to avoid Amanda. One day she was in the beauty parlor in Weston and a friend named Myrtle from Fairbury sat next to her while they waited for service. They discussed the usual political and social world at Fairbury, Weston and Hidden Shore which was so important among the denizens of beauty parlors.

"By the way, I saw Bill at the Tackleman's Restaurant a couple of weeks ago with this young blonde girl. Does he have a daughter?" Myrtle said.

"Bill and I aren't together any more." Mary told her.

"Well, this was just a high school aged girl. He sure found

one already I guess."

"I'd rather talk about something else." Mary told her.

They continued to talk about other items of importance like who was building what and where, and who was seen doing what to who.

"What did she look like?" Mary suddenly asked.

"Blonde, ratted hair. Not real pretty but they were being real cuddly. Remember that blonde that Doris hired to do her yard? She kind of looked like her."

"Oh! I know. I'll bet it was your niece." said Thelma from the other side of Mary.

"Couldn't be." said Mary. "What color lipstick was she wearing?"

"Pink?" Myrtle thought. "Definitely Pink. I remember it didn't look good for a blonde she needed to have red.

"Did she have a scar over her right eyebrow?"

"Didn't notice." said Myrtle

"What was she wearing?"

"I thought you didn't want to talk about it?" Myrtle went on.

"What was she wearing?" Mary repeated a little louder.

"Blue blouse with a fleurs-de-lis stitched in it."

When Mary returned to Hidden Shore she headed right to Amanda's house.

"Were you in Fairbury with Bill? she asked Amanda.

"Yah? He was hungry and invited me to dinner."

"How come you didn't tell me?" Mary asked accusingly.

"Hey! He wanted me to, you know, but I turned him down. He's gone anyway."

"Don't you ever come near my house again. I'm calling your mother and tell her you've been trouble. You need to go back home."

Mary stomped out of there in a jealous rage. Amanda never saw her Aunt again.

68

Hidden Shore

The summer of 1963 was much different for Jeff and Melody than the summer of 1962. Time heals many wounds and the argument between the two lovers was settled; but strains remained. They often argued over the smallest inconsequential things. Melody had matured and the upper classman boyfriend was now her equal in every thing but age. Jeff felt threatened by Melody's new found independence. Melody no longer lingered on every word that Jeff said.

They still had pleasing romantic encounters. There was a late low tide on the 13th of July and Jeff and Melody swam nude on North Beach. They made love as often as they felt inclined. Jeff became a bit more demanding making special requests such as oral sex when Melody did not necessarily feel inclined. She kept peace by spending no time at the camp and not inviting Jeff there. The catharsis that her trips to the camp meant no longer existed. She seemed to need to escape, let her hair down and enjoy friendships unencumbered by sexual overtures. Bill had ruined some of the camp experience for her. He added the sexual element to what had an appearance of being sex free. The sex she had with Jeff was consensual, Bill was a mandatory situation because it was unsolicited.

Mary and Bill were going to Disneyland starting on the fifteenth of July and would have taken Stan and Jeff with them, but when Bill left, the vacation was canceled. Melody went home again to San Francisco and remained there from the twenty-second returning the twenty-eighth. She wrote to Jeff each day but, of course, he could not write back. The day after she returned Jennifer sent Amanda packing and Amanda moved in with a girl named Trina in Weston.

On Friday August 2nd, Gabe came home and talked about a conflict brewing in Southeast Asia in a country called Vietnam .. He expected that he would be going along with quite a few other soldiers as advisers to the South Vietnamese government.

Melody spent that afternoon with Gabe while Jeff was at work just visiting and getting to know Gabe better. Gabe made one unfavorable suggestion that may be he and Stevie and Jeff and her might double date sometime and implied that maybe they could switch date. Jeff take Stevie out and he would take her out. This never materialized.

Jeff and Melody did stray from their commitment when they played strip poker again with Greg and Mary, but the fun had disappeared from the game after the girls were braless, they decided they wanted to play something else.

On Saturday August 10th, Amanda bumped into Clint again while bowling with Trina in Fairbury. The two girls took him home after he humbled himself to them and Clint began seeing Amanda on the side.

School began on September 2nd. Jeff became a Senior and ran down the aisle at a move-up assembly with Sharon. Melody became a Sophomore.

On September 15th, Greg showed Jeff a now camera he had just bought which took instant pictures so they did not have to send them to a pharmacy. Jeff took Melody to a deserted building north of town and took nude pictures of her. He kept them close to his bed and hidden away.

On November 1st, Jeff's Mother Mary was involved in a single car auto accident between Weston and Hidden Shore. She had been drinking and was arrested by Clint's father Steve Taylor for drunk driving.

On November 22nd, the town of Hidden Shore like the rest of the nation was shocked at the assassination of President John F. Kennedy in Dallas, Texas. Memorial services were held at the school and everyone packed before their television sets to watch the funeral the following Sunday.

Christmas 1963, was celebrated by Jeff and Melody as they had been the year before. For New Year, Melody and Jeff agreed to kiss only each other at midnight. The school did not hold the New Year dance again because of the lingering kisses the year before.

69

Hidden Shore

Jeff celebrated his 18th birthday on January 16th. Melody gave him a pair of motorcycle gloves.

On Friday evening January 26th, Melody went to a basketball game with Mary Woo because Jeff, who had found a weekend job mounting chalk board for Weston Construction, had to work. After the game, a group of the students and players went to the bowling alley in Fairbury. Mary Woo and Melody bowled with two of the boys from the basketball team. One was also a running back for the football team named Brian, the other was a boy named Jim. The girls had been promised a ride home when they went to the bowling alley with some of their girlfriends.

"We'll take you." the boys offered.

Brian had a new 1964 Mustang which was one of the hot new cars on the market. Jim sat in the back seat with Mary. On the way home Brian drove up to the cemetery at Hidden Shore to a spot that overlooked the Ocean. Melody felt a little uncomfortable with Brian and being so close to Jeff's house. Mary and Jim were going at it pretty heavily in the back seat and when Brian parked he leaned over to kiss Melody. She hesitated but she was excited about being with Brian. She allowed the kiss and he reached over and palmed her breasts as she responded with a kiss that included tongue play. His hands roamed freely but they were in bucket seats and when he reached between her legs she stopped him.

"Not now," she said, "I have a boy friend."

"I know but why be with him when you can have me?" Brian responded.

"I can't do this." Melody countered. "If you insist I'll walk from here."

Melody opened the door and stepped out and Brian got out and walked a while with Melody. Bryan put his arm around Melody as they walked. Mary and Jim were steaming up the windows of the Mustang.

"I have a girl friend too but it's not working out for us." Brian admitted.

"I love Jeff, but it's been hard lately." Melody confided.

Hidden Shore

They walked and discussed their situations. When they got cold, they returned to the car and Brian kissed Melody and then opened the door for her to get in. The boys took Mary home and then went back to Weston to drop Melody off.

"Can I have you phone number?" Brian requested.

Melody gave it to him.

That night Jeff called and Melody rushed him off the phone. Brian called twenty minutes later and they talked for three hours.

The next morning, January 25th 1964, Melody was awoken by her Uncle.

"Jeff's at the door." her Uncle Jim informed her.

Melody arose and went to her dresser as her Uncle invited Jeff in for a cup of coffee. She dressed and glanced at the chain with the locket and the heart which she had removed and deposited on the dresser. She did not pick it up and continued to dress.

"Hi, Jeff." she said to him as she sat at the table. Her Uncle was cooking breakfast and placed it before her and Jeff.

"Let's go for a walk." Jeff suggested.

"What for?" I've got homework to do." Melody responded.

"I just thought we could spend the day together."

Melody thought about telling Jeff she was too busy but thought better of it. Conflicting feelings were racing through her as she continued to eat her breakfast. Finally she condescended. to a small walk.

They walked over to the Library and stood outside by the swings that they had played on when they first met. Jeff wrapped his arms around Melody who stood stiff and unresponsive as he kissed her neck.

"Are you okay?" asked Jeff who was worried about the way she was acting.

"No Jeff, I've got a lot on my mind."

Jeff looked down Melody's cleavage as she turned to look away. He reached over to reach down her cleavage and Melody pushed his hand aside.

"What's the matter?" Jeff asked roughly.

"Jeff, I just don't feel like it today, it seems to be the only thing you think about." Melody argued. "I think I'm starting my period."

"Well that never stopped you before," Jeff responded but instead of leaving it alone he countered, "and where's your chain? You can't use the Mother excuse, I always have mine." he cruelly showed her his.

That is when the fight erupted. Tempers flared and Melody tried to walk away as Jeff reached for her. Melody began to run. Jeff pursued her and caught her and tried to hold her and she wiggled out of his grasp.

"I don't know Jeff, I think...." she stopped. She wanted to tell him that she needed some time alone. She wanted to scream and run away. She began to cry. Again Jeff reached out and she warded off his attempt to touch her.

"I'm going home now Jeff, don't follow me. Just stay right there. If you follow me you'll never see me again."

"Melody, what's wrong?" Jeff screamed. "Go. Just get out of here."

Melody walked away crying all the way home.

Jeff watched her as he paced back and forth until she was out of sight.

"Damn." Jeff yelled. He ran to his bike which sat in front of Melody's house. He walked around the block hitting telephone poles, mail boxes; cursing. He felt like someone was ripping his body apart. He screamed. He cried. He pranced. He kicked a curb and hurt his toes. He limped back to his bike again.

Melody was sitting on her front porch again. He was still hitting things when he noticed her.

She looked very dark. Very alone. Jeff stopped his fitful rage and looked at her. She looked helpless almost pathetic sitting there.

They stared at each other, neither knowing what to say.

"I love you Jeff." Melody finally said.

Jeff stood with his arms hanging limply at his side.

"I love you Mel." Jeff finally said.

"Just give me some time to sort out what's going on in my

mind. I'm confused. If you really love me you'll give me some time."

"I do love you Mel." Jeff said calmly and encouraged. "Can I call you?"

"Please do. I'll let you know when I want to see you again. Don't come over, in fact, let me call you."

"Okay." Jeff agreed. "Please call me at least once a day to make me feel better."

Melody's only thought was that even here was a demand from him.

That evening, Brian picked her up at seven. They drove to Fairbury and had dinner at the Italian Restaurant. She sat next to Brian as he held her. She felt comfortable and warm in his arms. After dinner they parked near the river at the Steelhead River Bridge. They kissed and Melody found his manhood and wanted to give something of herself. She mouthed and tongued him until he was relieved. She let him touch her breasts inside and out of her bra. She let him finger her out side of her panties but would not let him touch inside. She came from his gentle touching. She had not ever came for Jeff. It was electrifying. She kissed Brian hard and he held her afterwards.

Melody called Jeff on Sunday afternoon and they talked of nothing. She talked to Brian for two hours; they talked of nothing. The same procedure happened on Monday. At school Melody walked with Jeff at lunch and they talked of nothing. She talked to Brian after school for a couple of hours. She had to get off the phone to call Jeff. She called Brian back.

On Tuesday, Jeff and Melody were having lunch when Brian walked up to them with his girlfriend Carol.

"Hi Melody." Brian said. "You know my girlfriend Carol!"

Melody was gracious and introduced Jeff to Brian. Jeff knew Brian but he ran with a different circle of friends.

"Hey! It's nice meeting you." Brian said to Jeff. "Carol and I are going to Eureka Saturday, how about we make it a day the four of us."

Jeff looked at Melody. She shrugged a "why not?" shrug.

Hidden Shore

"Sure, we like to double date, right Mel?" Jeff answered.

Melody said: "That would be fun."

Wednesday night Melody called Jeff just before Brian picker her up. They went to the Midway Drive-in. It rained. They could not see the screen. They sat in the back seat. They weren't really interested in the movie anyway. Brian was satisfied.

Thursday, Melody called Jeff and he pleaded with her to let him come over and see her. "I'm tired and need to get a good night sleep." Melody told him.

Jeff yelled. He told her he was trying to understand but that it was hard for him.

"Let's go to the movie tomorrow night." Melody suggested.

"Okay, I'll pick you up."

"No, the movie starts at seven, I'll meet you there." Melody demanded.

They went to the movie and Jeff kept his arm around her throughout.

"I love you." he told her. Melody leaned her head into the nape of his arm. She let him fondle her breasts. Jeff felt encouraged. After the movie he left his bike at the theater and walked Melody home. Jeff kept his arm around her trying to warm her from the January chill. He felt that Melody was beginning to respond favorably. At her porch they kissed. He palmed her breast as she responded with passionate kisses. She broke the kiss.

"Jeff, I love you. I don't know how to make you understand that I do so much. I just don't want to make love to you right now. Just hold me a while." Jeff and Melody sat on the stoop of her house and he held her.

After Jeff left, Melody went to her room. She fingered her locket and heart and she opened the music box and listened to I Love How You Love Me. She took a piece of paper and a pen and tried to write a letter to Jeff. She wrote a few words and wadded the sheet and threw it away. The phone rang and it was Brian.

"Ready for tomorrow?" Brian asked. "We'll be over at ten to pick you up."

"Brian, I'm a little uncomfortable about tomorrow."

"It'll be okay." he assured her.

"I forgot to tell Jeff what time. I'll need to call him."

After leaving Melody, Jeff rode to Hidden Shore and felt like he needed catharses so he went past Hidden Shore and headed south. He opened the throttle and let the air pass through him. The cold January air was reviving to his senses. He returned home and his mother told him that Melody called and told her to tell him to come over for breakfast at nine o'clock because Brian would pick them up at ten to go to Eureka. Jeff tried calling Melody but the phone was busy. He finally got through at 12:30.

"You been on the phone?" he asked.

"No, I've been asleep," she lied, "maybe Aunt Peggy was."

On Saturday morning, Jeff arrived at Melody's promptly at nine o'clock. He remembered the precision timing he performed in San Francisco to pick her up at 9AM.

Brian and Carol arrived right after Jeff and Melody finished breakfast. Instead of going to Eureka, the whole group decided to hike the trail to Fern Canyon which was north of Eureka.

Unfortunately, the day with Brian and Carol was uncomfortable and Jeff and Melody argued about every little thing. After the date, Brian and Carol dropped Jeff and Melody off at Jeff's in Hidden Shore.

No one was home. Jeff and Melody went into his bedroom and made love for the first time in a long time for Jeff. Something was different, Melody appeared not to respond as she had at one time. Melody had hoped that the feelings would return, but they did not. Jeff seemed like just a mechanical toy not the warm boy she fell in love with one and a half years before.

They sat on the sofa and waited for Stevie to return home. Their talk was stilted. When Stevie arrived home Melody stood up.

"I love you, gotta go." she left and walked next door to Stevie's.

After a promise not to reveal anything, Melody filled Stevie in on all that had happened and what she planned. They talked out in front of Melody's house for a long time.

"Just always be my friend." Stevie asked.

"I will but I can't stay at your house any more." Melody told her.

Melody knew long before Brian told her that decision time had come. Brian called that evening and he and Melody made their pact.

70

Late Sunday morning February 2nd, Melody called Jeff.

"Hi honey, how are you." Jeff began.

"Jeff sit down, I need to tell you something."

Jeff was sitting. He asked her: "What's wrong?"

"Jeff, it's over between us. I've fallen in love with Brian and we're going together now."

Jeff exploded in disbelief.

"What? What about Carol?"

"He's dropping her today." she informed him.

Jeff went out of control. He erupted into a fit of tears.

"I need to see you. I need to talk to you. You don't mean it." Jeff was in denial. "I have to see you. You owe me that much."

"The decisions made." Melody snapped trying to be strong.

Jeff pleaded with her. She finally condescended and agreed to meet him at the swings by the Library.

Jeff raced in his bike and Melody was already there. He ran to her and she would not let him touch her.

"It's final. I simply felt you deserved to hear it face to face."

Jeff raised his fist as if to strike her.

"If that is what will make you feel better, just hit me." she said standing boldly before him.

"How do you know you love him? I thought we had something."

Melody thought for a second then she answered his question quite cruelly with the only thing she could think of and in the hope it would anger him enough to hate her so he would leave her alone.

"You know how I never liked giving you a blow job? Well, I like doing it for Brian so I must love him more."

"Well that's a shitty reason to love someone. Does that mean you have been cheating on me? Fucking him and not letting me know?"

"I don't have to tell you what I do, but I never have FUCKED anyone else but you if that's what you want to call it. I didn't want to do it until I ended it with you so no I have not 'fucked' Brian. But I'm gonna now."

She walked away. Again he reached for her.

"Touch me and I'll scream rape!!" she yelled.

She then ran home, with that same bounce of the back of her skirt that Jeff had always loved.

Jeff sat on a swing and bawled. He rolled in the sand at the foot of the swing. He ran to his bike and roared toward Hidden Shore. He considered running his bike into one of the cliffs.

Jeff wanted to die.

Melody went to her room and wept bitterly.

71

By the next morning, Jeff was out of touch with reality. For nearly two years Melody, like a third arm, had been a permanent part of him. There had been rocks on the road, there had been arguments, but there were times of warmth and affection. More warmth and affection than rocks. Jeff had felt confident that there were always rocks for couples, but he felt they were never insurmountable and that he and Melody would overcome all obstacles. He was willing to forge on and keep their relationship together through anything. Her sudden decline, though not without warning, devastated his confidence in anything. He had tried to give her the space she needed which she had requested. He had hoped that she would remember the good times as well as the bad times and was secure that she would work things out in her mind in his favor which he felt confident would be in her favor also.

Melody felt just as disjointed. The evening after she told Jeff, Brian picked her up and they went to the bowling alley in Fairbury again. Having spent so much time with Jeff as her constant companion it felt somewhat odd to suddenly slip into the arms of a different boy with the realization that this was the only boy now in her life. Doing things with Brian was easier. Brian had a car. This fact alone simply made things different. If she wanted to go anywhere, all she would have to do was to call Brian and he'd be there. Jeff had to either walk the four miles from Hidden Shore or ride his bike and then they had to make arrangements with someone else for rides. The wonderful feeling that she had felt with Jeff was now gone. She felt obligated to have sex whenever he wanted, not because she wanted, because she really no longer felt that early desire for Jeff. Brian made her tingle again. Jeff had become old hat. Like an old worn hat she needed to discard, she knew for her own sanity she needed to rid herself of someone who was holding her back. She needed to progress and saw no possibility of newness with Jeff. It was not that she felt no sympathy for Jeff, she still felt a caring for him; she did not want to hurt him. She did have to think of herself, if she was not happy with Jeff she knew she had to move along.

This was how conflicting the thoughts were for Jeff and Melody. Melody pulled herself up but Jeff fell into a well of self pity and hatred for everything around him. His brother Gabe was not home. Stevie could not help. Sharon simply told him he needed to forget Melody and go on with his life. Stan could listen but could supply no answers either. Jeff needed to sort it out himself, somehow. Jeff felt that Melody was the only one that mattered to him. He wanted no other girl but her. He wandered over to Greg's house but Mary had just dropped him so the two miserable boys could be of no help to each other except to curse all women and swear never to let a woman lead them around again; they became resurrected girl haters.

For three weeks Jeff reveled in his misery. He spent lunches alone at school. Melody spent lunches off campus or in the bleachers with Brian. Jeff saw Brian and Melody together at school from a distance and this hurt him. He called Melody twice but she was cold and aloof; she acted short and made every attempt to keep the conversation to a minimum. Jeff finally gave up deciding it hurt less because all she talked about was Brian in an attempt to make him wake up and move on.

He walked to a cliff above and south of North Beach one day and considered jumping. All he could do was cry and hate himself for not having the strength to end his own life. Self hatred became his weakness. All his confidence in anything he could do well was gone.

72

On February 22nd, Jeff and Greg, who had moved on without Mary, went for a walk to the beach. On arrival at South Beach there were several cars parked. A rusty old station wagon, an old Woody, and a Volkswagen without a rear window. On arrival at North Beach, there were six men on the beach. The word was out. The waves looked perfect pealing left and right. Southern California surfers had discovered the north coast. Skinny dipping on the beach would now become a thing of the past as North Beach was claimed by surf enthusiasts.

This was another loss for Jeff. No more running and screaming and playing. Boys just got in the way. Being eighteen this was fine. He had his childhood; however, he knew that future kids would be less inclined to spend their days on the beach. Television became the new draw as boys sat in front of that world of escape.

On March 1st, Gabe and Stevie were married and Stevie moved to housing on base. Gabe came home less and Stevie was now gone.

Jeff looked into joining the Air Force after graduation and scheduled a physical in Eureka for April.

Greg began to come around and spend more time with Jeff as they both looked forward to graduation.

On March 22nd, Jeff's mother married another Bill. This was her third Bill. This Bill was home most of the time. This changed the freedom of not having an adult around the house.

Clint never left Tanya. His relationship with Amanda was one of convenience. When Tanya was not around, he'd wander over to Amanda's. He became possessive with her. He expected her to be there when he wanted her. Amanda never was the kind of person to be there when demanded on her. This just made Clint more possessive as he tried to control her. Amanda was always uncontrollable.

On Saturday March 14th, Clint hit Amanda. Amanda told him never to come around again. He returned and was sent away.

A week later Amanda moved Carl in with her. Carl drove a truck and lived in Eureka but Amanda's house became a home away from home. He visited Weston but often drank at the Linger Longer Bar in Hidden Shore. He was friends with Mike, Gabe's boyhood friend.

On March 27th 1964, Clint went to Amanda's in Weston and beat her horribly. He left her and headed to the Linger Longer looking for Carl. Amanda called the police and was transported to Eureka and admitted to the hospital.

73

Late on the night of March 27, Clint's father, Chief Johnson received a call at the Weston Police office warning him that another tidal wave warning was in effect on the California coast and an evacuation of Hidden Shore was recommended. He sent his men all to Hidden Shore to help evacuate the elderly and any one else who needed help. There had been many other warnings and by now most people took these warnings with a grain of salt since nothing ever really came from any of them.

When Steve Taylor and the other deputies arrived, they discovered a fire had broken out at the Linger Longer Bar so they radioed for fire crews to put the fire out. While radioing, all of a sudden the tidal wave hit Hidden Shore.

74

Melody and Brian remained an item for only four weeks. Sylvia asked Brian to the Sadie Hawkins dance. When Melody asked Brian, he told her Sylvia had already asked him. Brian wanted to go with Sylvia. Melody had missed her period and was afraid she was pregnant with Brian's child. She was not but Brian did not care. He told her she would just have to deal with it. Melody dumped Brian. Sylvia had Brian's baby in December of 1964.

Saturday morning March 27th 1964, Melody was confused. She now knew she was not pregnant but she felt alone. Her thoughts wandered to Jeff. She knew she had devastated him. His friends and hers always told her that he was never the same after her. She needed to know how she felt about Jeff. She walked the full four miles to his house and arrived there at noon. She had the chain with the heart and locket in her pocket. When she arrived at Jeff's home she stood out front and tried to strengthen her will to knock on the door. This seemed so strange to stand outside the house where so much had happened but she had been away from there for so long.

The garage door suddenly opened and there was Jeff. She started to walk away but he called to her.

"What are you doing here?"

"I have your locket. I thought you probably deserved to have it back." she said.

"So I hear that Brian dumped you." Jeff informed her.

She wanted to tell him that his facts were incorrect but she felt it was better to let it lay.

"I really just thought we might talk. I need a friend." she told him.

"I've needed you for a long time but that didn't seem to matter to you." he shot back cruelly.

"Well, if your gonna be that way." she responded and began to walk away.

"I'm sorry." Jeff blurted.

"No...I'm sorry. I thought maybe we could still be friends at least." she countered.

"I have friends."

"Don't be cruel, I know I deserve it but... never mind." Again Melody began to walk away.

"You wanna go for a walk?" Jeff asked.

"Yes, I'd like that." Melody smiled.

Jeff and Melody began to walk. He did not even close the garage door he expected to be right back. They walked up to Railroad Avenue, to the Bridge, past the Mill, and to South Beach. They talked and apologized and began to become comfortable with each other again. They walked past the tide pools to North Beach.

"There's no surfers today." Jeff told Melody and then explained the invasion to her.

They sat at the knoll near the cliff and talked. It became cold in the March wind so Jeff built his best fort ever. They worked on it together. It was covered and when they were finished they hugged and kissed and made love within their little home on the beach. They promised themselves to each other again. They swore they would never again play the games with other people again. They exchanged vows and proclaimed themselves man and wife.

"Jeff, the only thing that has ever meant anything to me in the whole world since I first saw you was just that: you," Melody proclaimed to Jeff "It's a whole lot ridiculous that we allowed our special feelings to become so public instead of keeping our feelings so special and between ourselves. We killed everything. Perhaps it was inevitable that we needed to learn what really was important to us. I don't want any one but you; I want to spend the rest of my life with you. I want to have your children and I want you to always be there and protect me. I love you with all my heart and soul and will never look anywhere but what I find in you. We can't be sure that everything will always be this wonderful, we have seen the worst. Forgive what I have done and take me back forever."

"I give my love to you without hesitation and swear that you will never spend another day without me in your life," Jeff countered. "I will never allow my thoughts to wander toward anyone else the rest of my life. I will support you in anything you want and anything you want me to do. Please don't ever leave me alone again. Life without you would be the most empty thing I can imagine in life."

With these pledges, Jeff and Melody fell into each others arms and cried and sobbed uncontrollably.

It became dark and the tide came up. Melody and Jeff had no way to leave North Beach. They resigned themselves to spend the night. They made love and Jeff's head spun with the realization that the only thing he could ever ask for in life had happened. They laid together satisfied with the sudden turn of events.

About Midnight, Jeff had built a fire and they were cuddling by it to keep warm. Holding Melody again made Jeff cry. Melody joined him in fits of sobs and I'm sorrys.

After a short while Melody and Jeff began to become aware again of the world around them.

"It's so quiet." Melody noticed.

"That's strange I don't ever remember not hearing the surf." Jeff noted. "I've never heard it so quiet on this beach."

Suddenly; they could hear a rumble and without warning the fort built by Jeff and Melody was slammed by water.

"Jee-eff" screamed Melody.

That would be the last sound Jeff would ever hear.

75

After leaving Amanda, Clint first stopped at his home in

Hidden Shore

Weston and slipped his 38 pistol into the belt of his trousers and then drove to Hidden Shore. He knew that all his troubles with Amanda were because of Carl. He decided it was time to get even with that man who had tried to lay claim to his woman. He wanted to call him out and beat him even worse than he had beat Amanda.

Clint arrived at the bar at about ten o'clock that night. When he entered he observed that Mike and Carl were sitting at the bar playing the game of aces up with the bartender. There were about fifteen or twenty other people there. Clint walked to the other side of the bar and just stood. The bartender knew him and welcomed him but told him that he couldn't drink anything because he was not old enough yet but he was welcome to hang around if he wished; as son of the chief of police he was often allowed to do things that no other kid could do. Clint thanked him and sat quietly in a corner. He told the tender he just needed a warm place to sit and think because he had a lot on his mind.

Clint sat for a couple of hours until about midnight and the only people left were the three at the bar. The bartender considered many times calling Clint's dad and getting his advise about Clint because he had never seen him in the mood he appeared to be in but he thought differently of it because he remembered being in high school and he assumed that Clint had had a fight with someone or something so he just let Clint sit and stew.

Sometime after midnight, the bartender finally walked up to Clint with a coke in hand and offered it to him. The juke box was playing "For the Good Times" by Ray Price. As he stood over Clint, the teenager suddenly pulled his gun from his waist and shot the bartender killing him immediately, leveled it at Carl and killed him with one shot. Mike dived under the pool table just as someone walked through the door. The person at the door was Jack Purvis, the man who had scared Clint and Jeff with the chicken in the "Haunted House" years earlier. Jack ran from the bar as Clint shot at Mike who jumped at him and was killed from a point blank shot.

Clint went behind the bar and began to pour brandy all over the bar and the floor and lit it on fire with a cigarette lighter. The bar became engulfed and Clint then fled from the bar.

He made it home to Weston and went to bed.

Hidden Shore was slammed hard by the tsunami. The bar continued to burn even after the wave hit. After regrouping, the police and firemen were finally able to extinguish the fire but discovered the horrible scene within.

Jack Purvis was first arrested after he was identified as having been seen running from the bar just before it caught fire. He relayed to Steve Taylor what he had seen at the bar. The presence of Clint was verified by others who had been at the bar earlier.

Steve radioed to the Chief that his son needed to be contacted.

76

"Clint. Clinton. Your father wants to talk to you." Mrs. Johnson called after answering the telephone.

"Clint."

"Clint?"

Bang, the sound of a gun from Clint's playroom.

"Oh my God... NO!"

After Word

Jeff's body was found at about the same place the body of the girl was found over two years earlier. Melody was never found. Clint had been at the bar, but he was dead now. Tanya was at home in Fairbury. Mary, Jeff's mother, fled from work looking for Stan, Jeff and Bill. She found the house empty but the garage door open and fled to Weston. Stan had fled with Bill to Weston. Amanda was in the hospital in Eureka. Stevie was with Gabe. Melody's Aunt Peggy and Uncle Jim were at home and knew nothing of what happened until the next morning. They found Melody's bed unslept in. No one ever made a connection between her and Jeff because no one knew she had anything to do with him anymore; they simply never knew what happened to her. Greg helped Mary Woo and her parents evacuate. Clint's father John Johnson and Steve Taylor, who discovered the bar fire and called Clint's dad, were on the radio dispatching. Mike, Gabe's friend, died in the bar. Jennifer visited Amanda in Eureka and was there along with Trina.

In 1965, Gabe was detached as one of the first "advisers" in Vietnam. He died there.

Stevie, devastated by Gabe's death, returned and moved to Weston but later attended Humbolt State. While there she became a stripper at a bar and later she moved to San Francisco and became a Burlesque dancer. Her body was later found in a debris box behind the Old Mint at Fifth and Mission.

Mary divorced Bill no.3. She remarried and married Henry.

Amanda recovered from her beating, left Trina who moved in with Jennifer. She returned to Boston, married a born again Christian and raised seven children to be "proper Christians." None ever thought that their mother had been anything less than a saint her whole life. She never told any one of them about her past.

Greg met Franklin, his only true love, moved to San Francisco, turned hippie, and protested the Vietnam war.

Stanley became President of the Weston Bank.

Brian and Sylvia adopted out their illegitimate child and later married and had three children in wedlock, none of them ever knew they had an older brother.

Mary Woo married Jack Chen but died in an auto accident

Hidden Shore

while pregnant with their first child.

Mrs. Sanchez lived the rest of her life in her apartment in San Francisco. Carlos never got around to joining the Army and stayed with his mother. Mrs. Sanchez leaves a flower at Mr. Pruit's grave for Melody every Sunday. She never believed Melody just ran away. She was sure Melody died.

Today the name Hidden Shore is only found marked on maps as the road which runs from Weston to the coast: Hidden Shore Rd.